# Home of the Brave

# HOME
## OF THE
# BRAVE

## SOMEWHERE IN THE SAND

EDITED BY

## JEFFERY HESS

Press 53
Winston-Salem, NC

Press 53
PO Box 30314
Winston-Salem, NC 27130
www.Press53.com

First Edition

Cover design by Kevin Morgan Watson

Cover photo "Sunset over Kandahar" is a U.S. Army photo
by Staff Sgt. Ruth Pagan, 2nd BCT, 4th Inf. Div., PAO, and is in the Public
Domain. Neither the U.S. Army nor Staff Sgt. Pagan endorses Press 53,
this anthology, or the views contained herein.

Printed on acid-free paper

ISBN 978-1-935708-85-8

*For Chris Hartnett*
*Soldier, badass, father, old friend*

# CONTENTS

# INTRODUCTION

Hemingway famously said, "War is the best subject of all." And, Tolstoy wrote a memorable opening line that states, "...each unhappy family is unhappy in its own way." In many respects, this book is the crossroads of these two sentiments.

Being a book about the military, these stories naturally touch on issues of honor, duty, priorities, justice, camaraderie, and combat. While those battlefield elements make for exciting stories, a book that focuses solely on them misses the opportunity to explore the lives that exist beyond the headlines, behind closed doors.

We've all seen the footage of combat, images of flag-draped caskets, and pairs of boots with rifles stabbed into the sand behind them with helmets resting on their upturned stocks. I'm interested in those stories and the effects they have back home when "here" and "there" collide.

These stories provide glimpses into military life, marriages and other relationships—good or bad, even religion, as well as death, physical injuries, post-traumatic stress, and traumatic brain injuries. Displayed here are also the ways people handle grief, isolation, conscience, dissent, karma, impermanence, and support gone wrong. At the heart of every story here is an American affected by our country's military involvement in Iraq or Afghanistan.

As I began this project in the summer of 2012, a friend asked me why I would do another anthology of military fiction. He suggested that "Home of the Brave: Stories in Uniform" (which consists of stories from World War II through Iraq and Afghanistan) covered the topic.

My answer pointed to the events of our nation's military that have dominated the lives of millions of people almost every year of this century. There are an infinite number of stories out there that need to be told—each in their unique way.

When I began these anthologies, I didn't know what kinds of stories I'd want to include. I thought back to a panel discussion I attended at an Association of Writers and Writing Programs conference on the topic of who can write about war. The conversation that followed encouraged me because the panelists agreed that anyone who has been somehow impacted by war is not only entitled to write about it, but is encouraged to do so.

To find these stories, I called out as far and wide as I could to solicit submissions that somehow touched on America's military presence in Iraq or Afghanistan. I left the interpretation up to the authors. I also read literary journals where I found many strong possibilities, but only those that stayed with me made me reach out and contact the author to ask for permission to include it here. Almost every time, I was told yes.

Abraham Lincoln said, "Any Nation that does not honor its heroes will not long endure."

If this open call for submissions is any indication, our heroes are being honored in fiction.

The general submissions impressed me by their variety of approaches to the material as well as by their and quality. Many of the stories not selected could have filled another fine anthology. I wish it were possible to put all of them between the covers of a book as a way to share the lives of people affected, even in a distant way, by combat—veteran and civilians alike.

I had no plan or agenda. No ideology. No partisanship. None of these stories are about politicians or policies. Nor are all these stories seek-and-destroy stories. Even the ones that might be considered such are not just that. There's more to them. Few stories are ever simply war stories. Invariably there are other layers or aspects to them.

This anthology is for those who consider themselves pro-military and pacifist, alike. I wanted to give everyone an opportunity to engage various situations regardless of the side of the spectrum they may fall.

Here, you'll find stories about Soldiers and Marines, male and female, in the heat of battle, with all the surprises that come with the realities of combat. Of these, some take place immediately afterward, where the carnage is assessed and the injured are tended to, but no one is unscathed. Some of these brave men and women kill. Some are killed, others are wounded. Some stories detail the months that follow, or later, still, through the hardships wounded warriors face once they return home and the effects of their return or their absence on their spouses and their children, their mothers and fathers, their neighbors, a drone controller, and an unlikely pair of protestors. What unites them is their country's wars of this new century.

I'm no expert on the topic. I'm just in awe of these people. As a side note, I live fifteen miles from MacDill Air Force Base, which is the military headquarters for both Central Command—CENTCOM, and Special Operations Command—SOCOM. It's no secret that this is the nerve center for all operations "over there." Decisions made so close to home somehow make me feel involved. And, yet, while I type this on my patio looking at the shadows inching up my oak tree, it's hard to believe this is not a military town and that there are American military personnel dying in combat.

Halfway between my house and the MacDill base, is Raymond James Stadium where the Tampa Bay Buccaneers play. As large as that stadium is, it's just big enough to hold the 50,286 military personnel wounded in Iraq and Afghanistan. The remaining seats could serve as visual reminders of the 6,473 brave men and women who didn't make it home.

As tragic as those numbers are, they don't include the scores of others who deployed for one tour, or more, of combat, nor their families, nor the rest of the civilians. The brave men and women who served and all their families and everyone else who ever slept poorly at night because of combat, or the notion of combat, who could fill stadiums all across this country are heroic to me. We need enduring records of what the experience was like. And not just what these people experienced, but what they remember, relive, imagine.

Someday, people may look at these stories as a chronicle of our times. Perhaps younger generations will grow curious. Perhaps more of our current generation will come to realize that reading about a fictional character's life can actually offer more benefit than watching someone being voted off a television show.

Not coincidentally, there's a debate in literary circles about the viability of the short story. But luckily, there seem to be more literary journals, short story collections, and anthologies coming out every year. Short stories are a tremendous art form. What better way to experience a moment in another person's life? To witness their ambitions and their injuries, visible and invisible?

At an event for the previous Home of the Brave anthology, someone asked why I found it important to spend so much time on made up stories instead of "true, non-fiction."

I cribbed my answer from the great writer, Tim O'Brien, who basically asserts that facts aren't stories, facts are news or history. They're important, but it's only in fiction that one can get past the facts and reach a stronger semblance of the emotional truth. That's what interests me.

And, it's not just me. Many of you may be familiar with the New York Times article that cites international studies that prove reading fiction impacts the brain in an emotionally expansive way. In short, reading informs those unfamiliar with the situations in stories, and it comforts those who can relate personally. That seems an entirely worthwhile endeavor, to me.

A note about title: In the spring of 2009, as I'd been putting together the earlier anthology, I'd been struggling for a title. As I explained in the introduction to that book, I was inserting my American flag into the holder mounted on my house when the Star Spangled Banner flashed through my mind. It's embarrassingly cliché, but the last four words in our national anthem echoed in my head. I knew then that "Home of the Brave" had to be the title. I also knew it would need a subtitle so as to further define the content. "Stories in Uniform" encapsulated everything I thought about the stories and struck me as appropriate.

In May of that same year, upon the publication of Home of the Brave: Stories in Uniform, I appeared on the Dennis Miller Show. I'd been a big fan since his Saturday Night Live days and through his movie roles and stand up specials and it was a thrill to speak with him. I'd listened to his radio show as regularly as I listened to NPR and knew he strongly supported our military and I was nervous. During the interview, I described the book and used the statement, "Somewhere in the sand" to refer to the combat in Afghanistan and Iraq. Dennis stopped me right there and said, "I would say, *Somewhere in the Sand* would be your next great book title." My response was immediate. It seemed like a great idea to me then as it does now. Thank you, Mr. Miller.

*Home of the Brave* implies the American military. *Somewhere in the Sand* implies the desert conditions of both Iraq and Afghanistan, but also the mental state that the returning service members occupy periodically or perpetually once they return home.

Ultimately, this isn't a book just about war. It's about the idea of war, the threat of war, war itself, and the aftermath of war. This book is in honor of those who served their country as well as those affected by the aftermath. I hope readers will identify, be entertained, challenged, caught off guard, moved, and enlightened. These stories paint a complex portrait of America's military experiences so far into this new century. This is not just the book I wanted to read, but the one that I want you to read as well.

Jeffery Hess
April 2013

*"War is the best subject of all. It groups the maximum of material and speeds up the action and brings out all kinds of stuff you have to wait a lifetime to get."*

—Ernest Hemingway

# SOLDIER'S CROSS

★ ★ ★

*Caleb S. Cage*

The platoon leader sat in the front, right seat of his humvee, still tasting the watery eggs he'd had a few hours before and still feeling the sleep in his eyes. Even though they'd been out since early in the morning, he was sweating, the sweat just sitting on his uniform, reminding him every time he tried to move that he was still in Iraq. Only an hour or so before he couldn't tell how cluttered with trash the streets were—product containers, discarded clothing, food waste, anything that was unwanted inside the impoverished Iraqi houses right off the street. With dawn breaking now, he welcomed the visions of local debris if it meant his driver could avoid getting stuck in the trenches of human waste that coursed unapologetically through the village streets. Approximately 15,000 Iraqis called the village of Tahrir home, and they had seldom been friendly to his presence there.

They'd been on a scheduled patrol, a routine check-the-block sort of thing, since the early morning hours, looking for trouble and finding none. Right as his four humvees were about to finish serpentining through their last neighborhood, he received a frago, the dreaded call from battalion telling them that they were going to have another mission, a surprise. They were to go to the local Sunni mosque and see what they could glean from the daily call to prayer. It wasn't a terribly uncommon request, and it even made a little bit of sense—the Imam's daily prayers were key sources of communication in the largely illiterate and disconnected local community—it was the fact that it was a frago from a morning patrol that pissed him off. No one could anticipate what a frago was going to look like ahead of time, but he momentarily reveled in the fact that his bosses at battalion had been wrong in denying him the use of one of the battalion's Iraqi interpreters for his morning patrol. He'd long since learned not to argue, though, even after a recent frago had left the battalion staff so confused that another platoon wound up abandoned and pinned down, losing two young soldiers.

"Hey Mac," he said, in a quiet morning tone, to the young soldier who was filling in as his driver for just this patrol.

"Yessir," Mac responded.

"Those black trenches in the street? You know what they are full of, right?"

"Yessir."

"Then can you pull away from this one over here so I don't have to swim through it to get out, please?"

"Sorry, sir," Mac responded, still too nervously, and slowly moved the vehicle forward.

"It's no big deal, Mac," he laughed, trying to give Specialist McPherson a break. "Valdez does that to me on purpose all the time. I just figure I can train you a little bit since you are new to the job," he popped Mac lightly with the back of his hand to make sure he knew he wasn't in trouble. He smiled back at the platoon leader. "Just pull right over there so we can see front door of the mosque and hear the speakers, please." Over his platoon radio he told his platoon to set up security, get pointed down roads and alleyways in all four directions, and settle in for the morning prayers they'd been ordered to monitor without an interpreter.

Just days before, he had been in his native Las Vegas. He was on R and R, a trip that he never thought would arrive, and then vanished in an instant. He'd waited until the end of the deployment to allow for his soldiers to go home first, and now, he had only months if not weeks to go in his deployment. Growing up there, he had been used to avoiding the Strip at all costs, laughing inside as weekend warriors plunged into McCarran hungry, elated, high-fiving, and left three days later bloodshot, spent, and haggard. With his friends waiting for him, and plenty of arrangements made in advance, he was the one plunging into the airport this time, and he'd be staying much longer than most out-of-towners.

He only seemed to be awake at night when he was in Vegas. There was a night when his friends rented an airport shuttle to carry them from place to place, debauching, and admitting as much to themselves, enjoying every bit of freedom and excess that they could afford. There were nights when everyone else had to work the next day, forcing him to go out and play just as hard on his own or with a ragtag group without a clear mission. The results were always the same: he would wake up hungover and a little bit angry. There would be a slight tremor in his hands from the drinking and the smoking and the dehydration, too. But at least in Vegas he could sleep the day away and not have to worry about writing incident reports or chasing any of his commander's great ideas.

For nearly a year in Iraq, swimming pools had been the object of his daydreams, offering a singular and elegant solution to the constant heat and the filth, his two least favorite parts of being in Iraq. His friend's pool in Vegas didn't disappoint him in the slightest. They had gone out on a typical night and met some underage Canadian tourists. He was particularly fond of Samantha, a nineteen-year-old from Vancouver who found his twenty-five years to be irresistible. They drank and ate and smoked and laughed for hours. He and Samantha watched the sun come up over the valley by the pool when everyone else had long since gone back inside. Alone, they hit a sober stretch, streaking into the pool when they couldn't stand the tension anymore. He knew that such a scenario would have never happened to him if he had been living like a local.

In Iraq, the sun was coming up through the cloud and haze that seemed ever present in a country that was wedded to constantly burning fossil fuels, and divorced from the idea that it had any impact on their quality of life. The call to prayer seemed to be starting the same way, slow and subdued, probably heavy on the praise to Allah and light on the call for *jihad*. As the sun crested the horizon completely, finally powerful enough to burn through the morning haze, the Imam's lecture seemed to change too. The knock at his window startled him from the increasingly intense rhythms and yells coming from the makeshift minaret directly in front of him.

"So what are we going to do, sir," his platoon sergeant asked.

"What's that?" he asked, removing an earplug from his right ear.

"What are we going to do here?"

"We're going to sit here for a while. It's just going to be one of those mornings," he said, not allowing himself to say what everyone was thinking. "What do you think we're going to hear, Mac?" he asked his temporary driver.

"I'm guessing that we hear how great God is, and how it will all be done if it is God's will if we listen closely enough, sir," Mac said, referring to *Allahu Akbar* and *Inshallah*, the only two Arabic phrases that nearly all Americans could hear and understand if they listened closely enough.

"You're probably right," the platoon leader said, laughing. "They'll all be reminded that they are a religion of peace, then be ordered to kill all Americans."

"What the hell are we doing here, sir?" his second squad leader asked, walking up from his vehicle in the rear.

"We're listening to the mosque, sergeant. Following orders," he responded, smiling.

"Can't we follow orders better in the shade?" the squad leader asked, using his need to spit a wad of brown saliva as an opportunity to break eye contact from the man whose authority he was mildly challenging. "Or back on base where we don't have to smell the trenches?"

"I don't know, sergeant. I kind of see this as the devil we know. Battalion thought it was a brilliant idea to send us out here to listen to the morning prayers without an interpreter. I think that this is far less inconvenient than going back into the chute for whatever great idea pops up next. I mean, we're already dressed." He was going to go on, but he knew better. He knew that it was his job to relay the orders and shield his men from the chickenshit as best he could, not to prove to his men that he understood and even shared their collective grievance.

"And besides, listen to this guy get down," the platoon sergeant said, eager to change the subject away from his platoon leader's insubordination.

"What is going *on* in there?" Mac asked.

"I'm not so worried about what's going on in there, look at what's going on out here," the squad leader said, squinting under the sun, the frago causing him to be outside the wire without the sunglasses he would have preferred on a mission like this.

"Looks like *hajji* is actually answering the call to prayer this morning," Mac said as several dozen locals began milling around on the streets in front of them toward the mosque. "Is it some sort of *hajji* holiday?"

"No one told me anything," the platoon leader muttered, staring at the small crowd entering the Sunni mosque to their front. He made a report to battalion, letting them know what was going on around them: the gradually intensifying call to prayer, the growing number of adherents entering the mosque from the community, and his current position. "I wonder if they'll let me go in there with them," he said to no one in particular.

"Who? The Iraqis or battalion?" the platoon sergeant asked, still leaning against his platoon leader's vehicle and not taking his eyes off of the front door of the mosque. "I'm not sure the Iraqis could stop you from going in with all of us out here, but we can't go in their mosques unless we are directly engaged from them," he said, answering his own question.

"I'm a Muslim," the platoon leader said nonchalantly.

"What?" the squad leader asked incredulously.

"My dog tags list my faith as Muslim," the platoon leader said, still not breaking his stare.

"Really?" Mac asked with even more disbelief in his voice than the squad leader.

The platoon leader nodded, still trying to figure out what was going on around them and why there had been dozens of "military-age Muslims males" staring him down as he entered the mosque a few yards away from his humvee.

"I had no idea," Mac said, as if he was calculating the cost of all the offensive remarks he had said in front of his platoon leader about his faith.

"I'm not really a Muslim, Mac," he said, snapping out of his stare and keying the radio mic to talk to his other vehicles. "Let's try not to interrupt their morning prayer here, but let's dismount teams and get vehicles pointed down these alleyways," he told his guys. "Sergeants?" he said with a raised eyebrow, sending two of his senior NCOs back to execute the order he had just given.

"I still don't get the dog tags, sir?" the squad leader asked while the platoon leader got out of his vehicle.

"They wouldn't let me put 'Nevadan' on them when we were getting ready to come over here," he said, dismissing the squad leader as well as the long and personally frustrating process that had ended with him simply choosing to make a particularly timely joke about the "religious faith" line on his dog tag processing form.

"I have no idea what that means," the squad leader said, looking directly at the platoon leader, half distrustful and half confused.

The platoon leader couldn't tell if he was truly puzzled, offended, or just trying to delay getting his squad in position, but he could tell that he wasn't getting off the hook. "At out-processing, during the pre-deployment stuff. I didn't want to fill out the 'religious faith' line on the form. I tried to leave it blank and they wouldn't let me. I tried to write in 'Nevadan' on there, you know, as a joke, but the sergeant didn't think that was funny either. Finally, he handed me off to one of his fellow NCOs who didn't care what I put as long as it was on his list. 'Muslim' was on the list, so I chose it. Now, get to work," he said. "Mac, get pointed down that alley there and watch our front," he said.

"Does your dog tag really say that you are Muslim, sir?" Mac asked.

"Yes," he said, mildly exasperated. He pulled the chain out of his pocket to answer his question for good.

"You know that if you die, they are going to give you Muslim last rites, don't you, sir," Mac said. "That's how the Chaplain knows."

"Do you believe in God, Mac?"

Mac pulled out his own dog tags and held them out to show the "Roman Catholic" written across the bottom.

"What's that?" he asked, pointing to a medallion on Mac's dog tag chain.

"It's a medallion appealing to Saint Rose of Lima," he replied. "Sometimes I think it's the only thing that's kept me alive."

"Well then, I think you're superstitious enough for the both of us, Mac," he said, laughing. "Be sure and tell the Chaplain to get behind cover if you see him leaning over me during a firefight one of these days." Mac handled the explanation better than his mom had when he had a nearly identical conversation with her the week before in Vegas. She'd seen the dog tags on the kitchen table while he was in the shower and looked like a wounded animal when he came down later for dinner.

"You know, you are just like your father," she said, after he tried to explain his joke to her.

"You mean, I'm a heavy-handed moralist who's into younger women?" he responded quickly, meaning it as a joke. Being around soldiers all day had clouded his judgment with respect to humor.

"That's not funny," his mother said blankly. He could tell that she wanted to say more, to offer up some explanation for why his father had waited until his son was off at war to have his mid-life crisis. It wasn't exactly what he had grown to expect from the man who wouldn't even let his small family have a television because he didn't want to let the evils of the world into his home. He waited for her to speak, but she didn't. He knew that his mother wanted to talk about it. He knew that she almost certainly could not have figured out a way to work through it all by herself. He hadn't yet, but he also knew that he was only home for two weeks. When he thought about it, he hated himself for avoiding the issue. And when his mom told him he favored his father, he hated himself even more.

"How are you doing with all of it, Momma?" he asked seriously for the first time since he'd been home.

"I'm still pretty confused, Michael," she said, "but I'm fine. I don't think any of us saw it coming, but I guess worse stuff happens to people all of the time." She was staring past him now, but he could tell that the anger he had heard on the phone months before had started to subside. "I'm hopeful. I am still hopeful. I think that maybe he was reacting harshly to your leaving, and that this was his only way of dealing with it. He returned one of my calls the other day."

He was momentarily furious that it had become his fault, but he put it all aside and hugged his mother. There was no way his father was coming back, right? Everything he had lived for was a lie, and coming back groveling would take more humility than the man had ever shown. No, he'd moved on, and his son was going to deal with it all later. "I'm going to head out for a bit, mom," he said, kissing her on the forehead.

"I wish you'd get your dog tags fixed," she'd said, before letting go of his hand.

"It's just a joke, mom," he'd said, smiling halfheartedly as he left the room.

Hopefully Mac knew it was a joke, too. He slapped him on the shoulder, and pointed at the alley closest to their position. "Keep an eye down this alley, and use the wall for cover." The call to prayer seemed to be over now, but there were still rants coming from the speaker. It was a different voice, and although it was louder, he couldn't tell if it was more radical than before. They were to respect the call to prayer and other cultural customs, and nothing about four armed and armored humvees sitting out your front door seemed respectful. He wanted to leave. It was a lose-lose, he thought, but he wasn't in control. "What would you like us to do, over?" he asked into the mic for the battalion radio.

"Stay in position," he heard in response. It wasn't what he wanted to hear, but he didn't have many options.

"We're going to sit tight for a while, boys," he said into his platoon mic. "The idiots at battalion are trying to figure out how to tell us we shouldn't be here without having to say that they shouldn't have sent us here. Shouldn't be long now."

"Yeah, no time at all," a voice came back over the radio.

His platoon was in a good security position when they started to hear shooting. The shots didn't seem particularly well-aimed, and he couldn't tell where the shots were coming from. They were nearby, though, and not coming from the second or third stories of the buildings immediately next to them.

"Please tell me those shots are coming from inside the mosque?" his second squad leader asked over the radio, laughing. "I kind of want to see what the inside of one of those things looks like."

"Could you imagine the bloodbath if we went in there?" the platoon leader returned. The shots were even more sporadic now, and it became increasingly clear that they were coming from a block or two north of their position. They weren't hitting anywhere near them, but they were definitely being fired from nearby.

"Get back behind that wall, Mac," he yelled, leaving the radios alone to see when and how the shooting was going to stop. Mac's alley was only a few feet wide, not even wide enough for a vehicle, and Mac covered it in the prone. He was a right-handed shooter, and the position his platoon leader had given him to cover was also on his right, forcing him to expose more of his body in order to cover the alley. "Actually," he reconsidered, "switch sides. I think you've got better cover from this side of the alley."

"Are you serious, sir?" Mac said, looking up at him more confused than when he had been told his boss was a Muslim. "There's a trench there."

"Well," the platoon leader said. "Don't swim in it. But you've got to get better cover than that wall. You're hanging half your body out into that alley." Once Mac was in position, the platoon leader squatted down next to him, leaning against the brick wall and trying to figure out what they were going to do next. "You got anything, Mac?"

"Just the same shooting you're hearing, sir."

The attack seemed to be building, but it still wasn't much more than harassment fire yet. The Imam was still yelling loudly and fiercely, building to rhythms that the platoon leader had only heard during Ramadan before he went on leave. The platoon leader looked up when the Imam's words became more staccato, matching the random shots going from enemy AK-47s popping in the alleyways around the platoon.

"It's hot out here, isn't it, Mac?" He asked, the slowing speech and shooting causing him to notice for the first time.

Before Mac could answer, the Imam was yelling again, perhaps signaling the fighters to match his words with their actions, and they did. For the first time since the shooting started, they could see enemy maneuvering, streaming out of the far side of the mosque and trying to flank the stationary platoon through the alleys to their east and west. The platoon's vehicle gunners were well positioned, and the intensifying fire sparked off a vicious response from American machine guns and assault rifles. He scrambled to call in the report to battalion and ask for backup while his men killed tens of poorly organized and blindly assaulting insurgents. He was confident. His men had done this before, dozens of times, and very well. They had superior firepower, superior skill, and superior communication. He didn't wait to hear battalion's response before checking on his squads. He gave a thumbs-up to his nearest squad leader, and got two in return. He got the same from his other squad leader and his platoon sergeant at the end of their position.

"I think this ought to be over pretty soon, Mac," the platoon leader yelled, once he got back to the wall. "The shooting is dying down."

"What?" Mac yelled back.

"I think it's dying down," he said again.

"It sure sounds that way," Mac yelled, still sprawled out in the prone with only his rifle and eye peering around the alleyway.

"Did you shoot at all?"

"A little," Mac yelled, still concentrating on his alley. "You think they planned this attack, sir, or do you think we pissed them off because we were here during their prayers?"

"I think that the morons in charge still think this is the Cold War they grew up with. I don't think they have a clue, and they wound up putting us in the wrong place at the wrong time," he answered, not really caring too much about protecting the chain of command since the shooting started.

"Do they do that a lot?" Mac asked, staring down the sights on his issued rifle. "I mean, are most of our missions this—"

Their alley, the alley that had been the quietest avenue of approach for the enemy since the shooting started, erupted into a torrent of fire, and the platoon leader noticed rounds impacting the ground and walls near him. He rose to a half-squat. "You good, Mac?" he yelled over the fire, seemingly paralyzed by the rapid metallic clacking of the nearby AKs. "Mac, are you good?" he asked again, enunciating each word as loudly as he could. He wasn't able to tell if he was refusing to look down at Mac, or simply unable. "Mac, get up," he said, finally forcing himself to look down. Mac was fully slouched, his rifle was toppled under his weight. The growing pool of blood coming out of his forehead was already mixing with the black pool of human waste in the trench next to them. "Mac, get up," he yelled again over the concentrated fire that was still suppressing his position.

He grabbed Mac by his vest near his shoulders and rolled him onto his back. Evaluate the casualty like you've been trained a thousand times, he told himself. There was no responsiveness when he called his name. He wasn't breathing and there was blood streaming from his head. Everything else he was supposed to check for—the burns, the broken bones, the shock—were all irrelevant. "You're going to be okay, Mac," he said in a voice that he knew he couldn't expect Mac to believe.

Later that afternoon he sat in his room on his FOB, sweating and filthy in a camping chair that was nearly as broken as he was, thinking about saying goodbye to his mom when he left Vegas. They hadn't had any more conversations that mattered for the rest of his trip. She didn't push him on anything anymore, and he did his best not to flaunt the fun he was having. Their truce had allowed for a few distinctly good nights: a dinner at P.J. Clarke's, a visit to the Springs Preserve, and a movie night like they used to enjoy as a family.

On the last day before going back to Iraq he asked her if she wanted to say her goodbyes at home and let him take a cab to the airport. She allowed for it, but only after putting up a fight. When he walked downstairs in his newly-washed uniform, smelling like laundry soap and fabric softener for the first time in months, he could barely look at her sitting at the kitchen table. Her eyes were puffy and she was crying silently into a dishtowel, looking like a grieving widow.

"You know I love you, Momma," he said softly, pulling her head into his chest. "You know I'm not leaving because I want to, right?"

"I know that, honey," she whispered between sobs, her throat too swollen from holding back her screams to actually allow her a voice. "I just love you so much."

"I love you too, Momma."

"I know you do," she whispered.

"I'll be home in two months, Momma. Back in Germany. Then I'll be back in Vegas four months later. We just have to hang on."

"You know I can't lose you," she said, mustering all of her strength to hold onto her youngest son's torso and to voice the words they'd both been avoiding. She was heaving now, bawling. "I'm so sorry," she said. "I'm sorry. I know you don't need this, but I can't. I can't." Her body fell limp and she let go of her son, who had been holding tightly. "God, don't take my baby."

"I'll be home, Momma. I'll be home."

His cab arrived shortly after and it was everything he could do to leave. He hadn't mentioned it, but his mother had aged ten years in the year since he'd left. Her hair was grayer and her eyes were more desperate. How much older would she look when he came back next time? How much longer would she last if he didn't? Thinking these things actually offered him solace when he got back from Mac's death. Or maybe it wasn't solace, he thought. Maybe seeing his mother like that just hurt worse.

He'd heard that there were already investigations to establish guilt, there were certain to be rumors, too. He had plenty else to do, though, plenty else with outcomes that he could control. His immediate commander had directed him to have his guys make sure that Mac's personal effects were clear of anything that might be embarrassing when his parents received them, and also to build

Mac's Soldier's Cross for the memorial ceremony the following day. As much as he didn't want to move from his chair, he couldn't imagine delegating those tasks to anyone.

Organizing Mac's gear made him realize that although he had been Mac's platoon leader for at least eighteen months, he hadn't really known him at all. He knew that he was an excellent athlete and wanted to coach high school basketball when he got out. He knew that his father was a McPherson and his mother was first generation American from Peru. And, he knew that Mac was not the best soldier in the platoon, but he was probably the most beloved. He smiled when he found a diary with Mac's handwriting across the front: "Specialist McPherson, John Taylor, one each." The phrase was how he often introduced himself into any room or group, a sort of military-issued third person that spoke both to his sense of humor and his willingness to fully accept the identity that the Army had given him. His diary said that he loved a girl back in Germany, his wife and the mother of his son, and it held a worn and creased picture to prove it. It said that he was terrified of the war on a daily basis, and had handwritten prayers to his God to prove that, too. He found several extra sets of Mac's dog tags, too, that told him that he was blood type A-Positive, that he had the 573 prefix for his California social security number, and that he was a Roman Catholic.

The Soldier's Cross, a makeshift memorial for fallen soldiers on the battlefield, had a four-foot plywood cube as a base. His actual boots were filled with sand and laced up until they stood centered on the plywood as rigid as they did when he wore them. His rifle, with bayonet fixed, was sticking out of a hole in the top of the box behind the boots with the butt stock pointed straight up. The platoon leader used a toothbrush and a bucket of soapy water to make sure Mac's helmet was cleaned of blood and bone before resting it, canted slightly forward on the stock of the rifle, sitting just over the dog tags that hung around the middle of the issued rifle.

He could imagine it standing in the middle of the gravel lot in front of the headquarters the next day with the companies formed up around it. The company's first sergeant would stand at the podium in front of the formation and conduct a symbolic final roll call while the men stood at attention. When no answer returned from McPherson's empty spot in the formation, it would be turned over to the Battalion Commander, who, he imagined, would talk about how all of this could have all been averted. He'd probably even call the fallen soldier John, as if he knew Mac and had forgiven him the difference in rank. He was surprised at how impersonal the cross was standing in front of him. It looked just like every other one that had to be built over their time in Iraq, just like the one someone would be building for him if that day had turned out differently. The small Saint Rose of Lima medallion might have been the only thing that would have distinguished Mac's cross from his own, if he hadn't been instructed to remove it.

# Sand Trapped

★ ★ ★

*Roland Goity*

My wife would hate it here, she really would—the heat, the wind, the wavy mirages of the plain. This place cooks you all day, spits sand in your face at night. Cavernous in the way it makes you empty inside, carnivorous in how it swallows your every step. Casey would absolutely hate it; it's just like home.

Only here it's a little more interesting. Here I gotta watch out. Here a sniper might off me should I not maintain the same precautions and attention to detail for which I'm here—implementing security measures for Karzai's guys, *our* guys. If I'm careless I might take one in the back of the head or lose my legs in a street market from some whacked-out Taliban sympathizer's bullet or IED. The landscape may be dreary, but the hostile environment keeps you on your toes.

But my wife's back on the base with our son in Twentynine Palms, enduring a desperately hot and achingly isolated summer. No doubt fighting the recurring nightmare she gets, where she's being chased. I'm no Freud, but I can tell she feels trapped. When dreaming she says her escape route always involves fierce headwinds and running through sand. Twentynine palms. *Twentynine-fucking-palms.* That's where things started going wrong for us—and keep going wrong, for Casey. Some of it's beyond her control, but there's absolutely no reason to fuck things up like she has lately. She's gone 5150, completely upside down.

Casey and I met after I'd enlisted. I'd worked sales for an auto parts distributor and took courses at the local JC. But then 9/11 happened and I decided to become one of the good guys, a hero to my country. So I was molding myself into a man at Camp Pendleton while she was a San Diego party girl, 19, sharing an apartment with girlfriends and working at the Wild Animal Park. We met at a popular watering hole and dance spot one night along the Mission Beach boardwalk; Casey's fake ID had drawn interrogating looks and I stepped in to make everything better. She was striking—flaxen hair and bronze-skin, big shiny teeth unveiled with her dimpled smile. There was a certain electricity between us and it wasn't long before we made out in an alleyway. But, just as quickly, she slithered off with her roommates and I was left with a phone number that was likely no good, a red herring designed to lead me afield.

But days later when I rang Casey answered. We had our fun. Off base I loved to get lit, and she was always ready to drink with me—at the beach, at a bar, in the back of her Subaru. Plus, at the time, I was seriously into climbing. The skills it required were a perfect fit for my Marine training. There were a number of amazing spots within a day's drive, and so I turned Casey on to the sport, too. All the rappelling and belaying was something that she really dug. She felt that, more than the physical benefits we derived from the endeavor, we obtained a mutual trust in each other that represented our relationship as a whole.

And maybe she was on to something, for over the next six months we invariably coursed our future. She got pregnant and we soon got married—a budgeted wedding party for our closest family and friends. But then fate set in not much later and I got deployed. Casey, in her third trimester, practically tackled me before I boarded the ship. Once out to sea I discovered the blood drawn by her fingernails had stuck to and matted the hairs on my chest.

There've been several redeployments since, and such a circus never ends. Now, Ben, Jr., my three-year-old son whom I love but barely know, is learning about life from the confines of a Marine base in the California desert, and his mother is associating with ne'er-do-wells outside its boundaries. The physical and mental isolation has led to progressively poorer choices and now Casey seeks escape from all responsibilities with the "help" of dangerous drugs. It's a sad state of affairs, but there's not much I can do without the consent of my commanders. I've continually expressed my concern about how badly Casey needs me now, and have provided them her therapist's confirming, handwritten opinion.

We need you badly, too, they always say. We need you even more.

I rely on my friend, Riley, a staff sergeant who's stationed on home base many times I'm not. Reliable Riley, who—when I was first deployed—was undergoing a dirty divorce that no amount of drinking could cleanse. Back then my greatest worry was that he'd hook up with Casey. But those worries were unfounded. Now, years later, he's embraced a key role in keeping tabs on my wife and kid, and intervenes when necessary to keep her from going too far astray. Because of the drugs there's always the danger our marriage and her ability to function as a mother will bid adios. She could end up whiling her days in a jail cell—or worse, six feet under.

It's a difficult situation made near impossible with me overseas. Apart like this, there's not much I can do. I sometimes think if I had the right words, a letter or phone call could make a world of difference. I keep trying that angle but, so far, my words have failed me.

In Kabul, our unit trains the police and security forces of the Afghan government. Most of us have been here before or in Iraq (I did two tours there) and are itching to exchange our duties in this forsaken hellhole for life as we know it back home. Unfortunately only those "dying" to get back are making the trip. Two guys not yet of drinking age returned this week in caskets. They'd been manning a roadside checkpoint when some insurgents rolled up and opened fire.

Death is the way of life here. There's a cemetery outside the city high up on a hill that I pass nearly every day. It's a "sacred place," off limits for combat even if Taliban gather there. Headstones bloom like wildflowers, more and more each day it seems. I walk it sometimes but can't understand the inscriptions (my Arabic no better than that of most Marines). Yet I know most of the buried have been there for years, decades, victims of some armed conflict or another. This country's known nothing but war for far too long.

At times of leisure I stroll the street markets. It makes me reminisce of home—one of my wife's favorite weekend activities was attending the coastal farmer's markets and stockpiling on smoked fish, heirloom tomatoes and fresh-cut flowers. It's one of the few things she still occasionally enjoys, even when I'm not around. But Casey would be appalled by what's on display. Here, food and produce is dwindling by the day. Stale bread that in the past was sold for livestock feed is now eaten by the local Pashtun citizenry. The goats in these parts are emaciated like no animals I've seen before. But they're considered a delicacy these days, and are fetching a princely sum. There's not much worth buying here, and the only money the market claims from me is that lifted by young pickpockets who snake in and out of market aisles, and make mad dashes when chased by victimized merchants.

I observe the bartering and clamoring from my outsider's perspective, trying to gauge the mood of the people. We Americans are appreciated at times but not especially beloved by the Afghan people. Largely, the feeling's mutual. I'm not fond of the Afghanis, but have nothing against them. I'm indifferent, really. Most troops are. The way I see it, there's a cultural disconnect that's not easily fixed, and it goes far beyond language. When my brother first got into advertising he told me his agency didn't have a clue about what their clients actually did, but were more than happy to spend their money. That's the way I feel about our role here.

At least I'm with my Marine brothers, duty bound. I know what to do and where to go; I have orders to follow. What Casey follows is the trail to the dive bar off base where she scores crank from tweaker friends. She denied this fact when I confronted her about it on the phone, but Riley's kept me informed. And from the description of the man she's seen with, Casey's allied herself with, in her own words, the Devil.

The Devil! That was *the Devil*! exclaimed Casey.

We'd met someone subterranean or other worldly that's for sure. Had just dropped him off in the parking lot of The Oasis, a tavern

in town that appealed more to bikers than servicemen. He invited
us in for a drink, said he was a mainstay there, but we shook our
heads emphatically. The place gave me the creeps. I'd been in once
before, nearly blotto, and a fight broke out. Now, the crescent-
moon scar on my neck from a broken bottle is a constant reminder
of that night, and the intoxicated time I spent having a medic treat
my wound in the infirmary.

What a freak, Casey said. It's scary to think there are people
like that out here.

I shrugged my shoulders, but guessed he was one of many.
Your mind can short-circuit in the heat and isolation of the Mojave
Desert. As Marines, a sense of order and purpose was drilled into
us. For common folk living on the cheap, unable to make it
anywhere else, they must battle for themselves.

The sketchy character who'd disappeared into The Oasis, he
of the stringy hair, sepia teeth and cracking skin, had camped by
our site at Joshua Tree National Park the night before. Casey's
mother had come to the base from LA to care for her grandson so
we could enjoy a rare vacation—just the two of us—while I was
on leave between tours of duty. We'd brought our climbing bags
and ropes and carabiners for a few days of scaling towering boulders.
Just like old times. Somehow we'd failed to notice our campground
neighbor the previous night as we drank one beer from the cooler
after another, but in the morning the Devil woke us with a
thundering series of belches and coughs. He had a surprise waiting
for us when we opened the tent upon hearing a high-pitched buzz.

Oh my God, look at that guy! Casey had said.

Her future cohort and crystal meth mentor stood not a dozen
yards away, balancing a rattlesnake the size of a fire hose at the
end of a thick mesquite branch. The snake was by turns coiling
and unfurling, as if it couldn't decide whether to cling, jump or
strike. It shook its rattle and hissed like crazy. The man simply
laughed and laughed, undeterred by any sense of danger.

We made friendly and chatted him up—but only after he'd
returned the rattler to the maze of husks at the base of the Joshua
tree where it sought shade. When the Devil learned Casey and I

would aim for home in the direction of his very own stomping grounds, he coaxed his way into the backseat of our vehicle. We got rolling and he got talking. Oh did he talk.

He said he was a Gulf War veteran, but I wasn't so sure—he looked too old to have been a young recruit then, and didn't really speak the lingo when quizzed. But again: the sun, the heat, the parched desert. It certainly could have weathered him and advanced his age. Coupled with the combat, it might have even melted his mind. Something had, because as we motored on he made a scarier commotion than that rattlesnake he'd messed with. Talked about invisible winged beings—the size of humans—who hovered the air undetected. When we slept or weren't looking they stole from our homes, ravaged our women and children, and poisoned our crops and sources of water. Casey kept telling him to shut up and it was all I could do to keep my hands on the wheel and not wring them around his neck. His delusions, I realized then, were more likely caused by crank than PTSD.

And now knowing that he's opened the door to my wife's dark side kills me; I hope to hell little Ben doesn't understand what's happening to his mother.

I jolted awake the other day in such a sweaty fright I nearly caromed off my bunk. I've been having Casey's dream lately, running scared through endless drifts of sand. Only this time, as I fled from whatever was in pursuit (an invisible winged being?) I stumbled and fell flat on my face. Dusting off what tripped me I discovered someone's forlorn grave. Then I looked around and saw tombstone after tombstone, until another huge gust of wind came and covered everything up in sand, me included.

That one dream soured the pit of my stomach so badly I called home and called home, again and again. Finally, I got a hold of Casey.

A Marine buddy and Afghan translator wait for me at the bottom of the hill, take cat naps in the vehicle until I return. A furnace-like breeze sails past me, but today's one of my better days. I think of my son whom I talked to that morning. I miss you, he said, the very first words he's spoken by phone. Hearing him speak I could almost picture what he must look like now. What's more, to my surprise, my wife wasn't anxious and defensive at the sound of my voice. In her own way she confessed she has problems but lacks the power to overcome them on her own. Casey said she keeps envisioning the day we'll again be together, and says that's what she needs to turn her life back around. She asked when that will be and I told her not to think about it.

And now as I stand in the cemetery outside Kabul, one living soul in a sea of the dead, I finally understand what's written on the gravestones. No knowledge of Arabic is necessary to get the meaning behind the words. It's simple: I must get back to my family. Somehow, some way, I must survive this place. There will come a day.

# KILLING TIME IN KANDAHAR

★ ★ ★

*Thomas Vincent Nowaczyk*

My first tour in Afghanistan I was a lance corporal, you know, little badass Marine and shit. I wasn't responsible for squat and didn't give a damn about anything. My job was easy: hump ammo like a pack mule, kill shit, get shit done, and take shit from everyone up the chain of command. I was good at pack-muling and killing, so I didn't have to take much shit. At least not from our guys.

This tour I'm a sergeant, and I am just learning how good I had it back then. If there was any doubt about that yesterday, there is none today. Yesterday was easy; all the right people were still alive. Yesterday was fine. Yesterday was good. Yesterday was same old, same old; up before the rosy crack of dawn and out the wire before the light knew we were moving. By the time the light hit the wire, we had gone most ghostlike, whispering like a cloud across undulating rises and shady hollows, early morning in Afghanistan where gray gives way to beige like cool gives way to hard. This country has been the playground to more infantrymen than Valhalla. We take our turn, one step at a time.

We walk, one foot in front of the other, quietly, quickly, no sound but the gentle puff of dust rolling up from under the sole of a boot, one after another. We think there is a chance of mines or booby traps, so we follow, very literally, in each other's footsteps. I step carefully, as if crossing a stream on rocks where to slip and get wet means having your legs ripped and shredded when your body is slammed in the explosion.

We walk, and I listen to my own breathing, my own internal

movement. I listen to every sound I can hear: the faintest, the most distant muffled anything, measured against the closeness of a snapping twig or a dislodged stone, eye-fucking the area looking for clues, sniffing for danger, waiting for it to come, as it always does. As far as I can tell, we patrol to provoke a response. We don't even have to do anything, just show up. We're Marines. There are people out here who want to kill us, and we patrol until we find them, or until we wind up back inside the wire with a satchel full of information, the kind you can get only by going out and seeing for yourself what changed in the last 24. Whichever. It's all the same to me. That's why we're out here, making the scene with full magazines, boots on the ground, humpin' to please.

The only real difference on this patrol was we had the three new guys. That was the monkey wrench in the works right there. They just showed up the other morning out of nowhere. Replacements, their paperwork said. Fresh meat. "Winkin, Blinkin, and Nod" the gunny said as soon as he saw them. It kind of stuck. There was never any real designation of which one was which, and that became quite a source of amusement, even before Corporal Riggs came looking for a working party after late chow the other evening.

"Which one are you?"

"I'm not sure anymore, Corporal," said the first.

"OK, for now you're Nod."

"I'm Nod, Corporal," said the second.

"OK, then who are you?" Riggs said to the third.

"I'm Blinkin."

"Wait a minute, Sergeant Harper just said that I was Blinkin," said the first.

"You just said you didn't know," said Blinkin-the third.

"Blinkin, Linkin, shut the fuck up," said Riggs. "Just... you know what? All of you... yeah... all three of you go over to the mortar section. They need help digging a hole."

Sergeant Harper, our platoon sergeant—me and him enlisted together right out of high school, you know; we've been in this same platoon ever since. He wanted to keep the three newbies together in 1st squad until the "wet behind the ears" dried up a little. But the lieutenant—that arrogant, clueless little shit they sent to replace Lieutenant Bode—seriously, they replaced a guy who earned a Silver Star with a guy who got fired from a desk job at Division Headquarters, and he came in straight away thinking he's gonna teach us how. Right. So dipshit sent one to each squad, instead. You can probably guess how that worked out. No wait, let me tell you.

Last night when we made the road back to camp and came to the outskirts of Bumblefuck here, BOOM! The shit just absolutely hit the fan. There was one big explosion and then it seemed like every AK-47 from here to Kabul opened up on us. I mean we were like in it for real. And where's the last of the new guys? Way back at the intersection of Last Week and What The Fuck. Harper yelled at me and motioned us on with the lieutenant, then turned and ran back through the shit to find 3rd squad. As soon as he disappeared into the smoke it was like someone turned up the volume and then the shit got heavy, like hornets swarming past to the *pop-pop-pop-pop-pop* of a couple dozen AK's. Just like that we were cut off, and stayed that way all goddam night. Nobody could raise Harper or Corporal Riggs on the radio. Aside from the two of them and the one new guy, Blinkin, whose name is actually Dietz, we had a handle on everyone else. But no one could figure out where they were or what exactly had happened. Aside from the close air support from a couple Cobra helicopter gunships, everything else was just fucked. The pot shots from snipers and flare ups from the zealously brave lasted until sunrise. At first light we came out, unopposed, to find the bodies. And we did.

Like I said, yesterday was easy. Today is a motherfucker.

The bodies were in a long stone hut near a riverbed that ran water only in the spring, and it might have provided easy cover if the odds weren't so overwhelming. Overwhelming was exactly the right word. It was me, the lieutenant, Lance Corporal Jasper from my squad, and the platoon radioman, Corporal Thompson, who went inside the hut while everyone else took up the perimeter. As my eyes adjusted to the darkness, shapeless lumps became dead people. There were seven. Two of them were Marines. The floor was sticky and slippery, and it was a moment before it occurred to me that this was from all the blood. I had thought the hut was some sort of work shed until we stepped inside. There were curtains folded back from the windows, a table, a throw rug in front of the door… this was someone's home.

"Where are their rifles?" said the lieutenant.

"Here's one," said Jasper. "Bolt's locked back." He nudged it with the barrel of his rifle. "Fucker's empty."

"Does it have a Sponge Bob sticker on the magazine well?" I said.

"No," said Jasper. "Ain't Sergeant Harper's."

"Corporal Riggs is over here," said the lieutenant. He was standing over three bodies lying near the wall. Riggs was between the other two with a bloodless gash along the side of his face from his temple to his chin, exposed white bone gleamed beneath.

"Empty AK over here," said Thompson. "Maybe the gunfight turned into a knife fight."

"Hand to fuckin' hand," said Jasper.

"Aye," said Thompson.

"No shit," said the lieutenant. "Jesus fuckin' Christ."

"Sergeant Harper," I said, looking down at his corpse.

"Fuck me to hell," said Jasper.

Harper's Ka-Bar was still in his hand. He was laid out on the floor so quietly still, arms and legs spread like wings, staring blankly up at the ceiling, his skin some opaque mushy plastic stretched across his face after bleeding out into the ever-darkening floor. His eyes were dull, the pupils beginning to cloud over. We all just sort of gathered over his body. The sight of him stunned me like a kick in the throat. It stunned every one. You could tell by the silence.

Up until this moment Sergeant Harper was, or seemed, immortal. The man survived shit that would have killed the rest of us—snipers, IEDs—and he had the purple hearts to prove it. But even now, even here in this shitty little tomb, there was still the hint of that grin—that sarcastic crooked assed grin—like even in death he had something on the rest of us. And maybe he did, because unlike the rest of us, he had faced his. So we stood there like a bunch of lost idiots and faced it, too, and I felt like fate was mocking us: "Here is your friend, here is your leader, here is your savior, who will help you now?"

I cannot say what everyone else was thinking, but we all stood there staring at him. There was nothing, just a desperate and sullen silence, and I listened carefully to that, until it seemed that the silence itself had a voice. But this was a trick of my mind, I knew, because I thought I really did hear a voice, whispering.

"It's okay, baby, shhh, shhh, they're just looking for food or something. They'll be gone in a minute. Shhh."

I looked around the room, at Thompson, at Jasper, both with quizzical expressions. I looked at the lieutenant. He looked back at me and squinted, like "What the hell?"

"Dietz," I said. I had been so shocked by Harper and Riggs that I didn't even notice the little fucker wasn't here. Stupid of me, I know.

"Dietz!" the lieutenant shouted. We listened. There was nothing.

Then we heard a sniff, from under the floor. Everyone looked down at their feet.

I saw the rug first; it was behind the lieutenant, a small dark oriental rug with fringe on the edges laying right where it served no purpose at all. I gestured at it with the barrel of my rifle. The lieutenant looked down at it, then back at me. Everybody was, like the Brits say, ready, steady- waiting for go. The lieutenant reached down and yanked the rug away. Sure as shit, there was a trap door. The lieutenant clenched his jaw, whispered through his teeth "Shit, shit, shit!" and the whole goddamned war rose up in my belly.

I knew, I just knew, that if Dietz was alive down there, that door was not booby trapped. I can't explain it. But I still used my left fucking arm. I reached down, grabbed the dirty knot of rope used for a handle, and yanked the door open. The lieutenant had his rifle pointed straight into a hole that went down at least six feet. I saw movement at the bottom and squeezed the slack out of my trigger. Something strange and familiar stopped me. At the bottom of the hole I saw an American uniform in a pile of shadows.

"Dietz," I said.

The lieutenant shit a flashlight from somewhere and illuminated the hole with bright and instantaneous daylight. I squinted, as much from the light as the sudden stench of rot and decay that came up from that hole. "Jesus," the lieutenant said and covered his mouth and nose in the crook of his elbow to filter the air.

Dietz was in a heap of bloody garbage at the bottom, one leg at odd angles, his uniform bloody, I mean soaked bloody. There was someone else down there too, but I couldn't tell who or what. There was just too much blood, and the sight of it so sudden, so vivid, the deepest, richest red that I have ever seen, and hope to God I'll never see again, ever, the essence of life itself pissing all of its glory into cold, dead earth.

The cries went up immediately, "Corpsman, up!" I couldn't tell you if it was me or the lieutenant or whoever that started it, but people were still yelling "corpsman up!" even after Doc's pudgy little ass came huffing through the door, his eyes rolling in their sockets, scrambling for information. He looked at the hole. He looked at the lieutenant. He looked at me. Then he looked at Harper and stopped, and the color drained from his face. He took a deep breath, moved toward us, and looked into the hole.

Doc did not look like much but he could go all day and night and had his shit wired as tight as anybody out here. Doc was usually the measure of reason. He looked up from that hole over at Harper, and back at me. I saw shadows across his face and the plea in his eyes, and I felt dizzy for a second, like the weight of the world had shifted, and I was off balance.

"Fuck," he said, and looked away.

In a moment he looked back into the hole. "What's that fuckin' stench?" he said. "And who is she?"

The other person down there with Dietz was a girl, her body ripped by gunfire, her dress stitched by a needle the size of my finger, and the life all drained out of her through the holes. She lay bloody and limp with Dietz, wrapped in his bloody arms. They laid there together in the bottom of that pit, in a bed of sand which their blood had soaked into the consistency of used coffee grounds. He kissed the side of her head.

"See baby?" His voice was sincere, like a promise. "I told you. They came for us."

He stroked her hair gently. His hand was so frail... so white... so....

"What?" He smiled." No baby, no, those are just stories... they told you to scare you, I told you about that. We're gonna go... to America. You'll see. It's just like I said."

I looked at the lieutenant. He looked back at me. It was the first time I ever saw him look scared. I had been waiting for the day when his cocky ass would see the light, and that day had come at last. Now we were finally gonna learn who he was. He looked back down into the hole. When he finally spoke, his voice had a strange tone, like he wasn't sure what he had to do.

"Dietz?" he said, hesitantly, like he wouldn't get an answer. Dietz moved a bit. "Dietz? Are you all right?"

"It's good," Dietz said weakly, the side of his face moving under the girl's dark matted hair, his voice a notch or two above a whisper. "She hid me down here... they stormed the house... she protected me. We don't speak... the same... but we understand... each other... like we can... read... minds... I can't really... feel my leg." Dietz was panting from the effort of talking. I figured somebody else was gonna have to tell him his girlfriend was dead. I was done processing shit when I saw Harper.

I did wonder exactly how the hell we were going to extract him from that hole. Nobody was going to jump down six feet to land on top of them. But you know how Doc gets when shit's bleeding—that's exactly what he did, landing like a cat, gingerly pulling the girl off Dietz. Her head rolled back and her mouth opened slightly, pink tongue hovering between pale lips, glassy eyes beneath pale slits of open eyelid. Doc noticed none of this. He had his head down, lifting.

"Here, Dev, get a hold here," he said. I laid my rifle beside me as I knelt down and reached my arms forward leaning into the stench of the hole. Doc had the girl by the bottom of the rib cage, lifting her, pushing her upward toward me in such a manner that I was able to grab her under the armpits.

"I've got her," I said.

"You've got her," he said, and let go. I lifted. She was pretty light, maybe fifty pounds at the most. I pulled her up out of the hole and cradled her in my arms, as if she had fallen asleep and I was putting her to bed. But she wasn't asleep, and the fifty pounds might as well have been an unruly sack of potatoes. I laid her on the floor, a little ways from the hole. Her blue dress was soaked in blood, as were her matching blue pants. It was odd she was actually dressed like a girl. I'd gotten used to seeing girls disguised as boys—that's how fucked this country is. Yet here she was, in a pretty blue dress. You'd think that the blood would have turned the blue cloth some pretty shade of purple, but it was all a brown, rusty-looking mess. The blue *chador*, the little head scarf which was tangled in her hair, wasn't as bloody. I pulled the *chador* free and used it to cover her face. I wasn't sure what else to do, and hoped it was enough. I wanted to feel bad for her. But you spend enough time in this country and see what happens to these kids... maybe whoever shot her did her a favor. Maybe not. Either way, those bullet holes were from an AK.

Doc, who was still in the hole plugging bleeding gashes in a mad effort to save what was left of Dietz's life, started screaming for a stretcher. I turned around. Jasper was at the door, repeating the call. Thompson had taken his radio off and was leaning into the hole helping Doc with something. And the lieutenant was standing above them, holding the flashlight like a nine year old. Like there was nothing better for him to do. Like there wasn't a war going on. Like there wasn't a whole passel of Marines outside waiting for him to make a decision and give an order. Like everyone in this town didn't know we would come for our dead. Like they hadn't been busy reloading. Like if we dicked around here much longer we weren't gonna wind up as dead as Harper and Riggs. I wanted to bust the side of his head open with the butt of my rifle.

The lieutenant looked at me, but if he could read what was on my mind, he didn't let on. At least he didn't react like someone accused of being an idiot who just got a bunch of people fucked up and killed, including Neville Harper.

No sooner than I had that thought, I got this creepy feeling crawling up my back and around my throat, and I saw that this was all an irreversible process; that we all had to take a turn, and now it was my turn. And what I had to do right then was stow that hate and anger somewhere. So I swallowed it. It was like a large stone in my throat, sliding down my gullet, pushing against my heart so it skipped a beat, forcing air out of my lungs. When it finally settled into the pit of my gut, as hard and heavy as an old cannon ball, it brought with it the end of everything I had ever been before. This was my war now, and I took it in hand.

"Sir, we got this," I said. "You've got more important shit to deal with. Lance Corporal Jasper, get that light for the Lieutenant."

"Here, sir," said Jasper, relieving him of the flashlight. The lieutenant looked back at me.

"Right, keep me posted, Sergeant Devin," he said. "Corporal Thompson, with me." Thompson looked at me and rolled his eyes. He turned toward the door to follow the lieutenant out. I stopped him.

"Hey T, we got a medevac inbound, right?" I said, quietly enough that the lieutenant wouldn't hear.

"Fuck me," said Thompson.

"That's on him. Do it bro."

"Aye, what the fuck," he said, pulling the handset to his ear, making the call as he walked out the door.

The stretcher bearers, two other corpsman, had come in and looked briefly around the room. One of them got caught up staring, at Harper, I'd guess. I had not looked back at him since we found Dietz, and I resisted the urge.

"Here," said Doc. "This is bad. OK. Now let me get under him."

The two of them squatted down on either side of the hole. With Doc lifting from the bottom and the two of them each grabbing hold under Dietz's armpits as Doc hefted his bloodied mass upward, they managed to pull him, with some good effort, slithering out of the hole. Dietz was so weak he could not scream, barely conscious, moaning violently through the short, torturous process. The corpsmen rolled him onto the stretcher as Doc climbed out of the hole.

"What about the girl," one of the corpsman said.

"She ain't ours and she's dead," said Doc.

This set Dietz off, and he started moaning again and tried to roll off the stretcher, but the corpsmen held him fast. There was blood oozing out of him everywhere and I wondered if he'd survive the medevac.

"Stick him, get some fluid in him," Doc said. "Help me secure this tourniquet." One of the corpsman isolated a vein in Dietz's less-bloody left arm and slipped the i.v. needle through the skin while Doc and the other corpsman stifled the bleeding as best they could. He was all bullet holes and shrapnel tears, like bloody ground beef. Doc had wrapped half of Dietz's left leg with Gorilla tape—that shit that makes duct tape seem like tissue paper—and left it at that. By the time they had him secured to the stretcher, he was unconscious but still breathing.

Thompson poked his head in the door and yelled "Bird on station!"

"Jasper," I said, motioning to the stretcher, "grab the other corner."

"On three," Doc said. "One, two..." He and the other corpsmen lifted the stretcher. Jasper was still bent over, waiting for "three." "You fuckers," he chuckled, lifting up his corner.

As they maneuvered Dietz out the door the air was filled with the *whap-whap-whap* of a large helicopter descending rapidly, the noise reverberating in the stone hut as it drew closer. The thrashing changed into a choppy whirring drone when the chopper settled to earth.

Inside the stone hut it seemed that the earth was spinning as well. My whole world slammed hard, autorotating down like a chopper that took a hit, smoke and fire, trying to pick a soft spot for a hard landing, and I spun completely around, the soles of my boots twisting against the floor, my knees crossing, until I plopped right down on my ass, cross-legged in the middle of the gory aftermath in that room, another checkpoint on a six-month long trail of carnage that was not about to stop any time soon, and surely not about to stop here. And I knew I had to check that shit right there.

I used my rifle like a cane to push myself up, and I stood, breathing heavily in the heat and closeness of the hut. It was like breathing cotton instead of air. I looked at the girl and then at Riggs and Harper as I worked to catch my breath. I walked across the room to where they lay. I wondered briefly if they got to speak, and ten thousand other things. I kneeled beside Harper, facing the door, and looked at his face, crooked grin, sharp nose, cloudy eyes. I felt burning in my forehead, pressure in my throat. Shit that must be checked, shit that must be stowed. I swallowed hard.

"Neville," I said. My own voice sounded strange, an alien sound in an alien universe, and it felt strange, pushing up out of my throat, a limp warble, meaningless. I never called him Neville. Nobody did. Not his wife, not even his parents.

"Nev," I said. It came out so naturally, so life-like that I almost expected him to roll his head over and look at me, the cloudiness in his eyes evaporating. He did not move.

"Dude," I tried again, "what happened?" I was more sure this time that there would not be an answer. That Nev would not look at me. That Nev would not speak. That Nev, in all finality, was gone.

I sat there, helpless, and glanced around the room, at everything, at nothing, taking it all in, sorting it all out. What seemed like a puzzle was really simple. Dietz was hurt and Nev and Riggs dragged him in here for cover, and the fight followed them. I figure the girl was here and got shot for helping them. Then the ammo ran out. Riggs was killed in the knife fight. Somewhere along the line Nev put Dietz in the hole with the girl. Nev covered it with the rug. Nev did everything he could think of to secure a dynamic battle scene and protect the newbie as best he could, and having accomplished that, laid himself down here and died.

Outside, the engines of the helo rolled up and the *whapping* became louder, more forceful. The rotors beat the air, and then dulled a bit as the bird began to lift. The beating mellowed and began to fade as the medevac lifted Dietz up and away, to triage, to the morgue, who knew at this point? Which was even better anymore?

I listened for a moment as the sound grew faint, a barely audible chopping fading in the distance. There would be other helicopters returning, coming for Nev and Riggs, bringing ammo, and more ammo. It was going to get busy around here, as if it hadn't been already. I stretched my hand over Nev's face, and set my palm against the cold white skin of his forehead, and just like they do in the movies, pushed his eyelids closed. As soon as I did, I remembered the day Lieutenant Bode, our original platoon commander, and Staff Sergeant Jackson, our original platoon sergeant, were killed by an IED, and Nev was the one pushing Jackson's eyes closed. That was three months ago. Nev became platoon sergeant and we got the boot lieutenant.

"I feel like I'm gonna puke," I said to Nev. "Dude, I'm here with a boot looey who's fucking up, and now he's scared, just like you said. And what do I say to the guys who came in with Dietz? They've been here three days. The platoon's ripping apart. What's my play?"

Nev, of course, just laid there. I looked over at Corporal Riggs. I hadn't noticed before, but the handle of Riggs' bayonet was stuck to the hilt in the chest of some bearded bastard lying next to him. For some reason it reminded me of King Arthur's sword *Excalibur* sticking up out of that rock.

"Look at that shit," I said to no one. The sound of the chopper had faded to nothing, and it seemed to take with it not only Dietz, but most of the heaviness in the room. Shit to be checked, shit to be done. I started going through Nev's pockets. I took the platoon sergeant's notebook out of his shirt pocket and put it in mine. I collected his valuables, his watch, his wallet, his bloodied Ka-Bar. It took me a long time before I could take the wedding ring off his finger. I knew Renee, and I knew I was going to have to call her. I had no idea what I was going to tell her. Shit to be stowed. I removed the ring.

There was a shadow in the door. Jasper came back inside.

"You OK, Sergeant Devin?"

"Just fuckin' peachy, Jaz."

"Shit's hittin' the fan out here," he said gesturing with his thumb behind him out the door.

I figured his eyes adjusted to the darkness in the hut because he took a couple steps forward. Either that or he got used to being creeped out again. "Hitting the fan how?" I said. I hadn't heard any gunshots.

"Battalion commander is pissed. The Skipper's moving the company forward. Looks like we're going into the ass kicking business."

"I'm OK with that."

Jasper was silent for a moment.

"Lieutenant's got the shakes pretty bad," he said.

"Well that's nice," I said. "Remember it's the first time he's seen his own wounded. Cut him some slack."

"Aye," Jasper said, and again fell silent. It was a moment before he spoke again. "So, uh, you in charge now?"

"You think somebody's in charge of this motherfucker?"

"You know what I mean," he said.

"Yeah," I said. I wanted another minute to not think about it. I looked at Nev again.

"You need to get out of here," Jasper said. "They'll take care of Sergeant Harper. I know he's your bud and all, but…"

"Yeah, you think?" I looked back at Jasper. "Who are the other two boots who came in with Dietz? Andrews and who?"

"PFC Redding."

"What do you think?" I asked as I stood up from the ground. I gathered myself, and put my helmet back on.

"Tell you the truth, Andrews's a space cadet," Jasper said. "Shoulda been in supply."

"Great. The other?"

"Redding's a nut job. Fits right in." Jasper grinned, for the first time since yesterday.

"How's that?" I said.

"Redding's taking a piss. Andrews taps him on the shoulder, being a smartass. Redding turns around pissing all over Andrews' trousers and says 'What?' We all about died."

I laughed, but as quickly as it happened I felt guilty about it, I think because of Nev lying there like that. It creeped me out for a second, that I could laugh, but I shook it off.

"We've got to regroup," I said. "I'm giving you the squad and both of them. Keep them alive."

"You fucker," Jasper said. "I don't want to run anything but my mouth."

"That's Sergeant Fucker to you," I said. "And you're welcome."

"Platoon Sergeant Fucker," Jasper said, and laughed. His laughing was good, and it grounded me.

"Where they at now?" I said.

"Sitting outside where you left them, baking like little cupcakes, being afraid."

"Let's go fix that." I said, wrapping my head hard around what needed to be done. "Back my play."

"Aye," Jasper said, and followed me through the door.

Outside the whole bright sunny world was winding down from having yet another day. The sun was creeping down the last of its path to the far horizon. It would get cooler, then cold. We would freeze, and then those of us who were still here tomorrow would bake again.

There were vehicles moving, trucks, helicopters in the air, Marines digging in. One of the machine guns had been set up in the hollow corner of a broken stone wall overlooking the intersection where I had left the new guys, and they were still there. At least they had stayed put. Jasper followed me, trudging across the sand. We squatted with the others behind the wall.

"How you guys holding up?" I said.

"I'm OK, Sergeant," said Redding. "How's PFC Dietz? We saw when they brought him out."

"Hey, is Sergeant Harper really dead?" said Andrews.

I wanted to punch him in the face, but I stowed that shit again.

"Yes," I said, listening to the words come out of my mouth. "Sergeant Harper is dead. Your boy Dietz on the other hand..." I wanted to puke. I took a deep breath and forced the words. "Your boy Dietz is fucked up, bleeding like a stuck pig. But he's still alive. If you guys are half as tough as that little fucker you'll do all right. What went down in there went down hard, I won't lie to you. Ka-Bars and bayonets. Dietz went down swinging. He went down like a Marine. That's who he is. I expect no less out of either of you. You copy?"

"Yes, sergeant," they said, almost in unison.

"Now you know Lance Corporal Jasper here. He's your new fairy godmother. You stick to him like dogshit. He's always on top of the game. Right?"

I looked at Jasper who was nodding, staring at the ground, trying to look serious. And his face busted into that big stupid-assed grin, for the second time today. For a moment I thought that maybe, just maybe, we were gonna be all right. But that didn't really matter either, because it can't. When shit really matters, people have something to lose. People with something to lose live in fear. It never gets any better after that. Take a look around.

"All right," I said. "Coffee break's over. Let's get back to work."

# An Unlawful Order—Chapter 1

★ ★ ★

*Tracy Crow*
*aka Carver Greene*

Captain Chase Anderson was running along her favorite stretch of the base, glancing from time to time at the emerald, fluted Koolau mountain range. A windward gust off the Pacific, chilly even for October, surprised her, knocking her slightly off balance. She'd been too up in her head, distracted by her conversation with Stone. Since his death, she'd become addicted to running. Three-mile runs had extended to five, sometimes six. Once, she'd run nearly nine miles before realizing she would be late for her staff meeting with the general. She had called Sergeant North from her cell phone for a ride back. Lately, since Molly had started kindergarten, Chase found she had so much to tell Stone about all he was missing. So she ran. To an outsider, she might have appeared to be in training for a marathon. To those who knew better, she was running from grief. Chase was, however, running for her life— and for the only life she had left with Stone.

Today, she'd logged two miles, barely time enough to break a sweat, and was telling Stone about how Molly wanted to dress as a hula dancer for Halloween when Sergeant North showed up, slowing the military sedan to a crawl in the middle of the road. Chase ran in place, giving North time to lower the window. Behind his aviator sunglasses and the tease of a new mustache, North looked more like a police officer pulling over a hitchhiker. "Sorry, Captain," he shouted above the whirring of a helicopter now overhead in approach of the flight line. "We've got a crash."

Chase jumped inside the sedan and reached over a shoulder for the seatbelt as North made a wide U-turn for the office. "What's down?"

"Another 81, ma'am."

"Damn it," she said, and slapped the dash. The day she had learned of Stone's helicopter crash in Afghanistan, she was running within the perimeter of a desert tent city on the outskirts of Baghdad, daydreaming about him and Molly, when the colonel who was head of Public Affairs flagged her down. The combination of the news and heat had nearly caused her to vomit on the colonel's boots. Instead, she'd climbed into the colonel's Humvee and focused on the horizon the way she'd learned to do to combat seasickness aboard a ship.

"The media?"

"MPs at the gate are holding two crews already." Thanks to the media and their police scanners, bad news traveled fast.

The Marine-81 was their workhorse—and their problem child. Stone's crash, though, had been "downed by enemy fire," according to the investigation. These days, especially after the crash that killed the four National AeroStar executives, headquarters in DC was fielding lots of questions from the media about the helicopter's flightworthiness and about the new defense contracts for additional 81s. The crash that killed the executives was blamed on a faulty swash- plate duplex bearing, the part that changes the angle and tilt of the rotor blades. Headquarters grounded the fleet for a while, and the problem was supposedly corrected.

"Crash site?"

North nodded toward the ocean. "Five miles out. Another routine training exercise."

"Is there any other kind?" She glanced toward the placid Pacific.

"Colonel Farris is standing by for your call," North said and leaned over her lap for the glove box, retrieving a small notebook and pen that he held against the steering wheel while she scanned through her cell phone directory for Farris's number.

"The pilot?"

"No names yet, ma'am,"

The 81 squadron was Stone's last squadron, so Chase knew most of the pilots; some better than others. Some she knew only through their wives. As she waited for Farris to answer, her thoughts raced ahead to the women who, on this October Saturday morning, were most likely in the middle of their weekly shopping runs to the commissary or cheering their kids through the soccer tournament at the base field. Everyone so unassuming, just as she had been nine months ago before learning the news about Stone's crash. Even this morning, she'd awakened listening for the familiar rattling of his golf clubs she'd heard him retrieve from the closet by the front door so many times. She used to know by the zipping and unzipping of golf bag compartments—part of a checks-and-balances system her husband had put in play to account for tees, balls, a glove, even dimes to mark his ball on the greens—that it was sunrise without opening her eyes. Stone had always been an early riser. His body had an internal clock set for six, no matter the time they went to bed, no matter the time of actual sunrise.

The call to Farris dropped. Typical. Cellular service on the base was spotty thanks to radio interference between pilots and the tower. She tried again. This time Colonel John "Flyboy" Farris, Stone's former squadron commander, answered before the end of the first ring. His voice sounded measured, controlled, the way hers was, too, during one of these situations. The meltdown would come in private, much later. She asked the usual questions and jotted his answers into the notebook: nineteen dead, no survivors, routine training exercise with the Navy.

"Sir, the names?"

"The Chaplain's Office is making notification this minute." She detected hesitation in the long pause that followed. Finally, "The pilot was Tony White."

Three months before Stone's deployment to Afghanistan, the general had ordered Chase to arrange a dog-and-pony show for the media to prove Marines had confidence in their 81. White had been the pilot. Even then, Stone had objected to her flying in the 81, and they had argued. Arguments had become their norm then. Since reuniting after their first Middle East tour, Stone had become super protective of her and Molly. Never mind that Chase had been in combat herself, outside of Fallujah. Since their return from the Middle East, Chase couldn't go to the PX without Stone checking on her.

"Skipper," Farris said, "I trust you'll handle this delicately." *Skipper* was the nickname for the rank of captain and generally used to convey a sense of familiarity, which told her Farris was reaching for an ally. As squadron CO, he knew which fingers would be pointing toward his pilot and crew and who would be questioning his leadership. Colonel Flyboy Farris had another fine mess on his hands, and Chase was swelling with sympathy.

"By all means, sir."

Harry Truman once said the Marines had a propaganda machine nearly as good as Stalin's. As a public affairs officer, Chase was never more aware of her role in disseminating that propaganda than in the moments following a helicopter crash. At twenty-nine, her job for seven years had been to tell the Marine Corps story in ways that were sure to increase recruitment and retention. Therefore, all accidents happened during routine training exercises; all accidents were under military investigation; all names were withheld pending notification of next of kin; and all other information was deemed "inappropriate for comment," the Defense Department's kinder, gentler approach to *No comment.*

Back in her office, Chase zipped up a flight suit and laced her boots. She had wanted a shower, but there was no time. According to North, all the local media were now waiting at the gate for her statement, and the wire services were expecting callbacks. In the small mirror of the wardrobe, she checked her reflection. After Stone's death, she'd chopped off her long dark hair for a cut with a more utilitarian purpose, but she hadn't returned in months for a trim. She tucked the unruly pieces behind her ears and up into her cap. Her face was still flushed from the run and, judging from her heart rate, from having to face the media. She considered calling in the others on her staff, but Cruise was hosting a birthday party for her son at the Koolau Ranch, which was where Molly was as well, and Staff Sergeant Martinez and his wife, if they'd kept their plans, were sightseeing on the big island. Lieutenant Thompson had deployed a few weeks earlier, and his replacement hadn't been named as of yet. The others, two Pfcs and a lance corporal, were too green to call.

Today's tragedy would have to be hers and North's to manage. Nothing new. They'd been a team for years. Sergeant Harrison North was also twenty-nine and had joined the Marines a week after graduating from high school. The added years of experience he had on Chase made him appear older, or so Stone had said during the only conversation they'd had about North's infatuation for her. Why did it have to be infatuation, she'd asked Stone one evening while putting away the dishes after dinner, when a man followed a woman into combat and something altogether different for those who followed a man? "Human nature," Stone had said, handing her a stack of warm plates from the dishwasher. "I can't speak for women, but a man can't be that close to a woman without thinking about her sexually." She could have said the same held true for women, but Stone would have continued to unfairly suspect North when the suspicions belonged elsewhere.

Chase slipped on her dog tags and tucked the cold metal beneath her T-shirt. "Okay, North," she called out. North knocked anyway before entering and handed over a draft of a media release. He set the three-inch binder containing their entire file on the 81 on the single empty corner of her desk.

"Next of kin?"

"Notifications still being made, ma'am."

She read over the release, mentally checking off time, date, and place. She rang up headquarters, and Major O'Donnell, the G-1 officer for General Hickman, answered. "This is what we get for coming in this weekend to catch up on paperwork," he teased.

"No rest for the wicked, sir." They'd known each other since their combat tour in Iraq, and O'Donnell's had been the first familiar face she'd seen in Hawaii.

"General Hickman's on the line with Colonel Farris," he said. "I'll notify him you're holding."

Brigadier General "Wild Bill" Hickman was not the first Marine Chase had had to win over. He was a Desert Storm veteran who had the distinction of having flown more combat missions than any pilot on active duty and he'd made it clear he didn't have much use for female Marines. He let her get halfway through the reading of the news release before he interrupted. "MPs tell me the gate's overrun with media. Who told them about the crash?" At the accusatory tone, she instinctively glanced up at North who was now standing in front of her desk, awaiting her next order.

"Most likely they picked it up from scanners, sir—"

North read the situation and rolled his eyes. She continued, "I understand they were at the gate before my office was even notified."

There was a click, and it took a moment to register that the general had actually hung up on her. "I'll take that as a yes on the statement," she said, dropping the phone in the cradle and forcing a smile as North held out a wad of pink telephone message slips.

"He's a piece of work—"

Chase held up a hand to stop him. She took several of the phone messages for herself and handed back the rest. "Remember, don't let these guys draw you into any speculation about the 81 or the cause of the crash. And hurry. They're waiting for us at the gate."

"Aye-aye, ma'am." North excused himself and disappeared into his office. A few seconds later, he was identifying himself as a Marine with Public Affairs who was calling with a media release about a helicopter crash. At times, their voices broke into unison during the reading of the release; other times, a morbid musical round.

She finished her calls first and flipped through the folder North had prepared to the page buried in the back, the list of dead Marines, the top of the list for the name of the pilot: Major Anthony White; 33; home-of-record: Chevy Chase, Maryland; next-of-kin: Kitty White, 2 children.

She didn't know Major White other than the time she'd flown with him, at least not in the sense of knowing that brings shock and grief. General Hickman had instructed her to orchestrate a media day for the 81. Her job, as Hickman put it, had been to *show them we're not afraid to fly in the damn thing*. Chase and her staff invited local and national media to ride aboard an 81 during a training exercise that would demonstrate just how efficient the helicopter was at lifting heavy equipment such as trucks and howitzers.

The night before the media circus, however, Stone could no longer hide his true fears about her flying in an 81. How often she looked back on that argument, replaying it word for word, with the sense that Stone had foreshadowed his own fatal crash. "They should ground the entire fleet," he had said that night, pacing the kitchen, "until they can figure out what's wrong with the swash-plate bearing." Chase had been stir-frying vegetables in the wok. She pressed a foot on the lever of the garbage can and tossed in the spines of red and green pepper. Ginger, sesame oil, and soy sauce were filling up the kitchen and making her eyes water. She had glared at Stone and nodded toward Molly, who was coloring in a book at the kitchen table, and Stone had dropped the subject until the next morning.

Since their return from the Gulf, and on learning six months later that Stone was headed back for a second tour, he had vacillated between an almost cavalier lack of concern for her and Molly to one of over concern. He had never been one to resent her status as a military officer, not like other husbands they knew with military wives. But nothing had been the same since they'd been torn apart for that year. Then again, few Marines on the base had returned from this war unscathed. Any hint of post-traumatic stress disorder grounded a pilot indefinitely. She had stopped attending the wives' club events because the air was too thick with denial.

Stone's solution had been to drink—when he wasn't scheduled to fly. Chase came to prefer the evil of his flying to the evil of his drinking. What had started with a beer or two every night led to his hitting the hard stuff they stored in the small cabinet above the refrigerator for the friends who used to drop by. During his first tour, Stone had lost his best friends when the 81 he was flying went down in a hard landing on the desert floor. His crew chief, Mouse, and copilot, Hammer, had been like brothers. The bird had bumped hard and flipped on its side, Mouse and Hammer's side. Chase had tried often to talk to Stone about survivor's guilt, but his eyes would dim. The one night she suggested he talk to a doctor, he had thrown a glass so hard into the kitchen sink that it shattered, sending glass clear across the kitchen. He had crunched across the shards on the way to the front door. How Molly had slept through it all, she couldn't imagine. Maybe the poor child had been so frightened, she just pretended to sleep.

The way Chase had seen it, Stone would eventually fail the flight exam. His blood alcohol level would be too high, and then what? What scared Chase most was her fear about whether she'd still love Stone if he were grounded. More than anything, she hated the stigma of failure in any form, and she hated herself for thinking she might not have it within her to love him enough in his weakest moment.

But on the morning of the media day, Stone had again tried to talk her out of flying with Major White. He had been guiding Molly out the door and to the car for the ride to preschool and whispering over the little girl's head, "You're really going to do this?" Chase had nodded and gone about buckling Molly into the backseat, breathing in the cloud of baby shampoo and mint toothpaste. When she straightened, Stone was still standing in the driveway behind her. Chase cinched her robe. "You do this to me every time you fly, you know."

"At least I have some control—" And he had stopped. Everyone knew helicopter pilots rarely survived a crash. In an Officers' Club on a Friday night, drunken pilots might even joke about feeling expendable. Surprising how many people assumed that when a helicopter failed it simply rotored on down. Truth was, it fell with the aerodynamics of a grand piano.

"White's a good pilot," Stone had stammered. Chase lifted on her toes to kiss him, but he turned away, muttering as he walked to the driver's side of their Jeep, "You'll be fine."

That morning, General Hickman hadn't shown up for the flight. Neither had Colonel Farris, but the assistant secretary of the Navy was there to show the Pentagon's support for the helicopter. Even a National AeroStar executive showed up. Hickman had pull when he wanted to use it.

While the mechanics, copilot, and crew chief were making preflight checks that morning, reporters and their photographers had nervously joked about karma and about how they'd all be different sorts of newsmakers that evening if the helicopter crashed. Maybe White had heard all this. He was zipped into a flight suit, helmet swinging by one hand when he walked over from the bird. He polled the group for how many had flown in a helicopter. Besides the Pentagon official and the guy from National AeroStar, only Chase and Paul Shapiro with the *Honolulu Current* newspaper raised their hands. White had broken into a smile, clearly loving all this. With his helmet resting against his left hip under the weight of an arm, Major Tony White exhibited a quiet confidence. He spouted stats about the 81 and about how vital the bird had been during Desert Storm and current Middle East operations. He confessed his number of missions, smiling through it all, and Chase had appreciated how his confidence calmed everyone's nerves, including hers.

A few minutes later, the group ran behind her, hunched under the spinning blades. She paused outside the bird until everyone had climbed aboard, then signaled a thumbs-up to White. Inside, the crew chief was passing around headsets. She had reached overhead for hers, heard the crackling of air broken into bits of chatter between White and the tower, and then the nose of the bird lifted. When the theme song for *Hawaii 5-0* filtered through their headsets, the spread of smiles, thigh slapping, and thumbs-up gestures had filled her with assurance for positive press coverage. And the rest of the trip couldn't have gone better. Major White had acted as if he were a paid tour guide, pointing out Diamond Head and the house portrayed in the television series *Magnum, P.I.* and hovering over Sacred Falls for photographs of the breathtaking eighty-seven foot wall of water that belonged to a beloved part of Hawaiian folklore. He had flown low over the canyon where *Jurassic Park* had been filmed, and then he'd flown over the Dole Plantation, pointing out the world's largest maze. Next came a fly-over of Pearl Harbor. *Yes, the positive press for this dog-and-pony show,* she'd thought, *will be well worth all the hassle with Stone.*

Chase stared at White's name on the list. She couldn't conjure much more about the man other than the charm he'd affected over the media those months earlier. What she could conjure, however, was the face of a woman in a crisp photograph Major White had wedged into the corner of his curved windshield just after Chase had given him the thumbs-up for take-off. There wasn't anything particularly unique about the woman. She was pretty enough, with regular features and dark hair. It was the idea of the woman, Kitty White, there in her husband's cockpit that had caused Chase to make a mental note of asking Stone whether he flew with a photograph of her, or of her and Molly. And if so, why? Sure, she wanted to think of herself as being there with him always, but not when he flew. He needed a clear head for flying, one for the ethereal side of life, not the earthbound one. But in the flurry of the media circus and its heady aftermath of accolades; Chase had forgotten to ask Stone.

Now Major White was dead, and the photo of his wife, Kitty, lost at sea.

North appeared in Chase's doorway with an armful of media releases and the car keys. Halfway down the stairwell to the lobby, they heard a pounding on the locked front door.

"What the—?" North raced ahead as if to preempt whatever danger might befall his officer. By the time Chase reached the lobby, he had already unlocked the glass door and was ushering in the woman who looked as if she'd just climbed out of Major White's photo.

"I've seen you on TV," the woman said to Chase. "You're taller in person."

The woman in her jeans, flip-flops, and white tank wasn't dressed at all the way an officer's wife was expected to dress outside her home. Yet under these circumstances, who could blame her?

"I'm Captain Anderson," Chase said, "and this is Sergeant North." The woman pressed a bony hand into Chase's but ignored Sergeant North's.

"I'll get the car," North muttered, and then sprinted down the sidewalk toward the parking lot.

Chase hadn't noticed the purse in Mrs. White's hand until the woman pulled the strap over a shoulder and unzipped the bag. "I know there's been a crash," she said, "an 81."

Chase silently cursed the media and their scanners. "Yes," she said, glancing out the window. North had parked the car at the end of the sidewalk and was running around to the passenger door to open it for her. She willed herself to look stoically back at Mrs. White. In seven years, Chase had tap-danced her way through dozens of press conferences, soft-shoeing past the questions that might have landed the Marine Corps before a Senate hearing, but never had she faced this situation. It wasn't as though she wasn't used to hearing from the next-of- kin. After all, whenever a helicopter went down, it seemed every mother of a Marine tearfully called Chase's office and every other Public Affairs office in the country, even if her Marine was stationed a thousand miles from the scene of the accident. Now that the Associated Press had been notified, she knew the voice mail would be full by the time she and North returned. They would have to refer the anxious mothers to the Chaplain's Office. But here was Major White's next-of-kin in person. Chase's face was growing hotter. She knew she was sweating. She nodded toward North in the parking lot.

"They're waiting for me at the front gate."

Mrs. White seemed awfully young to be the mother of two children, one a preteen, but she had the dried out look of someone who had spent too much time on Waikiki. When she began rifling through her purse, her hair fell across her face. "It's Tony, isn't it?" she said, behind the heavy curtain of hair. Chase resisted the impulse to tuck it behind an ear.

She'd never had patience for someone whose eyes she couldn't see when talking to them.

North was still waiting beside the open door of the sedan. "I'm sorry," Chase said, "but all names are pending release until the next of kin have been notified." The woman was still rifling through her purse. "I really need to go," Chase added.

"No, wait," the woman said, grabbing Chase's wrist, fingernails pinching flesh.

Funny how many thoughts can speed through the mind in less than a second. Maybe it was true what people said about how your whole life flashed in front of you before you died. Had Stone's before his crash? It wasn't as if Chase felt in this moment she were about to die, but Mrs. White's fingernails digging deeper and deeper were causing Chase to imagine Major White's last seconds. The photograph of this woman flashed through her mind. She saw the background behind the woman's face and imagined it being taken on that stretch of Perimeter Road where the jungle creeps down the cliff to the shore...or was that a photograph Stone had taken of her and Molly before his deployment, the one still under a magnet on the refrigerator door? Chase imagined White's eyes fixed on this woman's face, this face before her now, as he and his bird fell from the sky like a stone. Chase pulled against the woman's hold.

"You need to go home, Mrs. White."

"I'm not—you've got it all wrong," she said. The woman twisted Chase's wrist and wedged a set of dog tags onto her palm. "I think his kids should have these." Releasing Chase's wrist, the woman stormed off toward the parking lot.

Chase was still staring at Major White's dog tags when she and North pulled up to the front gate. When the MP, a young female corporal, saluted, Chase returned the salute, and slipped the dog tags into the breast pocket of her flight suit as North steered the car to the shoulder. Reporters were milling about, some talking on cell phones. Paul Shapiro, with the *Current,* spotted their car and was already walking toward them with his long spindly legs, easily ahead of the pack. He looked about the same age as she, maybe a year or so older. He was newly assigned as the paper's military beat reporter. North slowed the sedan to a stop, and Shapiro walked around to Chase's door.

"Jackals," North whispered as Chase opened the door.

Shapiro shouted above the noise of a news helicopter that was flying overhead in small circles like a bird trying to catch the thermals. "Is it true, Captain Anderson? Another 81?"

The others were catching up and shouting, "Are there plans to ground the 81?"

"Are there any survivors?"

"How many casualties?"

"Do you have the names?"

Chase held up a hand and waved everyone toward the base's welcome sign. "Let's do this once," she said. Reporters signaled to their photographers who had been capturing images of a larger-than-usual Saturday morning anti-war protest. The protestors were hamming it up, hoisting anti-war signage and shouting chants she refused to decipher.

When they were finally gathered in a semicircle around her, Chase read North's media release, punctuating *routine training exercise*, *under investigation*, and *names being withheld pending notification of next of kin*. She asked for questions: She always did, though everyone knew by now she had nothing more she could add other than general statistics about the helicopter. Paul Shapiro blurted, "Can you confirm Major Anthony White as the pilot?"

"I cannot."

"Is that a denial?" Shapiro was glaring.

"That's neither a denial nor a confirmation, Paul."

His pen hovered above his pocket-sized spiral notebook. "I have it on good authority that the major was drinking in a bar off base last night, Captain. Any comment?"

The urge to tap her breast pocket for assurance of Major White's dog tags was nearly impossible for Chase to suppress. The reporters, who had been scribbling furiously after Shapiro mentioned Major White, looked up as if Chase had commanded them to do so. For a second, she feared they could see through the pocket of her flight suit at the imprinted information on the dog tags that included Major White's full name, social security number, O-positive blood type, and Catholic religious affiliation.

"It would be inappropriate," she said, willing herself to look relaxed before the cameras, "for me to comment on anything beyond our statement at this point."

"You Marines," Shapiro said, shaking his head, "always taking care of your own."

Chase pretended not to hear the comment and waved for North who was standing off camera. "Pass out the info sheet on the 81."

At home that evening, an exhausted Chase whipped up waffle batter while Molly worked out arithmetic problems at the kitchen table. Since when were kindergartners expected to know addition? Chase wondered, *What's left for first grade?* "Try not to use your fingers, sweetie." Molly tucked both hands behind her back and searched the ceiling as if she expected the answer for two-plus-one to materialize there. Chase chopped three round slices of banana and set them in front of her daughter. "Watch this," she said, sliding two slices a good distance across the glass tabletop from the other one. "Two—plus one, right?"

Molly nodded. "So, count the slices. What's the answer?" Molly smiled, showing off two rows of pretty white baby teeth.

"Three."

Chase smiled. "You want bananas or blueberries in your waffle?"

"Blueberries, please."

Molly always chose blueberries, just as Stone would have. Chase preferred bananas and pecans. Waffles had become their Saturday night tradition since Stone's passing. When Stone was alive, the tradition of waffles on Sunday morning had been his doing, his treat to his girls, he'd say. Molly was too young to remember any of that, and Chase too respectful to encroach on what had been his precious territory. Since she was home every Saturday night anyway, she'd altered the routine. Molly thought it special to have breakfast for dinner.

Darkness came early to this side of Oahu, even earlier this time of year. The sliding glass door was open, letting in the cool breeze. Normally she enjoyed the music of wind in the palm fronds, but given the events of the day, she thought the sound mournful, lonely. Poor Kitty White, no doubt this minute surrounded by a throng of sympathetic officers' wives, unless she was heavily sedated in bed. Other more fortunate wives would look after Kitty's children tonight and in the days leading to the memorial service. Kitty would have the rest of her life to deal with being a single parent, just as Chase had.

She turned on the small television mounted under a cabinet and channel-surfed to the local news station, then thought otherwise. Molly didn't need to hear her mother talking about a helicopter crash. She found a cartoon channel instead. Molly looked up from her homework and smiled, causing Chase's heart to lurch. Molly was the ultra-feminine version of her father.

Later, after the waffles and the dishes, after Molly's bath and storytelling time, Chase curled up in Stone's recliner in the den and pulled her mother's crocheted afghan over her lap. She waited for the eleven o'clock news. She was holding White's dog tags. She didn't know why. Her fingers hypnotically traced the grooves of punched tin. If Stone would only walk through that front door, she thought. "So sorry about Tony White," she would say.

When her face appeared on the television screen, Stone would say, "You look good, baby."

Just then, a camera cut to the mob of anti-war protestors. An off camera reporter asked a woman to comment on the helicopter crash and the nineteen dead Marines. "I only feel bad for their families—I mean, who's thinking about the families in Iraq? Nineteen fewer baby killers, if you ask me—"

If Stone were here, she thought, he'd ask about the dog tags. "They're Major White's—given to me this afternoon by a woman—not the major's wife." And Stone would probably say something like, "Tony was a good pilot before Iraq. Too many close calls—and you know how they treat an officer who can't keep his family life together."

"So you think this investigation will reveal pilot error instead of something mechanical?" Stone would defend his friend. *Engine failure, probably. Over open water, so who knows?* Maybe he would add, *I was a good pilot, Chase.* Stone, the combat helicopter pilot. Stone, the rock of her life, that is, until his drinking. Now—Stone who had fallen from the sky.

"I never got your dog tags," she would say to Stone if he were here. "And I can't give Tony's dog tags to Kitty. She doesn't need to know her husband apparently had a mistress."

"Best to let everyone believe they were lost at sea," she could hear him say, and he would be right.

Chase climbed out of his recliner and shuffled to the kitchen. When she reached the garbage can, she pressed the foot lever and gave one final squeeze before Major White's dog tags slipped from her hand, like a burial at sea.

# KILL BOX

★ ★ ★

*Jack King*

His plane soaring through a clear night sky above a country he would never set foot in, Doug Davidson (Double-D to his friends) was focused on the moon. His cockpit was in a rectangular room in the basement of Building 1304 at Nellis Air Force Base, Nevada, while his plane, a Reaper unmanned aerial vehicle (or UAV), was 17,000 feet above Kandahar, Afghanistan. His console was made to resemble a cockpit with a control stick and throttle and multiple displays showing the instruments. The center screen displayed the forward camera in the nose cone of the UAV. A half-moon hung above the mountains to the east and night shrouded the landscape below. Under different circumstances he would've considered it beautiful; the lack of lights from civilization made the land appear black as a bottomless abyss, and the cloudless sky glowed with the kind of brilliant starlight he'd never seen with his own eyes. Beneath the UAV hung a cluster of sensors with acronyms like FLIR and SAR, acronyms which sounded to Double-D like exotic venereal diseases rather than sensitive electronic equipment. The screens to his left and right showed the world through light-sensitive lenses, infrared imagery, and computer-generated topography, revealing miles of open scrubland with the occasional clusters of colored yellow and red blobs which marked the heat signatures of living things.

"This is Delta Two One Nine," he said, broadcasting to everyone on duty. "The skies are clear."

Technology had become his friend despite his inability to understand its peculiarities. He could not, for instance, hyperlink within e-mail, or transfer files between folders, and if someone asked his IP address, he was just as likely to provide the serial number to his monitor as anything else. And yet technology had given him the chance to fly, years after retiring.

Double-D had been trained on the flight systems for a number of UAVs. As an operator (not *pilot*, because pilot was reserved for those who sit in actual airplanes) his job mostly entailed patrolling the skies and recording video for later analysis. Even as a contractor he was responsible for providing the occasional close air support for soldiers in the field, and today was such a day. The shift commander, Major Keller, had asked all operators to track the movement of a combat patrol returning from a mission in the foothills that bordered Pakistan.

Double-D's headset squawked to life and Isaac, the mission's operation specialist (seated ten feet away), spoke in an apathetic tone that more befitted late night talk show radio hosts than a surveillance operator. "Delta Two One Nine, this is Delta Four Five Five. I'm tracking the package"—a phrase which meant Isaac had sight of the combat patrol. Isaac read off a series of coordinates, and Double-D banked his UAV to the east. He sometimes caught himself leaning with the control stick, as if he could feel the momentum of the plane as the horizon on the camera tilted.

As he watched the distance to target tick off, his hands began to shake with a kind of anticipatory dread of what was to come. From the first time his father took him to the air and space museum, Double-D had dreamed of slicing through the skies in fighter jets. A swimming incident when he was ten rendered him unsuitable. His older brother held him beneath the surface of Grove Park Swim Club's largest pool on a cloudless June day, held him until Double-D released his grip on a glow-in-the-dark pirate ship he'd found in a cereal box that morning. Unconsciousness left him with an inner-ear condition, and when he failed the g-force test in flight training, he was deemed unsuitable to pilot large and expensive fighter jets, but perfectly suited to pilot cargo planes filled with large and expensive equipment. The world, as he knew it, was filled with these kinds of ironies.

"They're at it again," Delmar Garcia (Delta One Eight One) said. His operator station was on the far side of the room, but his UAV was in the patrol box that bordered Double-D's. Delmar's internal radar seemed tuned to find trouble. The man had no filter and had, in the past year, identified and recorded and reported on several dozen couples engaged in (as he put it on the official reports) fornication. The list included an interlude between a man and a goat. Most recently, he had identified a group of women who bathed by moonlight, which sounded alluring until Double-D learned the women were of an age when gravity had begun to take effect on loose skin and breast. This didn't seem to bother Delmar in the slightest.

"Check it," Delmar said, broadcasting his main camera to everyone.

Double-D couldn't help but switch his main display over. He saw a zoomed-in riverbank, the green-scale screen capturing the barest hint of light and amplifying it until every wrinkle, every hair, every scab, and every bruise were visible in detail he could do without. The women stood together in waist-high water, their clothes spread out on nearby rocks.

"I bet they were hotties in their day," Delmar said.

"Dude," Isaac said, "you need counseling or something."

"I feel like I'm watching my grandmother," Ron Beller (Delta Four Five Five) said.

"But you're *watching*," Delmar said.

Double-D switched his main camera back to his own UAV. "What the hell do you get out of that?" he asked.

"Women bathing? That's hot no matter how old," Delmar said. "It's the kind of thing that makes you realize men have nipples, too."

Isaac said, "I can't even begin to tell you how wrong that is."

"You didn't have to look, but you did," Delmar said.

No filter, no restraint. Delmar had been reported and written up and reprimanded, and Double-D didn't understand how the man still had a job.

Focusing on his instrument panel, Double-D noted his fuel level was sufficient to last another twenty hours, well into the next operator's shift. For seven months, he flew patrols inside his box—

the map coordinates that marked off the airspace he was responsible for. His box was a cube in the same way an egg was a sphere. It came to a sharp point at the Afghanistan/Pakistani border, sloped down at an angle to the south, and then swung west along a lonely stretch of road for two hundred miles before connecting northward following a rugged line through the mountains. Within this patrol box were several dozen villages and two towns (which were identical to villages with the distinction that they had a well and a road). In the villages and towns were several dozen people. Double-D preferred to view them through the infrared camera which displayed vaguely human-shaped blobs of red and yellow. Even though he could use high-fidelity lenses to pick out faces, he vastly preferred the thermal imaging because it allowed his imagination to fill in the missing details. Double-D had come to recognize heat signatures of individuals and could pick them out as they farmed and hunted, repaired buildings, held parties, ate, slept, and carried on with their lives. It was like watching his son's ant colony, and gave him a godlike sense of power. He invented names and stories for them. The fat blob in East Village became George, and his daughter Lisa was sneaking off to see Bernard late at night. The blobs of Hector and Richard were always arguing nose to nose, until one day Hector knocked Richard down and he didn't get up again for many hours. Double-D thought it might have something to do with goats, because Hector gave Richard's family two goats and the arguing stopped. Twice a month, men from a village in the north would come and everyone would dance around bonfires late into the night.

Double-D snapped to attention when Isaac announced: "I have eyes on a target moving to intercept the package." He relayed a grid references to all of the UAV pilots on shift.

"Copy that," Double-D said. His pulse fired up and his hands became instantly sweaty. He closed his eyes and recited the phrase he'd learned in flight school: *maintain an even strain, maintain an even strain*. A simple rhyme to calm nerves and ease tensions.

Sometimes it would even work.

He swung his UAV lower and closer to the Pakistani border

where the land was broken by rugged and rocky ground. The group of colored blobs he'd identified as the combat patrol was following another group of colored blobs. His main display captured faces and analyzed them and identified several POIs, or Persons of Interest, which could mean anything from confirmed terrorists to people who threw shoes at political figures. The computer wasn't specific. "Positive match on targets," he said. "I have POIs inside the kill box."

Moments later, the view crackled with flaring white pops that designated muzzle flashes—weapons were being fired.

The most troubling thing about viewing combat through the lens of a UAV was the loss of senses. You had sight, based entirely on the available sensors and cameras, but no real sound or smell or touch or taste. No tangible connection to events happening on the other side of the world. Double-D feared the loss of control, feared firing on the wrong target.

Voices of other pilots sounded in his headset, their UAVs flying above or speeding toward the target area. Major Keller, who sat in the control room one floor above them, relayed information between the operators (not pilots) and the operatives, who were soldiers on the ground. *Operative* and not *Soldier*, because soldier was too harsh a term. It implied killing, and operative was innocuous and implied working, even if that work happened to be killing. Calling suspects POIs was a politically safe way to say terrorist. It allowed *operatives* to *execute orders* without declaring active combat. Double-D thought war was easier before political correctness sunk its fangs into the vocabulary of fighting. He wondered if being politically correct was a way to distance the emotional responsibility of pushing a button.

Major Keller's voice was sharp and calm, "Delta Two One Nine, engage targets on my mark; I'm activating the kill chain."

The kill chain referred to the long line of authorizations needed to fire a UAV-mounted weapon. The situation was being relayed through analysts and commanders, through mission coordinators and contractors, through men and women with long-winded job titles whose sole purpose was to ensure the right people were killed when buttons were pressed. The kill chain was meant to minimize accidental deaths and civilian deaths, and it was as effective in doing this as the Grove County Swim Club's lifeguards were at preventing older brothers from holding the heads of younger brothers under the water.

Double-D flicked a button on his control stick and heard a subtle tone in his headset indicating the UAV's Hellfire missiles were armed and ready. His stomach did several quick shudders that resembled the flutter he often felt when watching his wife emerge from the shower, her skin glistening and dripping. His tongue was numb and his mouth was dry.

"Call in," Major Keller said.

"Operatives are engaged in active combat," Double-D said in a voice that didn't sound like his own. The POIs on his main display were surrounded by tiny red squares as the targeting computer tracked them. They retreated in a group, laying down heavy fire behind them, and crossed a field toward East Village. It was three in the morning there, and everyone would be asleep.

While he waited, he thought about secrets. Double-D was very good at keeping secrets, which was why people were always telling him things he didn't care to hear. *Kelly Jenkins is cheating on her husband. The Wilkersons bought a time-share in Tahoe, but they can't afford it. Sharon Conely's youngest daughter is addicted to cough medicine.* As an Air Force captain, he had access to more secrets than he wanted to know. The best way to handle secrets was to forget them, which had the undesired consequence of trust and reliability and the eventual revelation of *more* secrets. And the more he tried to forget, the more he remembered. *Steve Korelli got his secretary pregnant. Wilma Willard has cancer, and her husband is leaving her. Darnell Jostler was in jail for assault.* Over time, he had used these secrets as a barometer for the health and well-being of his own life. His wife was healthy and (as far as he knew) faithful, his children were bright and outgoing, his lawn was always cut. These were the traits which made him suitable for classified work.

He often wondered what secrets were kept by the colored blobs in the villages and towns he watched. He suspected they weren't terribly different. A secret, when revealed, couldn't be taken back. Words can't be unspoken, and the dead can't be un-killed. He was bothered that he knew nearly nothing about the people he watched.

"Stand by," Major Keller said.

Classified work came with a price; secrets needed to be kept no matter how troubling they were, or how much the images stayed with him, or how tense he became. He watched the infrared monitor where the POIs and the operatives were fighting. *Maintain an even strain, maintain an even strain.* He was breathing shallowly, and his body felt numb.

Fighter pilots were given stress training after combat operations. Soldiers were given days, sometimes weeks, to decompress at the end of their duty tours. Contractors were given free coffee.

"Stand by," Major Keller said again.

The operatives, visible on the low-light screen to his left, had gathered behind a stone wall that marked the A-22—a highway that cut through the village. The POIs had taken cover near the house of George in West Village. Double-D imagined the rattle of gunfire, could almost smell the smoke. His hands trembled.

*Maintain an even strain.*

He thought about the glow-in-the-dark pirate ship. He thought about his older brother and the swimming pool. If only he could've stayed conscious during the g-force test he could have been a fighter pilot. Fighter pilots can fire and forget. UAV operators had to linger and record the aftermath. If only his brother hadn't held him underwater, or maybe let him up sooner. Seconds, maybe fractions of a second. That was all it took to change a life.

*Maintain an even strain.*

"Kill chain confirmed; you are go for weapons hot," Major Keller said.

A reflex: Double-D had pulled the trigger before Major Keller finished speaking.

The center display changed to a camera in the nose cone of a Hellfire missile, which was releasing itself and igniting its engine and twisting through the cool night air. Millions of calculations were performed using trigonometry and telemetry and physics, pre-calculations performed by men and women who had never seen a Hellfire missile. The weight of a falling object and the angle of attack and the ambient air temperature and other factors Double-D knew nothing about were calculated within hundredths of degrees of precision which, to the operatives on the ground, would never be precise enough.

The display zoomed in on the POIs before flashing white and switching back to the forward view.

Isaac said, "Impact on target. I have eleven out of action."

"Copy that," Major Keller said. "Ground team moving in to verify."

Double-D watched as the operative blobs scaled the stone wall, crossed the field and spread out among the ruins of a building.

"Nice kill," Delmar said. And though Double-D didn't like to take credit for work that wasn't his own (it was, after all, the computer that calculated and guided the missile), he said, "Thanks," just the same.

Double-D's fingers were numb and his body shivered.

Maintain an even strain.

For nearly an hour he circled and scanned and photographed and recorded. As his shift finally ended, the voices of new pilots chimed in.

"Delta Two One Nine, this is Delta Eight Zero Seven assuming control in three—two—one."

"You have the conn," Double-D said, when he felt his control stick slacken. The second-shift pilot would fly the UAV for the next twelve hours.

"Hey, Isaac," Delta Eight Zero Seven said, "how'd your date go?"

This was the portion of the day Double-D usually enjoyed—the shift-change conversation which (as nearly all of the operators were male) invariably turned to sex and the details ranged from vague descriptions to detailed accounts of fluids and contortions and fetishes. Double-D suspected most of the details were complete fabrication. Those who actually had something to brag about were often the most silent.

Today, he found the conversation annoying. He pulled his headset off, shut down his console, and walked slowly out of the room.

At his desk, he sat and began typing an after-action report into the computer. He clicked the box that read *confirmed kills* and typed *11* beside it.

"Hey D-man," Delmar said, "You coming to Flynn's with us?"

The after-shift drinking was always at Flynn's Pub, where Double-D's bar tab had been soaring to new heights. The thought of a stiff drink was welcoming. "Yes," he said, nodding.

"Good man. First rounds on me," Delmar said, which is what he always said but never carried through.

Double-D picked up his phone from the storage locker outside of the secure area, where no outside electronics were allowed. He saw two missed calls from his wife, and he smiled as he dialed her number and strode through the lobby and out the glass doors into the afternoon heat.

The sky was streaked with contrails like white ribbons. His eyes stung from the intensity of the light. The Nevada heat was dry and comforting. He imagined himself in Afghanistan, basking beneath a burning sun.

His wife answered on the third ring. "Hey babe," he said.

"Sam's soccer coach wants to talk with us," she said. "He missed practice again."

Double-D switched the phone to his opposite ear and balanced it while unlocking his car. "What time and when?"

"Today," she said. Bammer was barking in the background. The little terrier was named because of his penchant for flatulence when excited, and Bammer was almost always excited. "Shut up, Bammer!" she yelled. "Can you make it by four?"

He closed his car's door and started the engine and turned the air conditioner on full. "I have some paperwork to finish up."

There was silence before she said, "I guess I could cover for us both."

Feeling guilty, he said, "I'll pick up some Chinese for dinner."

"Don't forget Megan's rice thing."

"Right." His daughter's latest political statement was to protest rice, which she believed was better served in third world countries where cheap food was essential. Double-D didn't know where she got her facts, but arguing with a fourteen-year-old only made his head hurt. Reluctantly he agreed to stop eating rice in a show of support, though secretly he was glad third world countries didn't need bacon or cheeseburgers.

A choice: He spoke before he realized he'd made up his mind. "I can do this paperwork later. I'll meet you at Sam's school in half an hour," he said.

*Maintain an even strain.*

"Thank you," she said. "I love you."

He hung up and sat behind the wheel, letting the air conditioner cool him. In his mind's eye, he saw his son's soccer field viewed from above through infrared imaging, saw his son's team as colored blobs, red and yellow.

A reflex, a choice, a lie; these thoughts occupied his mind, drowning out all others as he pulled out of the parking lot and onto the road that led out of base.

# MOURNERS OF THE DEAD

★ ★ ★

*Brooke King*

There she was, kneeling down and crying beside the dead girl in the middle of the street, next to the five-ton cargo truck and a shell-shocked Private Ramirez, who was still pointing his rifle at the girl's lifeless corpse. The woman lifted her head and looked at Ramirez and then to the heavens. She was dressed in a full-length black abaya, but the hijab that had been covering her head loosened and fell to her feet, exposing long curly black hair. Ramirez stood next to her there with his shaky trigger finger still paused in the trigger well. He had shot her in a crowd of local nationals who had been standing by a 5-ton cargo truck waiting for supplies. The shot echoed through the street, turning it into an empty aisle of abandoned water bottles and food rations. The locals fled back to the buildings and alleyways from where they had come, leaving no sympathy for the grieving woman who sat crying over the girl. Our humanitarian mission to a local market in the Karrada District had become an utter failure.

Staff Sergeant VanCamp and I sat fifteen feet away in our humvee staring at Ramirez and the girl. Lowering his head, Staff Sergeant VanCamp whispered, "Fuck."

He opened the door and held onto it for support, as he threw his legs out the door and rocked himself up out of his seat. He stood up and rubbed his knee.

"I'm getting too old for this shit," he said, as he glanced up at me. "Do me a favor, Miller. Sit tight, don't move, and keep an ear to the radio."

I nodded, eyes fixed again on the scene in front of me. Staff

Sergeant VanCamp walked up to Ramirez, grabbed hold of his shoulder, and walked him back to our humvee. He opened the back door of the humvee, shoved Ramirez into the cab, looked at me, and said, "Keep an eye on him."

I nodded again. I turned and looked at Ramirez, who sat in the back seat with his helmet pressed against the seat in front of him, his eyes cast down at the humvee's floor.

I turned back around and watched from the driver's seat as the woman lifted her hands to the sky and bellowed foreign words to the heavens. She rocked back and forth, crying over the dead girl, her curly black hair just long enough to graze the blood-soaked ground each time she rocked forward.

Staff Sergeant VanCamp walked towards the scene. He looked down at the girl lying dead on the ground and shook his head. He knelt slowly, lowering one knee at a time towards the ground. At forty-three, his body looked more like a sixty-year-olds. Watching him now, I knew that this would probably be his last deployment.

As he knelt next to the girl's body, the woman looked up at him and their eyes met. Staff Sergeant VanCamp lowered his head. I watched the woman and Staff Sergeant VanCamp, as they both knelt there over the girl. The radio crackled to life, making me jump. Through the static, I heard the convoy leader giving the command to mount up, signaling that it was almost time to head back to base. The convoy trucks rumbled to life, each gunner crawling up into the turret of their humvee, taking their positions behind a machine gun. I looked at Staff Sergeant VanCamp, who still had not moved from his position on the ground. Wiping my bangs out of my face and tucking them back behind my ear, I opened my door and looked back at Ramirez, and said, "Don't fucking move."

He didn't look up from his gaze at the floor or say anything. He knew, just as well as I did, that he was fucked. I grabbed my M4 that was lying on top of the radio box, got out of the humvee, and walked towards Staff Sergeant VanCamp.

As I made it to his position, he placed his right hand over his heart, closed his eyes, and whispered, "Our Father, who art in heaven..."

I stood over the girl's body, there in the middle of the street while the smell of fresh blood burned my nostrils and filled my mouth with the taste of iron, like licking a dirty coin. I looked at the dead girl, who looked as though she could have been young enough to be my little sister, the woman crying beside her, and Staff Sergeant VanCamp praying. I looked away, but I couldn't help looking back at the girl again. She was my first dead body.

Her lips had already turned a soft shade of lilac. Blood had crept out the sides of her opened mouth, making it look as though her face was drawn open in a deathly scream. Her cheeks and nose were lightly freckled. Her eyebrows were thick and dark brown, and matched the color of her hair. Her hair, it had a soft wave to it and was half up, pulled behind her head and fastened with a barrette, but was matted together at the ends from a pool of blood that had spread out from underneath her shoulders where the bullet had exited out her back. Her ribcage was sunken in and slightly misshaped; the bullet must have bounced around her chest cavity before it exited. Parts of her white blouse and blue jumper were saturated with a crimson stain. Her arms were thin, one cocked slightly in and the other cocked outwards, but her legs canted sideways off to the right and were somewhat muscular at the calf, the telltale signs of a soccer player. She looked several years younger than I did; probably still a teenager. Her book bag lay next to her splattered with blood; she must have been walking home from school. The woman didn't touch her, but sat there crying beside her body, her hands pressed together against her forehead, her eyes now cast down.

I looked at the girl again. I clinched my hands together, digging my chipped and jagged clear-polished fingernails into my calloused palms to keep myself from crying. Up ahead in the distance, I heard the convoy commander shouting orders at soldiers, doors slamming shut, boots shuffling around as they busily rushed up and down the lined procession of trucks in the convoy. I saw nothing but the dead girl in front of me.

"Miller, stop staring," Staff Sergeant VanCamp said, as he peered up at me and nudged my leg. "You act like you've never seen a dead body before."

Tears began to well up in my eyes. I couldn't look away. The girl's eyes looked fogged, like a sort of milky haze had casted over them. Her limbs looked like deadfall littering the street. The blood on the ground was a brown muddy mixture that caked together in lumps around her hair and neck.

"Stop staring, Miller."

My lips began to throb from pulling them in tightly against my teeth and then pursing them out as I stood there looking at the girl's body. My tears surfaced faster the longer I looked. Her body lay almost entirely in the sun. The blood around her body had begun to turn a purplish brown. Her hair was matted with dirt, speckled with pollen, congealed with blood, and was a sopping mess about her neck. Her mouth gapped open, her front teeth covered by her bloated tongue. Her eyes wide, her eyelashes touching the top lids. Her cheekbones, drawn thin in a line and sunken in. The freckles on her nose and cheeks looked faded in the midday sun, her complexion now a lighter shade of desert brown. Spattered blood had crusted dry in her eyebrows, making them misshapen, and the hair out of place.

Staff Sergeant VanCamp lifted a knee and leaned against it as he said, "Miller, don't tell me this is your first dead body."

I nodded.

Still peering up at me, he said, "Don't worry, it won't be your last."

The creases of my eyes were filled almost enough for the tears to crest over my lower lashes and trickle down my face. I straightened up and grabbed a hold of my combat vest collar, pushing it down towards my collarbone as Staff Sergeant VanCamp stared at me.

"Shit, Miller. You're not crying are you?"

Still looking down at the girl, I nodded. A slight wind had blown a strand of her hair away from her cheek where her dried salty tears had smudged them with a tinge of white. Her ears were pierced, but she wore no earrings, only small slits where a pair of studs could have been. The skin on her neck sagged slightly, revealing a burn mark; it looked like the one I had on my neck from a stray bullet casing. A small pool of blood gathered at her collarbone, soaking the first two buttonholes of her white blouse with a deep crimson stain. Her thin arms were slightly freckled and covered lightly with golden-tipped brown hair. Her delicate wrist held a small gold bracelet. Her long slender fingers were crusted with dried blood; her fingernails, well-trimmed, had blood and dirt underneath them. My tears filled my eyes. I could no longer see the girl at my feet.

"Suck it the fuck up, Miller, I mean shit." He paused. "You can turn wrenches, smoke non-filtered cigarettes, talk shit, and curse like a man, but you can't handle a dead body?"

The tears finally spilled over onto my cheeks and I sobbed softly with my mouth closed, tucking my bottom lip inward. Staff Sergeant VanCamp shook his head and sighed as he said, "Shit, Miller. At least it's good to know there's still a woman underneath all that tomboy bullshit you front."

He softly patted my left leg, which broke my concentration on the girl's body. I wiped the tears away with the sleeve of my ACU top. Sniffling, I sucked the snot back up into my nose and tried to compose myself enough to relay the radio chatter.

"Sarge," I said, as I bent down, "We have to leave, the convoy's going to roll out soon."

"I'll be there in a minute," he said, as he lowered his head.

I was about to turn and leave when the woman raised her head suddenly, as if she had finally realized that I was there. She reached up from her knelt position and grabbed my forearm.

"Sarge," I said, as I tapped his shoulder.

"It's okay, Miller."

With tears in her eyes, the woman said something to me in Arabic that I couldn't understand. The hysterical expression on her face startled me and in a panic, I tried to take back my arm and pull myself away from her, but she held tightly to me as she cried.

I tried to pull my arm back again as I turned to Staff Sergeant VanCamp and said, "Sarge, she won't let go."

He just looked at me and said, "It's all right, she's not going to hurt you."

This is far from all right, I thought.

I tried to yank my arm back, but she clenched harder and yanked me down towards her. She wept as she spoke in a saddened tone the same foreign words. As I tried to jerk away, I imagined that she was telling to me get out, to leave this place before I ended up like the girl. I kept trying to yank myself away from her by standing up, but she wouldn't let go of me.

"Let go, please, let go," I said, as I tried again and again to take back my arm.

Gripping to it tightly and yanking me towards her until I was half knelt down, she spoke the same phrase over and over again. The words rambled out of her mouth too quickly for me to comprehend. I heard the compassion in her voice, the sorrow in her inflection, and it was her words that filled the street with pain. The woman reached out with one of her hands and pointed to the girl. I looked at the girl and then back at the woman as she yanked me closer and continued to speak the same desperate words as before.

"Sarge, she won't let go." I said, as tears spilled over my cheeks. A panic rose in my chest, making it heavy, like rocks weighed down my ribcage. My throat grew taut, my breathing labored and raspy. Frustrated and upset at the woman's hold on me, I grabbed her firmly with both my arms, looked at her, and pleaded through my tears in a shaky tone, "I don't understand what you're saying, please... let go."

She looked at me and I saw the suffering that filled her eyes. Staff Sergeant VanCamp put his hand on my shoulder and used it as a prop to get up. As he rose to his feet, he said in a soft whisper, "Let's go."

The woman looked down at the girl and then back at me. Turning her head slightly, tears ran down her face, as she spoke again. I looked at her. My lips quivered, as I said softly, "I'm sorry... I'm so sorry, but I have to go."

I glanced at the girl and in a fleeting moment, it looked as though she were only daydreaming. The slowly sinking sun cast the woman's shadow over the girl, like a marble statue in a graveyard. I turned away from the girl and looked back at the woman. With my hands around the woman's forearms, I embraced her gently, smiled half-heartedly, and though I knew she couldn't understand me, I mouthed, "It'll be okay."

With no other words spoken between us, she nodded and slowly began to let my arms slip out of her grasp. I stood, looked at the woman, and nodded. I turned around to leave, but as I did, I noticed that Staff Sergeant VanCamp had waited for me. I walked up to him. He patted me on the back and we walked to the humvee together, but as I approached the humvee, I turned around one last time and saw the woman looking straight at me. The sadness of her stare made my eyes well up with tears again. Clenching my jaw, I forced them back and kept walking. Staff Sergeant VanCamp was sitting in the passenger seat of our humvee with the door open, Ramirez in the back; both were waiting for me to get back to the wheel. Staff Sergeant VanCamp signaled me to mount up. He taped the top of his helmet and said, "Let's go."

When we got back to the base, I didn't bother taking off my gear, even though my combat tactical vest, still loaded to the teeth with ammo, weighed more than I did and made my back ache. I propped myself against the side of the humvee, pulled out a cigarette, and watched as Military Police hauled off Private Ramirez.

"I'm going to need you to come into company headquarters," Staff Sergeant VanCamp said, as he walked up next to me, "and fill out a personal statement about what happened out on mission."

I was looking down at the ground, moving the gravel around with my combat boot. I nodded my head, but said nothing.

"You okay, Miller?"

I looked up to see Staff Sergeant VanCamp peering at me. I looked down at the ground again, inhaled and exhaled a puff of my cigarette, and said, "To tell you the truth Sarge," I raised my head with tears in my eyes, "I don't know."

"You want to talk about it?"

I said nothing.

"Miller," he said, as he leaned up against the humvee next to me, "There aren't a lot of female soldiers that can handle what you've just been through, seeing a dead body and all."

I didn't speak or move. I just stood there looking at the ground.

"I know how you feel right now." He paused a moment, and then said, "Well, maybe not, but I've been through a similar situation before and can understand what you must be going through."

I sighed and pulled a drag from my cigarette.

"You need to talk to someone about this, Miller, or it's going to eat you up on the inside."

Tears flowed openly now.

He pulled out his Kodiak can from his pant pocket, slammed a wad of dip into the side of his right cheek, wiped his hand onto his cargo pants, and looked at me. The smell of his dip, wintergreen mint, filled the air around us, making my nostrils twinge from its pungent odor.

"Miller," he said, as he spit a brown stream of tobacco juice onto the ground, "There isn't anything you could have done for that girl, and as for that woman, well; there wasn't anything you could have done for her, either."

"Easy for you to say," I said, as I wiped tears and snot off my face with the sleeve of my ACU top.

"Look at me for a second," he said, as he turned to me. I raised my head. "Now, I'm not going to sugar coat it for you and tell you that everything is going to be okay," he said, as he spit a stream on the ground, "but what I am going to say is that if you don't get your shit together, and I mean soon, this deployment is going to get real hard, real quick, you hear me?"

I nodded.

"Good," he patted me on the back, "Now, come on."

He spit another stream onto the ground outside the humvee and then started to walk towards the company where the military police were waiting for his statement. I put out my smoke with the heel of my combat boot, wiped away the rest of my tears, and walked beside him, shuffling my feet through the gravel. My M4 felt heavy in my arms, but Staff Sergeant VanCamp seemed to walk at ease with his in his hands.

"Keep your head up and I'll see you tomorrow at formation."

I walked towards the hooches, but stopped and turned to look at Staff Sergeant VanCamp, who was halfway to where the military police stood with Ramirez. I shouted to him, "Hey Sarge, what about the personal statement?"

"Don't worry about it," he yelled, as he stood tall, giving no reprieve to his rickety knees, "It's not going anywhere."

The sun had started to set in violent reds and oranges that seemed to scatter the sky in a bloody mess of colors, like watercolors bleeding together on paper. I still felt conflicted over what had happened that day and felt a sort of hollowness inside, as if I was somehow one organ short. As I walked to my hooch, the remains of the day filled my head with reeling images of that bloody scene, like an endless war movie in my mind. Walking down the long line of tin-roofed hooches, I forced one foot in front of the other and grappled with my heavy combat vest. I made it to my hooch, tore off my vest and threw it onto the ground, set my rifle up against the front door, pulled out my pack of smokes and lit one up, inhaling the first couple of puffs deeply. My shoulders ached from wearing the vest all day. Putting the cigarette in my mouth, I leaned my back up against the door and stared down at my hands that, after only three months deep into a deployment, no longer looked like my own. They had been cut, burned, calloused, and worked into uniformity, but as I looked down at my hands, I knew the smallest cruelty was that I would never again be able to look down at them and know them as my own. I pulled the cigarette out of my mouth, and as I blew out the smoke as if I was letting out a sigh, I listened to a strange quietness that filled the air like a moment of silence for the dead. After a while, I heard music and chanting off in the distance; an out of tune zither playing in the background as a stern-voiced man beckoned his people to go to the mosque. It was the adhân, the Islamic call to prayer, being chanted through a crackling loud speaker. I watched the sun slip out of sight, but even as I stood there looking beyond the hooches towards where the road met the horizon, I thought, "Another day down, a hundred more fucked up days like this to go."

# HALF-SMILES

★ ★ ★

*Daniel Taylor*

"Our greatest foes, and whom we must chiefly combat, are within."
—*Miguel de Cervantes Saavedra*

In Honor of Staff Sergeant Juan Luis Rivadeneira

NORTHERN IRAQ: 2006

Sergeant Thompson smacked Connor Lambert hard on the shoulder, his ebony face inches from Connor's sun burnt and peeling nose. "You okay, Lamb?"

Connor's adrenaline had bottomed out. Reality was settling in and he wasn't sure how to feel. The rounds and the screams still rang in his ears; and the rusty smell of blood still filled his nose.

Connor shook his head and smiled, "Jesus, Sergeant, I never knew you had such fuckin' fragile female sensibilities, not for me any who."

"Yeah, well, now that Daddy's left us bastards, Mommy's got to step up, ya know. Come on, Banner is awaitin'."

The soldiers stood on a once-sprawling, Iraqi tarmac designed for military helicopters and small fixed-wing aircraft. A few scattered observation towers, well-worn from wind, sand, and neglect had been left to decay in the middle of nowhere since their abandonment in the nineties. The tower's original white paint was faded and marred by black blast strikes and bullet pock marks. The area had been well placed to strike at Iranian forces and to resupply Iraqi troops during the country's long struggle with its neighbors. Now, American resources and ingenuity had brought the desolate place back to life. The airfield was a hot bed of activity as soldiers scrambled everywhere, trucks rolled on and off the flight line, and medical helicopters lifted soldiers in and out.

Connor and Thompson hurried off the flight line to get back with the rest of their comrades. Heavy body armor and combat kit, still tightly strapped against their sweat soaked chests, barely moved as they quick stepped. Connor glanced back at the dust storm kicked up by the medevac helicopter as it lifted and soared away with their wounded buddies. He couldn't believe he had just loaded his Platoon Sergeant. They weaved through concrete barriers and guards to get to their armored vehicles parked in the sand across from the medevac area. The American base surrounded and expanded out from the flight line. Some original structures from the Saddam regime still stood, but most everything else was from American build-up. Roads and motor pools were built, or in the process of being built, all over the base with tons of small rock. The grays of the gravel roads were in stark contrast with the golden browns of the natural environment.

Connor and Thompson removed their Kevlar helmets as they approached their Stryker armored vehicle. Private Nathaniel Banner sat in his driver's seat with the hatch door in the locked and open position. The driver's compartment was inside the front, left side, of the vehicle and sat next to the giant engine block. The soldiers called this area the "hellhole." In combat Banner had to close the hatch, and secure himself completely inside the green beast. Banner grabbed onto the rim of his hatch and pulled himself up. The driver's hatch was about six feet off the ground and Banner was made even taller as he stood up in his seat.

"How's Sergeant Smith?" Banner yelled down.

"He's weak but good," Connor answered.

"He looked fucked up—"

Thompson cut Banner off with the wave of a hand. "Any word on the rest of the Company?"

"The C.O. said that they have already secured the site. Hold on," Banner pressed his radio headset tighter around his ears and listened intently. "The Commander's comin' in the wire now."

Connor and Thompson nodded in relief. Connor looked up at Banner. He was a short Ginger who fared miserably under the furnace of the Iraqi sun. Pudgy by infantry standards, Banner was working hard in the gym with Thompson; he was losing the flab with the goal of shredding up. Thompson was what infantrymen looked like on the recruiting posters. He was tall and muscular but not bulky. The bulky body builder types were a big sign of a Fobbit, people who had the luxury of endless hours in the gyms and access to all the powders and shakes. Whereas Thompson was tall and Banner short, Connor was just plain, an average wiry infantry carbon copy. Whatever their physical differences, each man had a kind of "hard" look about him. Sergeant Thompson was fond of saying, "An infantryman in combat walks around like a cocky rooster; he just does it without the showmanship." Connor thought of it as a kind of quiet confidence. It was an authentic, devil-may-care attitude that was often mistaken for, and teetered on, arrogance.

Their Lieutenant stood in the center of the other men with his Kevlar at his feet and a handheld radio stuck in his ear. He called for Thompson and the other leaders. "Be back with orders," Thompson said and then jogged over to him.

The other soldiers in Connor's unit waited silently for the next set of orders, or the "word" as they put it. They smoked cigarettes and drank water out of plastic bottles with foreign labels as they cooked under the sun. *We all look the same,* Connor mused to himself. Some of the soldiers were taller and some were shorter, but when they stood next to each other, it was hard to discern any distinguishable characteristics. Connor always thought that they all looked like a bunch of gray ninja turtles with their bulky body armor and Kevlars on. Their ESS and Oakley eye-pro pulled double duty as both sun shades and small fragment ballistic protection. The loose, powdery dirt, that the men called *moon dust*, clogged every open pore and covered every inch of their ammo pouches. Each man had various patterns of white blotches staining their uniforms, caused by sweating out so much salt. They were all just dirty, sun burnt faces with short cropped hair.

Connor watched as Banner dropped his head set and climbed down the vehicle, using the slat armor that was bolted on the outside. The slat armor was designed to catch rocket propelled grenades and essentially, was a big cage made up of long horizontal bars. Named after two Medal of Honor recipients that shared the same last name, the Strykers were eight-wheeled, 24-ton vehicles designed for speed and mobility. The angular front of the Stryker had an insect look to it and, overall, the vehicle looked like a big green monster. They could hold a nine-man infantry squad in the back and utilized a back ramp for rapid deployment. They were quiet and well-armed, perfect for raiding and therefore, perfect for Iraq's unique urban fighting; just as were the soldiers that rode inside them. *They're not scared of the Strykers; they're scared of the soldiers that come out.*

Banner carefully stepped between the gaps in the bars and found some footing on one of the tires. Both to Connor's amusement and disdain, Banner jumped down without the slightest touch of gracefulness, and kicked up a cloud of moon dust. He stretched his back with a grunt and smacked futilely at the dust that clung at his wet skin. Connor, without being asked, stuck an Iraqi cigarette in between the slit in his freckled face. Banner twitched in surprise. Connor had grown used to the strong and poorly named *Miami* cigarettes because he just couldn't beat paying some Iraqi kid five or ten bucks to get him a carton. But he still coveted his American cigarettes whenever he could get his hands on them. *They might be called Miami's but they taste like New Jersey's.* Their attentions were pulled to Sergeant Thompson speaking with the Lieutenant.

"There you go, BanMan," Connor said softly as he lit Banner's cigarette without ever taking his eyes off of Thompson.

Connor inhaled deeply, smoke drifting out his nostrils. Connor had been a young buck, a new private at Alpha Company, when Thompson arrived from the famous 101st Airborne Division. Thompson wore a Combat Infantrymen's Badge (CIB) on his uniform, the mark of real infantrymen. The CIB consisted of a silver model 1795 Springfield musket that lay in a rectangle field of blue that was on and over a silver, elliptical oak wreath. It was the most beautiful award Connor had ever seen. He smiled to himself at the thought that he, too, would receive a CIB, whether he lived to see it pinned on or not.

Thompson jogged back over and said, "K, we are standing down for the rest of today, no patrols, no raids, no nothing. We're going to have an A.A.R. later on at the motor pool. We need to get the trucks fueled and prepped and then we can hit chow."

Banner hopped back up in his driver's hatch while Thompson and Connor went in the back. Hydraulic chains thick as his wrist pulled the ramp up and there was a distinct whistle of air as it sealed itself shut. The floors and walls were made up of white Kevlar plates, everything else was green. Two bench seats ran along both sides of the interior and computer screens hung from several points of the vehicle. Thompson peeled off his body armor and let it fall with a thud. Connor followed suit as they bent down to get to their positions. *There may not be enough room to stand up in, but at least it's long enough to cram guys uncomfortably together,* Connor chuckled to himself. The gunner and commander seats were located by a wall at the end. Behind the wall were the driver's seat and the engine block.

The smell of JP8 fuel made Connor a little light-headed as they refueled, using long hoses connected to giant fuel bladders that sat in the sun like bloated slug bellies. They hit the supply sergeant next and he unlocked a small makeshift shed with an aluminum door. Connor and Banner pulled cases of MRE's out and restocked the truck as Thompson hustled the supply sergeant for more AA batteries. They had done this routine a thousand times and Connor did his tasks without much thought. Fuel and supply went like clockwork but by the time they had parked and locked their vehicle up in the motor pool, it was time for dinner chow. Connor's stomach growled and he wanted a shower but he knew better than that. Weapons maintenance took precedence over their needs and would be cleaned before the men cleaned themselves. They walked back to their living area which was made up of a latrine and shower facility, very similar in shape and size to a Conex shipping container, and uniform rows of wooden B-Huts raised by floor trusses. Connor laid out an Army poncho on a rickety picnic table that they had made out of mismatched pieces of scrap wood. The three men went to cleaning their weapons.

"Holy fuck! So that's what combat is like," Banner said.

Thompson looked up, shook his head, and went back to his weapon.

Connor got a whiff of the blood, heard the gunfire and screams.

"Then my fuckin' heart was poundin' in my fuckin' chest, bro."

Connor barely listened.

"When you guys breached that first room, it got fuckin' crazy."

Connor shook his head.

"Damn Lamb, you were the man!"

Connor could almost taste a bit of the adrenaline again from when the bullets were still flying. It wasn't the same rush as the real deal but it was the next best thing. Connor couldn't help but to smile as his cigarette bobbed up and down between his lips. They laughed together and for once, the stress was gone. Some life even danced around in their otherwise tired and shadowed eyes.

"I was just driving but it was still fuckin' crazy! Sergeant Thompson here was lighting dudes up with the 240, and man, that I.E.D.," Banner wiped his forehead with the back of his hand. "Fuck man, that was intense. And even before that, too," Banner trailed off, wild eyed. "Wow."

"It was fuckin' nuts inside, alright. We stacked up and cleared room by room, man," Connor said.

Banner took a pull off of his cigarette, "Then we heard that fire after Sergeant Smith and 'em went in. Heard the chaos over the radio. Man, Lamb, you were a hoss up in there!"

"Thank God for fools with luck," Thompson mumbled, without looking up from his rifle.

Connor's smile vanished. Sergeant Smith had been laying in the prone, bleeding from multiple gunshot wounds by the time Connor had made it to the room. Sergeant Smith's weapon had been utterly destroyed by fat AK-47 rounds. He was desperately reaching for his side arm but he wasn't going to make it.

"Yeah, he was all fucked up. Seemed like he took rounds every damn place." *If I would have been a little slower, shit,* Connor thought. "He was smiling when we loaded him up in the bird. He was fuckin' smiling," Connor said and took a slow pull from his Miami and looked at the ground.

Thompson nodded for several long moments. "Remember when

Bravo team loaded Barton up on the medevac bird last week? I heard he's back in the states now, but he might lose his leg."

Connor looked up in shock. "What?"

"Yeah, I'm no fucking doctor," Thompson said. "But he took three A.K. rounds to his left leg, and, and it was just fuckin' shattered, bro', fuckin' shattered," Thompson said.

"Holy fuck man, Maria is goin' to have a heart attack."

"And yeah, when Bravo team got back, that POG First Sergeant, the mothafucka with pressed D.C.U.s and shit, yelled at them for comin' off the flight line and not immediately puttin' their head gear on."

"Yeah, they still had armor on, for Christ's Sake," Banner said.

"And they were covered in Barton's blood. Remember that shit?" Thompson asked.

Connor's jaw clenched and he whispered to himself, "Yeah, I remember."

Connor, Banner, and Thompson walked across the dusty graveled base to the chow hall mumbling about the POG First Sergeant. The men had their rifles slung across their backs. Connor and Banner walked with cigarettes in their hands.

"Hey soldiers. There's no walkin' and smoking," a male soldier they didn't know called to them from five feet away. "We need to stay disciplined in combat."

For a minute, Connor thought that was all there was going to be to it. It looked like the stranger was going to keep going but then he did a double take. The guy power marched in their direction. *Oh shit, a super Fobbit, this is going to get fucked.*

He carried an M-16, the older model rifle issued to non-combat arms soldiers. The men referred to it as *the musket.* Connor touched his own weapon slung behind his back. His M-4 carbine was a shorter, modern version of the M-16. It was designed for easier maneuvering within a vehicle and in urban operations. Connor kept his sling a little loose so that it was ready to be swung in firing position if something unexpected happened. The stranger's sling was so tightly strapped to his body that Connor didn't believe it could come off.

The stranger made sure the rank on his chest wasn't obscured by his sling. He was a Sergeant like Thompson and he wanted that fact clearly visible. Thompson just looked at him, half-smiling.

"And you, Sergeant," the stranger said, pointing his finger. "Look at how un-squared away your guy's uniforms are. I guess your unit doesn't give a fuck about standards."

Thompson snatched Connor's cigarette right out of his mouth, and pointed it in the stranger's face. "You know what, mothafucka? We actually just got back from killin' the fuckin' enemy! You know, the whole reason we're fuckin' here, you pasty faced fuckin' faggot! Meanwhile you're walkin' roun' fuckin' with real soldiers like we're back in garrison so you can feel fuckin' tall!"

Thompson went to snuff the burning tobacco in the other man's eye. Connor and Banner grabbed their Sergeant, struggling against the force of the man. As Connor strained, bloody images flooded his vision. He couldn't shake the hours old memories of Sergeant Smith's bloodied body, or that of Barton before him.

*Why am I holding him back? I should let him go and help him! We should make a fuckin' example out of this POG and leave him broken and naked,* Connor thought.

The other Sergeant took off.

The three soldiers sat on the hot gravel with their backs against the Hesco barriers, making a second use of the large collapsible boxes filled with dirt, placed to protect against enemy explosions. Their unit's motor pool was ringed with double stacks of these barriers, taller than two average people. The entire company waited inside this great ring, their Stryker vehicles parked in neat, uniform rows. The soldiers waited around for their Commanding Officer (C.O.) and their First Sergeant to give them a brief.

Thompson looked at Connor and shook his head. Connor smiled with warmth and crushed his cigarette, letting the smoke drift through his teeth. Connor leaned back against the Hesco barrier and closed his eyes. *I can't believe I just loaded up my Platoon Sergeant on a fuckin' medevac bird. We were fuckin' jokin' around as he was bleeding out. He was smiling....*

Connor recalled Sergeant Smith laying on his side, his destroyed rifle on the floor, weakly, desperately reaching for his pistol strapped to his leg. The insurgent in his white man dress was there too. He saw that thick Sunni mustache and the twisted scowl that went with it. He watched himself, raising his own rifle and squeezing the trigger.

Connor opened his eyes just in time to see and hear Banner reading a letter from his girlfriend, Stephanie. "First off babe, thanks for the pictures, you look so sexy," Banner smiled to his audience. "It's tough here without you but I'm strong because I know that you need me to be strong. I look forward to our life together when you come home…"

Tears formed in Banner's eyes and he tried not to bring any attention to them. Connor noticed his wet, dust covered cheeks anyway. *I wished I had something to cry over*, Connor thought.

"I'm sorry, Soup, but I don't want to hear this shit now," Thompson said. He violently spit a stream of Redman chaw that splattered the powdery gravel. Connor studied his Team Leader, watching his furrowed brow furrow even more. Thompson chomped down on his thick plug noisily and looked away from Banner in a telling way. It was the kind of look that said, "There's no need for reply."

"How's Kelly, Sergeant?" Banner asked.

"I just said I don't wanna' talk bout my fuckin' wife, Banner. She's a fuckin' bitch, and she's a whore, what the fuck else is new for fightin' men?"

Connor looked away. *Yeah, my ex couldn't even stay faithful while I was at Basic.* The hour had grown late and the sun had almost set when the C.O. and the First Sergeant came into the motor pool. The C.O. was a tall and thin West Point officer. He ran at least six miles a day no matter how hot it was. To Connor, the barrel chested First Sergeant was the scariest man he'd ever met. He was a Ranger and a veteran of the Battle of Mogadishu. He was the only man that Connor knew that had a star on his CIB. The First Sergeant called the men to stand in formation by platoons. The men put out cigarettes, spit out their dips, and assembled quickly.

Connor listened as the C.O. addressed the men and told them that all of their wounded comrades made it to the hospital okay. He told them how proud he was of them. So proud in fact, that he was pushing their CIB ceremony to right then. After a short speech the C.O. individually pinned black enamel versions of the awards on each soldier. As tradition dictated, the First Sergeant followed after to drive the badges metal spikes into the chests of each man. They started with the medic, Doc Rivera, who received the rare and highly respected Combat Medical Badge. Connor sure as hell appreciated knowing that there was at least one man competent enough to save his life.

He waited for his turn, wishing he could see the First Sergeant coming. He needed something to do to pass the time. Connor recited the Infantryman's Creed in his head. *I am the Infantry. I am my country's strength in war, her deterrent in peace. I am the heart of the fight, wherever, whenever. I carry America's faith and honor against her enemies. I am the Queen of Battle.*

"Good job, Specialist Collins," Connor heard the C.O. say.

"Thank you Sir," Collins replied.

Just earlier that day an insurgent had raised his A.K. at Sergeant Smith. Connor had raised his own rifle and put his sights on the man's chest.

*Never will I fail my country's trust. Always I fight on, through the foe, to the objective, to triumph over all. If necessary, I will fight to my death...*

"Excellent work, Private Wilson," the C.O. said.

"Yes Sir...ooof!" Wilson sucked air in before composing himself. "Thank you, First Sergeant."

Staring straight ahead, Connor felt the C.O. getting closer to him and could hear the First Sergeant's congratulations with every loud thud his fist made.

*I yield not to weakness, to hunger, to cowardice, to fatigue, to superior odds...*

Connor had seen that Sunni man hovering over Sergeant Smith. His thumb had instantly switched his rifle's selector lever from safe to semi-automatic. His finger had tightened around the trigger.

*I forsake not my country, my mission, my fellow comrades, my sacred duty. I am relentless. I am always there, now and forever...*

BAM, BAM, BAM, BAM, BAM and the Iraqi man had crumpled.

*I am the Infantry. Follow me.*

The C.O. finally stepped in front of Connor, for his turn. *Lead the Way.* The C.O. pinned on the most coveted badge in the Army. Connor barely registered his First Sergeant's bear paw of a fist smashing into him; all he could think about was the bloody Sergeant Smith, and the crumpled up dead Arab.

*I killed him, I fuckin' killed that guy.*

The awards ceremony concluded and Connor watched Collins and some other men pick Doc Rivera up in congratulations. Doc smiled big but Connor was sure he saw pain in the man's eyes. After all, he was the one who had to put them all back together. It was lame and unpractical to wear pin-on badges in a combat zone so the men took theirs off. Connor rubbed the left side of his chest where his CIB had been punched into him. He stared at the CIB in his hand and smiled. *Goddamn, I can't believe it. I actually got one.* A small amount of blood from one of the badge's spikes smeared into his palm. Connor's smile slowly faded into a smirk, and then into nothing. He placed the backings on the pins and put the badge into his pocket.

Connor, Banner, and Thompson walked together through the darkness, unworried. They were quiet, each in their own head, but they were still together, still immortal. They ended up at the phone and internet area. Thompson veered off into the internet shack.

Banner and Connor waited by the phones. "You know, they'll make you team leader and you deserve it," Banner said.

"I'm goin' to get out, I think. I'll tell them to give it to you," Connor said.

"Thanks, Lamb, you know that means a lot to me," Banner said looking down. "But they'll never give it to me. I'm the fat body, remember. You know how it was back at the unit. How fucked up I was." Banner sighed and looked up. "When I first got there, Sergeant Thompson took one look at me and said, 'Private Banner, you are more ate up then a sloppy soup sandwich, aren't ya?'" Banner sighed. "You're the only one who never called me Soup."

"You got through on heart, BanMan. I wouldn't have helped you if I thought you were a shit-bag. You got more heart than all those fucks. They just were born naturally athletic; you have to work hard for every goal and every achievement. You *were* a fat body, now look at ya.' I'd rather have will over skill, any day. And you got both. Nobody I'd trust more goin' through a door."

Banner embraced Connor and told him he loved him. Connor, genuinely, told him he loved him back. More soldiers filed in. A Sergeant walked by and told them to get clean uniforms. Some soldiers stared at them, some snickered.

"You POGs can kiss my ass," Connor said.

The other soldiers waiting for phones scowled and flipped him off.

"Nah, kiss my ass," one said.

"Yeah, yeah, you Stryker guys are so fuckin' cool," said another.

"I hear Stryker guys all got small dicks."

Banner smiled. "Yeah, we got small dicks!"

Connor laughed and just stared at them. The other soldiers opened their mouths to speak but ended up just turning away. *They don't look like they know what's what now,* Connor thought.

Banner was called and went to his assigned phone. Banner talked to his beloved Stephanie without the slightest hint that it would be the last time. Connor remained in blissful ignorance as well. The future (along with a lightweight, close-in support 60mm mortar) had not yet robbed him of another friend.

The shack held twenty-two pay phone style booths and phones.

"You got twenty minutes on phone four," the soldier in charge said as he looked at Connor's dirty uniform and his high speed M-4 with disdain. "And you better not go over, 'cause I won't hesitate to throw violators out of here."

Connor ignored him and walked to his phone. He punched in some numbers from his phone card. There were several rings. He was just about to hang up when his mother answered.

"Hey Mom."

"Oh Connor, it's been so long," her strained and low voice replied.

"I know Momma, I know."

"You know I'm hearing more and more about this P.T.S.D. on the news."

Connor barely heard her. *Just tell her about the Ali Baba with the Saddam 'stache. You need to tell someone.*

"I'm okay, Momma. Don't worry, stop watchin' the news, they never say how it really is," Connor said. *Just ask Sergeant Thompson.*

"Well, Theresa's son came back angry, he had the P.T.S.D. He got help from some doctors."

Connor couldn't help but to smirk at that. "I don't need some shrink, Mom. They can't help anyone. It's not like I'm seeing real stuff like the Vietnam Vets did."

"Fifteen minutes," the soldier in charge called out.

*Fuckin' POG, shut up.* His mother talked a mile a minute and his phone time ticked away just as fast, but all Connor could hear in his head was "Get down, motherfucker," "Platoon Sergeant's team's hit," "room cleared."

*I killed someone...I should tell Mom, got to tell someone.*

Connor thought of his father, a Vietnam Veteran, telling him something before he deployed. His father had said, "Son, I went out in that jungle one night and I saw the Devil. He scared me so bad that when I came back out, I wasn't scared of nothing else ever again."

*Goddamn it, Connor, forget telling Mom, forget it, it's selfish to say shit that worries her, forget about what happened. Talk to your mom and go back and clean your weapon again!*

Connor buried it.

*Jesus, did the phone guy just call out time is up? There's no way I've been on here that long.*

"I just worry about you, that's a mother's right you will never understand," his mother said.

Connor listened to her but saw all of all his dead friends, the dead civilians, and the twisted face with the mustache.

*I killed someone...*

Connor felt the tears welling up in his eyes. He started to cry but he kept his voice steady, "Love you Mom."

"Love you too, baby."

"I said your time is up, four," the soldier called out again.

Connor hung up the phone and stared at the wall behind it. "I killed him," he whispered.

*Everything has changed. Nothing is going to be the same.*

"I said time is up, four!"

*What the fuck is that POGs problem? These bastards care more about what's happenin' inside the wire then they do about the enemy outside it.*

"SHUT THE FUCK UP, POG!"

Every phone conversation in the place halted. A few soldiers stood up in anger. "I'm talking to my kids, asshole," a soldier shouted.

Many more became aggressive and a First Sergeant, in a very clean uniform, jumped up and took control. The First Sergeant pulled Connor to the side and the soldiers went back to their phones. As Connor was being berated and threatened with jail time, he could feel his CIB pressing against his leg from the inside of his pocket. The left corner of his lip slowly curled to his ear.

"I'm sorry, First Sergeant. I've just been excited about my unit's big firefight earlier," Connor said as he assumed a respectful position with his hands folded in the small of his back. "But you know what combat's like, I'm sure…First Sergeant."

*Well, he's looking at me like I owe him money. Maybe he'll punch me.*

Instead of getting punched in his face, he heard "You're a disgrace" and "You Stryker guys are nothing but thugs."

"I hope you like being a Private, again. Be damn sure that your unit will hear about this," the First Sergeant flicked Connor on the Specialist rank that was centered in the middle of his chest. "Now, get the fuck out of here."

Connor walked to the exit of the shack, the Arabian night quiet and black before him. His half-smile became a scowl and he thought, *The enemy's not outside the wire, the fuckin' enemy is here! The C.O. is going to have my ass.* Connor's hands curled into fists. He shut his eyes tight, took a deep breath and adjusted his rifle sling. When he opened his eyes again, he had his smile back. Before Connor stepped out into the darkness, he thought, *Fuck it Connor, don't matter, forget it. Everything is fine.*

# RANGERS LEAD THE WAY

★ ★ ★

*Zoey Byrd*

In sleep she looked sullen and darkly beautiful. That was Rose di Cristo Sanchez-Garcia.

Her husband, Paul Freedman, liked watching her slumber. It was a quiet moment with his wife of one year. They'd met in high school in Waco, and although Paul had a wandering eye, he was solely an introvert and didn't have the 100% wherewithal to act on his fantasy of bagging the Tiffany Whites or Brittany Greens—the blonde, buxom cheerleaders who swished up and down the halls all tits and teeth. Either one would have done, both at the same time even better.

Rose was a cheerleader too, but didn't go by Rosie, and never *Rosa*. She was flat-chested and carried herself as if her heart were encased in a lead drum, her head lifted high, much like a martyr, red lipstick announcing full lips. At homecoming senior year, she burst through the banner first, beating the defensive line—black hair bound in a tight bun at the nape of her neck. It was then that Paul took notice.

Rose's mother was a di Cristo Sanchez, one quarter Italian which made Rose one eighth, her father a Garcia. She grew up as Rosa Garcia until she met Paul and told him straight out her name was Rose.

"The men in my family are fighters, defending their women to death," she said

"That's cool," said Paul.

It was then that she started letting her hair hang loose and putting *di Cristo Sanchez-Garcia* on her papers. "That's a typo," she told the teachers when they called roll and said, "Rosa?"

★ ★ ★

Paul joined the Army after high school with Rose's claws dug in deep. It was one way to shake a girl—put on a uniform and disappear. Uncle Sam owns me now, baby. Ft. Benning, an Army post in an armpit town in a crotch-rotten corner of Georgia. That should have scared her off.

Paul had had this plan ever since he'd seen pictures of his father dressed in black pajamas and grease paint toting all sorts of outlandish weapons. He begged for more stories of choppers dropping dark ops teams into Laos and Cambodia—forbidden AORs. "We were American. We were Rangers. No one knew what we did. It was pretty neat." His father was Tom Sawyer floating down the Mekong whistling a swell tune, flying low level over verdant triple canopies, lustful with wonder. Disneyland, and the kids armed to the teeth with carbines, rifles, mortars, machine guns, claymores, and grenades. AKs taken off the enemy dead. Fighting evil, saving the day. Touching down in an LZ, communing with the Montagnards. Tribal brothers, enmeshed souls.

"*Denial.* Not a bad way to spend the war," said his father.

And so Paul became a Ranger, too. It was 2005. He would deploy to a combat zone. He was in his element one hundred per cent and then some.

How Rose hated the military. In spite of her claim to honor and glory via her Italian and Hispanic heritages, she thought Paul should have studied to become a lawyer or doctor in order to make money, marry her, build their dynasty, and ensconce her in a two-story castle, with two kids, stainless steel appliances, granite countertops. His war should have been a day-to-day grind, a clogged freeway in San Antonio, a golf foursome on Sundays. These things were attainable—a pot of gold at the end of the rainbow, a Florida vacation, a two-car garage. Not sign up for poverty, a room in the barracks. It was disgraceful. Her hatred of what he had done stirred her loins and made her crave his wrongness with such fervor that she swore her breasts grew from a size A to a B cup during the thirteen weeks he was in basic. She was pregnant.

"You make me laugh," said Paul, the first time he bagged Rose. It was the night before he shipped out to basic. It was her virginity he took and now he owed her. He had a distant look in his eyes as if there were someplace else he needed to be. "This was just fun. This is good-bye."

To Paul, she said, "You're a black man but God changed his mind at the last minute and turned you white and that's how you ended up in your mother's womb."

Paul smiled. His yellow blond curls were so tight and compact that the thin helmet of hair on his head looked permed. Rose felt disgust at the girlishness of his locks, jealous of his green eyes flecked with gold, white teeth small like little pearls, high cheekbones. His strong, aquiline nose made up for his prettiness.

At Fort Benning, a million miles away, he told her over the phone, "Sure, I miss you."

But Rose wasn't buying it. *Sua Sponte* was a thorny crown he had put on to shun her. "You have to marry me." Her seriousness was the edge he needed, the salt in his coffee, peculiar and fascinating.

"You should see me now," said Paul. The Army was quick to shave his head. Shorn of his curls, he had a fantastic feeling. His father was right. The Army would break him down and build him back up.

At basic Paul met Seth Raderstorf, and it was instant. They arrived in their civvies looking like fags with their scruffy hair, slouchy stances, and T-shirts with tough words—*Wrangler, Def Leppard.*

"This is some fucked-up shit," said Seth.

"I signed up for this," said Paul.

"I hope I die," said Seth.

"We're teammates now. You can count on me," said Paul.

"Typical jock. *Texan*," said Seth. "Nice belt buckle."

Paul said, "Listen, Man, we're going to move farther, faster and fight harder than any other soldier. You'd better go Ranger. Make your parents proud," said Paul.

"Bringin' on the heartache."

Seth had graduated from a private school in Connecticut where he'd been on the debate team. Both his parents taught psych at a college. They had given him nothing to live up to.

"Professors of Monotony," said Seth.

"That's cool," said Paul. "Plants and things."

"Jesus, you're so dense it comes off as *gravitas*."

"I have no idea what you say 99% of the time," said Paul, "but I've got your back."

"Hence, I need friends like you."

"Man—*hence*—don't talk like that. It's embarrassing."

"Sure, man."

"Stick with me. I'll show you how this works," said Paul.

"Livin' the dream," said Seth.

"I'm proud of you, Son," Paul's father said at graduation from basic.

Paul saw the sadness in his father's down-slanted eyes. "Thanks, Dad," he said.

Paul had carried the flag.

"I can't believe this," said his mother. Her eyes were red from crying.

"Chill out, Mom. It's only the Army."

"Been there, done that," she said. She'd divorced Paul's father when he got back from Vietnam because "he'd changed" and then married him again ten years later because he was the love of her life, and vice versa. She was 44 when Paul was born, her only child. They lived on twenty-five acres outside of town for a reason.

After Paul enlisted, his mom sat in a rocking chair, not rocking, looking out the window at a live oak in the backyard, drinking salted coffee while his father read in *National Geographic* about ancient tribes like the Masaai, going deeper into the past than Vietnam, into a world where the weapons could be dropped and turned back into earth.

"Why didn't your parents come?" Paul asked Seth.

"They think I ran off to play in a rock band, stay up all night, drink and do drugs."

"Didn't you tell them about your ability to adapt and improvise weapons systems to fulfill a narrow requirement that has resulted in improved equipment across the entire Army?" said Paul.

"Are you serious?" said Seth.

"They don't teach that in college, do they?"

"I'll send them a field manual," said Seth.

Paul got permission to come home after jump school and marry Rose. It was the right thing to do. She wore a white dress at church and changed into a red satin mini with short, puffy sleeves for the reception. The wedding wasn't big but the backyard at her parents' house was. They put up a circus tent. They had a punch bowl that the boys from Benning—Grice, LaPlant, Sachs, and Rouser—spiked with 100 proof Southern Comfort. The mothers were appalled. But they liked the uniforms. It gave the event an importance, the magnitude of a *roman-fleuve* in the making. Sexy and honorable.

*Conquistadores*, said Rose's mother.

Rose's brothers were the stalwarts, each taking on a task as if serving the queen of utopia. They didn't drink the punch, rarely smiled, worked the reception like waiters and body guards, and spoke Spanish only to their father, cajoled their mother in English, and chided Rose in both languages calling her princess, not because they normally called her this, but to remind Paul and anyone else from the outside that Rosa di Cristo Sanchez-Garcia belonged to them and always would.

Paul liked Rose's brothers. They were respectful to him. He was an appendage that didn't need to be removed as long as he remained agreeable.

"I'm cool," said Paul.

"We've noticed. That's why you fit in here."

Paul hadn't known he did. He was pleased.

Seth was miffed. He was best man and could see that Rose wasn't the love of Paul's life or vice versa. He should have stood up when the priest said, ". . . or forever hold your peace," but he was already standing.

"How do you marry a chick you don't like and who doesn't like you?" Seth asked.

"My advice is to start drinking heavily," said Grice.

"Excuses are like assholes. Everybody's got one," said Rouser.

"Rejoice O young man in thy youth," said LaPlant.

"Okay, I got it. Shit, I lost it," said Seth.

"Hey, SoCo for anyone?" said Sachs.

"No, you dick, but I will have a Southern Comfort. Actually, come to think of it, I'll have a JD," said Seth.

When the band started to warm up, Seth grabbed Rose by the hand. She glared at him but didn't pull away.

"All I feel is heat and flames and all I see are dark eyes," Seth said to Rose.

"Ow," said Rose to nothing.

"Paul's supposed to be first," said LaPlant.

Grice, LaPlant, Sachs, and Rouser pushed Paul forward.

"Everything by the book until the shit hits the fan," said Grice.

"She's all yours," said Seth.

Paul danced awkwardly with Rose, shuffling his feet from side to side and gripping her too tightly.

"You're not leading," said Rose, smiling a big one for the photographer who circled them.

Paul didn't know which way to go. He looked to Seth.

Seth gave a thumbs up, and Rose glared at him, the glint of light in her eyes appearing a tad mean-spirited, but not unwarranted.

"Now that's what I'm talking about," said Seth.

"Do what?" said Grice.

"This ain't no party, this ain't no disco," said Sachs.

"This is fucked-up," said Seth.

"Better get used to it," said Rouser.

"Stop saying 'fuck,'" said LaPlant.

"He said 'fucked-up,'" said Grice.

"My bad," said LaPlant.

After that, Seth drank himself stupid. He was supposed to be the designated driver.

"Fuck, Seth," said LaPlant. "What the fuck?"

"A total lack of discipline," said Rouser.

"I can see I have to cover your ass as always," said Grice.

"Rich boy," said Sachs.

"*Venni, Vetti, Vecci,*" said Seth.

"Yeah, man. Seth, you're shit-faced, speaking Spanish and all," said LaPlant.

"That's messed up," said Paul.

Seth muttered something.

"He said, 'You're both wrong,'" said Sachs. "It's Latin."

Seth heaved out the window all the way back to the motel, hallucinating that the dotted, center line flashed cards of missed opportunities in his face. If he'd stayed in college he'd be a junior by now.

Hence, Paul and Rose tied the knot. Rose didn't change her last name to "Freedman." She didn't move to Fort Benning. She gave birth to twin girls, held her ground, stayed in Waco. After six months, she moved to San Antonio to live with her eldest brother who purchased a two-story house with all the fixtures. The neighbors thought they were a couple raising twins. Rose didn't correct them.

*How does a year go by so quickly? How does it?* Seth wondered.

All Paul wanted was to be a good soldier. Seth did, too. And there they were, hurtling through time and space, training and more training—so tired, but a good tired. They graduated from Ranger indoc and earned the tan beret. And then, oh yeah, family. Paul turned 19. He was lucky. Rose had seven brothers, a slew of aunts, uncles, and cousins. They took care of Rose and coddled the twins—Faith and Hope. How Paul hated those names. They chided him, pointed out his absences, and accused him of wrongs he could never right.

Paul's first instinct when he had time to make a phone call was always his Mom and Dad.

"Hey, it's me. Checking in."

"Paul, Paul," his mother said, trying to conjure up the boy, but he wouldn't let her do this.

"What's up? Same old, here."

Truth was, everything was new every day. The sky a cobalt blue, the field a chartreuse green—moving through this cinematic wonder was Paul, he and his squad tightly bound.

Seth felt bad. He thought Paul a fine soldier, but a fool when it came to women. What was he doing with a wife, kids? If girls, women, whatever you were supposed to call them, were so on top of it, why did they get pregnant? Logistics, planning, out the window. They let the shit hit the fan, twins born, and then started to organize. It was backasswards. It was ephemeral, hazy, beautiful, fucked-up.

*Love? How does a guy do that without giving too much away?* Seth wanted to know. They would deploy in thirty days. They were hanging out in Grice's room in the barracks and no one had money. They were drinking Bud Lite. Sad, pathetic.

"Infiltrate or penetrate, employing a seamless integration of one's assets. That's how," said Grice.

"Grice, you're so strac," LaPlant said.

They were playing video games.

"If you can't defeat them, retreat. Doing it the hard way will only bring you death. Don't pray that Lady Liberty will watch over you on the battlefield," said Sachs.

"The bullets don't know who you are. Only retreat will give you a chance to look for the possibility of rising again, cradling a weapon," said Rouser.

"What are you talking about?" said Paul. He'd slipped out for bible study.

"Call of Duty," said LaPlant.

"Modern Warfare," said Seth.

"Hell, yeah," said Rouser.

"Marriage is hell, but being alone is a worse hell," said Grice.

Paul ignored Grice. "I'm going to pray for you, Seth," said Paul. He carried a New Testament, now.

"God as your feudal overlord," said Seth.

"You have to save yourself, Seth," said Paul. "I can't do it."

It was their first deployment to a combat zone. No clear front line. Pockets of trouble and resistance.

Paul had ten days leave before he left. He went to Waco. Seth flew to Connecticut. His parents wanted to drive to the city and see Ground Zero. Seth wanted to stay home and read. It was the end of summer. Classes would be starting soon.

In San Antonio, Paul circled Rose and the twin girls, and the house not his. The leather and brass furnishings were garish and foreign, the stainless steel appliances space-age in form. The flat screen TV, huge with surround sound, was not his. Once downrange, a barren moonlike outpost would look more familiar to him than this.

At night, Paul watched Rose sleep. She was beautiful and composed, like a page in a magazine. He went into the girls' room and stared at them. He felt guilt, but it was fleeting. The nightlight illuminated their eyelashes which made him wonder what he could buy them before he left that would make up for his absence. They seemed to have everything—toys, clothes, and pink things he couldn't identify scattered around the hollow house. Rose was irritable, bored with his demands for sex, holding back from him in revenge for what she imagined he owed her. Paul had no training for this. *Family*. His squad was it.

Back in Waco, Paul stayed with his parents, Rose and the girls with hers.

Paul called Seth.

"Are you still in 'Wacko'?" said Seth.

"I need to be gone already," said Paul.

"You sound old."

"I can't sleep," said Paul.

"That sucks," said Seth. "I met a girl at the bookstore."

"That's cool."

"I gave her my e-mail."

"Hoo-ah," said Paul. He wished he could meet a girl.

"Hoo-ah, for real. Someone to cry for me when I die," said Seth.

Rose was livid. Paul would miss Faith and Hope's first birthday.

"You won't be in the photos," she said.

"I'm a Ranger," said Paul. He left out "first."

Not to be defeated, Rose staged a birthday party—a cake, candles, hats, presents, Care Bears music—*Oopsy Does It!*—and all of Rose's brothers, their wives, children, cousins, her parents, grandparents. Paul's parents were there, too, looking as out-of-place as they had at the wedding. Rose's family embraced, held on and rocked—an armada taking everyone within reach across the great ocean to a new world. Paul wanted to go, too, or so he thought.

Miraculously the twins rolled from their tummies to their backs, squealing, gurgling and cooing. It was perfect—flashes going, blinding them, scaring them and making them cry. The crying made more sense to Paul than the rolling. The movements were too easy. No one's first time was that grandiose. Everyone clapped. Paul reached for the girls. He liked holding them because they were warm, compliant, pleased by his mere presence. Rose eyed him suspiciously. Later, when they were alone, she would be quick to come up with more demands, complaints, and admonitions. She mistook his quiet manner for weakness.

"You're selfish," said Rose.

"I have to go. It's my duty."

"Your duty is to family."

All Paul could think of was his parents and they were cool. The best part of his wedding had been hanging out with his friends. It killed him that they had driven all the way from Benning non-stop.

On his last day in Waco, they drove to the *Foto Familia*, a shop owned by Rose's uncle. Paul, dressed in his greens, tan beret, and Rose, wearing a black halter dress and spike heels, sat on a carpeted block, angled toward each other—Faith in Paul's lap, Hope in Rose's. But that wasn't enough. Rose wanted shots of herself sprawled on a fake lawn with a colonial-style mansion and picket fence in the background, horses on a bluegrass lawn. It wasn't Waco, Fort Benning, San Antonio or anyplace else he'd ever been. Rose asked Paul to pick out the best proofs. He said, "Whatever you want." He was impatient, anxious to go help his dad clear the yard of dead tree limbs, and sit with his mom in the back room. That was love and he didn't have to say it.

Paul took the girls outside in their stroller, while Rose stayed in the photo shop talking to her aunt and uncle. Roxane, Rose's cousin, followed him to the car. She took both Faith and Hope's blonde dolls and held them out to Paul, and then pulled them back. They smiled at each other as if old chums. Roxane was more petite than Rose, her eyes set wide apart, an invitation to come closer.

"Wanna hang out later?" she asked. She lived in the apartment above the store.

Later, they went to a club and drank Baileys, Peppermint Schnapps, and wine coolers. Anything for her, thought Paul. "I am a sacrifice unto thee." With some girls it was like that—a déjà vu in the flesh, a fair trade agreement.

"Huh?" said Roxane.

"I'm just with you here and now," said Paul.

"Don't talk stupid."

With Roxane that night, Paul sank into a blank oblivion. She smelled like cigarettes and cotton candy. Her fingernails were sharp. The next morning he woke up with a splitting headache, scratches on his back and neck.

"Get out of here. Hurry," said Roxane, pushing him out of the bed, scratching at him some more. Paul drove home and his mom made him a cup of coffee. The salt took the bitterness away.

"This hits the spot," said Paul.

"I'm worried about you," said his mom.

"The beans are from Africa," said his dad.

"Africa's a continent, not a country, Dad," said Paul.

"You got me there."

"Oh my God," said his mom. "The beans are Ethiopian. I've never even left the lower 48."

Paul thought his mom a little nutty, the repercussion of having a mother who gave birth late.

Deployment. Dust. The journey wore Paul out. And then waiting for nothing for days wore him down even more. He tried to stay pumped-up, inspired, but he was depressed. It wasn't Disneyland, it wasn't neat. While Paul sulked, Seth stayed psyched. For him, this was the real deal—cleaning his weapon, working out, training in abandoned compounds, waiting for the proverbial shit to hit the fan. He was glad he'd dropped out of college. He was fit. The baby fat on his face was shed. He was tanned and lean.

"Rose, it's me," said Paul. He was calling from Afghanistan. His was a bleak existence. At the end of the day, he was a faceless Ranger, a body, a number, a cot in a row of other cots in a hangar, a seat on a Chinook.

"Where are you?"

"Here," said Paul.

"You don't even ask about Faith and Hope."

"Asking," he said.

"I wish you were dead," said Rose.

"Christ—," said Paul. He wanted to hit her, shut up her cruelty.

"I hate your guts," said Rose.

"Rose, I have to go."

"Go then."

Paul's mouth was coated with sand he couldn't get rid of. The odor of burning shit hung in the air. His head hurt. He wasn't drinking enough water. He was constipated. Why didn't Rose understand this?

"It was the worst phone call you can imagine," Paul told Seth.

"If your horse dies, I suggest you get off," said Grice.

"Pull yourself together, Freedman," said Seth.

Paul glared at Seth. Seth ignored him.

That night their sergeant ordered them to write the "in case" letter. No one had done it. No one wanted to do it.

Grice said, "That's morbid. Bad luck."

"Do it anyway," said the sergeant.

Seth approached it as if a term paper. He titled it, "Death Letter."

"I love you because you're my parents and I'm supposed to," wrote Seth. They'd like the irony.

"Don't worry—we are practically bulletproof," said Rouser.

"Now you're talking!" said LaPlant.

"We need to see some action," said Paul. He folded up a blank piece of paper and sealed it in an envelope.

"You didn't write anything," said Seth.

"I didn't come here to die," said Paul.

"She's still your wife. Rose. Her name is Rose."

That was the last straw for Paul. He jumped Seth, flipped him out of his cot, went for the throat, his two hands clamped down and squeezing—"I'm going to kill you, man." Seth's eyes bulged. Paul slammed his head into the plywood flooring, and Seth passively took it, ready to die. His letter was done. The squad had to pull Paul off Seth.

Grice kneeled over Seth and patted his chest. "You can't fight worth shit."

"You're wrong," said Seth.

Paul stood behind Grice, fists clenched, eyes small and mean, jaw clenched. Seth gave him the finger.

"You got no honor," said Paul.

"This is bullshit," said Seth, getting to his feet, pushing Grice's help away.

Everyone looked at Seth, stunned. They expected him to jump Paul back or at least counter with a smartass remark. Instead he fixed his cot, grabbed a book from his locker, and walked off to use a phone. His head felt heavy and throbbed with pain. He had a minor concussion. He called his Dad, who answered on the first ring.

"I've been thinking about you," said his dad.

"You would be," said Seth.

"Ha," said his dad.

"Where's Mom?" asked Seth.

"I'm here," she said from the other line. "I haven't touched your room."

"How are you?"

"I'm scared sick."

"Suffering makes you remember it better," said Seth.

"Hey, that's my line," said his dad.

"You two," said his mom.

Seth had forgotten how much his parents liked him.

That afternoon they got their mission—an infil on the outskirts of a village in response to something. It wasn't clear if the LZ was hot. They geared-up in a rush, filed onto the helo, their bodies heavy with kits. Their minds pinged with the words: just go, let's go, lift this bird. The platoon leader told the two squads of Rangers to watch their fires coming off, because of the friendlies operating in the area.

*This is no 'Nam*, thought Paul. *No slogging through swampy jungles for days on end eating shitty C-rats; this was the 21st century—quick reaction forces, hit and run*. Seth looked at Paul seated across from him, their eyes met. Paul nodded. Seth shrugged. Here it was, their glory moment. The ramp lowered. They touched down on the rocky terrain outside a village to a barrage of fire, an RPG tore one of the engines starting a fire. *Shit*. They'd been diverted to the wrong coordinates; the ridgeline was manned. Seth was eerily calm. Time slowed down. Bullets tore through the fuselage. There were shouts of *Go, go, go*. Seth charged off the Chinook. Paul followed at his heels. He was faster than Seth and stepped on Seth's heel. Seth tripped and fell at the bottom of the ramp, head first, knocking himself out cold.

Paul lept over him, exploding through the back of the helo first. He was greeted by machine gun fire. He took a bullet in his bicep and kept running, not knowing that the first sting of the metal piercing his skin was real. It was a shame Rose would never see him in this moment of unabashed fury.

Seth remained face down at the bottom of the ramp.

The two squads dispersed, took cover and began a counterassault on the ridgeline. No friendlies were in the area; the intel was wrong. Seth came to and crawled forward, towards Paul, gravitated to him like he had that first day in basic. "Freedman's down," he yelled. Bullets snapped past Seth's ears and cracked against the rocks. It was louder than the movies, louder than any live-fire training they'd done.

Grice covered him. "Where's your fucking weapon?" he shouted.

Seth didn't have his weapon. Paul was carrying the big gun, the 240, and so Grice ran to him, flipped him over and took it. He unloaded Paul's weapon on the ridgeline, while Seth fed him ammo.

Seth kept his head down. He was seeing stars. At some point Grice ran to Rouser under heavy fire and dragged him to cover. They fought until air support arrived. It was snafu all the way. But they survived. Paul was the only casualty. This was a shock. He was their poster boy. He wasn't supposed to die.

Paul was buried in the national cemetery in San Antonio. The rest of them had to finish their tour before they came home. They had a memorial ceremony for Paul in Afghanistan. It was rushed. Seth wanted to pray but he'd never done that before. His head throbbed. He would have to be medevac'd. The squad would carry the guilt of the survivor. They didn't talk about it. All of them separated at the end of their enlistments except Grice and Rouser, who'd earn their Ranger patches.

"Cocksucker," said Seth, whenever he'd think of Paul, which was every day. "He was my friend." Seth went back to college, carried his pack to school on the days he felt down.

On the first anniversary of Paul's death, Seth traveled to San Antonio to visit his grave. Sachs and LaPlant came too. Grice and Rouser were deployed but sent their regards. Rose met them at the cemetery with the twins, Faith and Hope. They all hugged each other half-heartedly. It was awkward. No SoCo or JD. They weren't the boys from Benning. They weren't *conquistadores*. It was sad, pathetic. It was a formality to get through. It didn't solve anything.

Rose's family had been afraid Rose would do something dramatic, but in a year's time she became happy, fat, and contented. She had had her tragedy. Seth looked into her eyes and saw a steely, cold reserve that had always been there. She had command and control of her children and all other aspects of her life. She smiled at him in the end, and kissed him on the cheek. It was "good-bye."

Seth's memory of the Army became sepia-toned, except for that bright moment in combat, pure Technicolor at its best—bullets flying past his face, the smell of disaster: fuel, smoke, cordite, blood, the fresh cold air of resistance, blank and beautiful. You don't get over it; you learn to live with it, they told him at the VA. *Hence*, wondered Seth. *Hence*.

# The Idiot, or Life in Wartime

★ ★ ★

*Fred Leebron*

I.

It was hard to wrap the chains around himself as he sat in his car in the parking garage, and even harder to account for the baby. He hadn't planned on the baby; the baby had been the great invention of his unconscious; and now as he turned it around and around he could see the many ways the baby would work to his advantage and the definite ways he would not.

He thought of how prisoners were sometimes shackled like this, twined around both groins, encased at the waist. It was an art he had had to study just so that he could walk.

He levered himself from the car. He must now weigh thirty more pounds, but he'd lost thirty pounds for this (how thin you're getting, Claire had said. For you, he'd replied, and kissed her.). And he'd stood in front of a mirror and practiced with sissel rope while downstairs the baby napped.

"Oh, honey," he said, gently reaching in and unbuckling Sam from the car seat. "It's time to go see the White House."

"Mommy coming home?" Sam said. It was what he always said whenever he woke from a nap.

"Soon," Walter said. After all, if he said five minutes or five hours, the response was always the same—the baby howled. But soon—soon always worked.

He'd allowed enough space to fit the baby within the chain metal net, and now he dipped him in. Sam was snug against his chest. He could feel the rapid heartbeat against his sternum, and Sam's head sunk deeply into his shoulder. It was only yesterday that, inexplicably, as Walter sat on the couch reading the newspaper the baby had climbed up into his lap and started kissing his face, like a moment of conviction, as if he'd finally decided he loved him even if he wasn't Mommy. Where would they be in ten hours, in twenty hours, in twenty months?

Up in the waning light of late afternoon, he clanked along with the baby, his oversized winter coat making them look like a harmless genetic mistake huddled against the cold. Sam was an act of genius. Without him, no doubt, Walter would have looked like he was carrying a bomb.

He was careful not to bump into anyone on the wide sidewalk of Pennsylvania Avenue. The White House fence went on and on. On one hand it looked like he could stop anywhere, flick the fist-sized padlock from his pocket, and install himself in an instant that would change everything for him once and for all.

And then would they slip the baby from him and fade so easily from his reach, or had he secured Sam enough?

He gave a frantic tug on the loose draw.

Sam whimpered but did not raise his head.

"Okay, baby," Walter soothed him. "Okay."

They passed the east entrance, moving as naturally as the two of them could move. He concentrated on staring straight ahead, past the concrete dividers and the thick metal pylons, to the next section of continuous fencing.

Somehow, thirty years ago, this kind of gesture had seemed significant, it had had an impact, but now he was beginning to see it as empty, futile, self-indulgent. Here was the fence, here was he, all he would be at most was a man with a toddler chained to a fence. To have any effect he'd need to stop the flow of traffic, but to do that would require twenty or thirty people. He didn't know twenty or thirty people he'd want to do this with. He wasn't political enough. Was it too late to turn political? Whenever his daughter, now thirteen, proclaimed that she was going to be President some day, he'd wonder, "Whatever would you want to do that for?" "Because I'm going to," she'd say, glaring at him as if not only were he simple but weak. He sighed heavily and leaned back against the fence. How ironic the ease with which he did this, right here on Pennsylvania Avenue. This had been his plan all along. Evidently it wasn't much of a plan. It didn't threaten anyone.

The truth was he didn't want to threaten anyone.

But power without the threat of violence wasn't power. It was nothing. That was what the whole problem was about. He was nothing. For years he'd accepted that he was just another professor at just another small college in the hinterland, while his brother had gone on to become a nationally renowned intellectual and his oldest friends had left him behind for Hollywood and Wall Street and Capitol Hill. Even now he didn't mind that he was nothing. What he minded was the war. He was sick of the practically casual and apparently acceptable violence, he was sick of watching some of his students go off so willingly into it. He'd sat with them in his office and watched them say that they wanted to go, that they were all for it, that it was a duty, an honor, something that they understood might happen from the beginning, before there even was a war. There always was a war, but he knew what they meant.

Tracy had been one of his favorite students. She had talked in class. She had handed in work before it was due, just to get a response and have a chance to make it better. She worked at the one bar he sometimes went to. She was six months from graduation. She changed the color of her hair every few weeks, it seemed. Even her boyfriend tried to persuade her to somehow resist. What was there to resist? Half of Tracy's platoon was going, and if she was in that half, that was absolutely fine by her. She was twenty-one years old. Now she was gone.

And then, just this morning, there was the kids' swim teacher from the Y, a skinny red-headed guy who looked fifteen or sixteen, but when Walter heard the news of the helicopter crash off the African coast, he instantly had a sick feeling in his gut, and at noon when he drove through the town square the flag was at half mast, and in the grocery store someone told him it had been Tim on that helicopter. Tim who had coaxed Henry into the water when nobody else could, Tim who had put the tentative Jordan on his bony shoulders and engaged in a tender chicken fight during free swim. Damn that kid had been a nice kid. Walter hadn't even known he'd gone to war.

Goddamn it he was crying. What kind of man was he to stand here tearful and chained. A nonviolent man in a violent world. An idiot—a private person, a person without political affiliation—in a world where everyone had chosen sides. He'd never believed in choosing sides. He'd believed that there were always more sides than could be chosen. He'd always told his students in writing their papers that there were no rules, only principles, and every choice they made as arguers, as writers, involved weighing the principles against each other. Tracy had nodded her head at this. He liked being attracted to students—it gave him energy—but he'd never felt attracted to her. Now she was his first thought when he woke every morning, and his last thought when he tried to fall asleep each night. You couldn't stop her. You couldn't stop anything.

"Sir?"

He looked up. It was an officer in a white military cap with a black brim.

"Sir, I know the baby's sleeping, but you have to move on."

Goddamn they were so polite, goddamn they were so civil while they were off killing and being killed.

"I understand," Walter managed. He tried to smoothly separate himself from the fence but the weight saddling him—the weight of the baby, the weight of the metal, all the weight he'd been feeling for these last long goddamn years—gathered itself around him and pushed him back against the fence. He heard the odd mechanical sound just as the officer did. The brim turned surely back upon him and just as surely Walter whipped the padlock from his pocket, caught the draw chain in his other hand, and as if he had practiced his whole life for this one meaningless gesture, locked himself into place on the White House fence.

"Sir!" the officer said sharply as something dull and black stuck its long snout at Walter. "Move away from the fence."

For the first time all day, all week, all month, all year, Walter felt absolutely clear-headed. He could see her again. Her hair was henna. He could see his wife in the kitchen, standing over the sink, wondering where the hell he was. Upstairs his daughter lay in her bed in her willfully chaotic room, reading a Tamora Pierce book with an i-pod attached to her ears. Across the hall his son was playing Star Wars on Play Station, his back tensed, his anger ready to launch itself against any intruder. Walter imagined he wouldn't be hearing that awful game for a long, long time. He loved his children but he wasn't crazy about tending to them. Maybe he thought he'd get a rest in prison.

"Sir!" the officer commanded, and now there were a half-dozen officers with him, and Walter supposed he was to raise his hands or shout something vile or blow himself up. He looked for fear, in himself or in the young officer within three feet of him or within his colleagues grouped to either side of him, but there was no fear anywhere, even within him, which surprised him, though soon he imagined he might feel quite lonely and depressed. Soon he would feel worse. But not now. Not yet.

"I can't," he said.

There were sirens in his ears and sirens in his eyes, there was the baby's sleepy breath against his neck, there was all this metal he'd trussed himself up with. He was rooted to the spot. Everything felt a little tight. He tried to measure the baby's breathing. He was breathing fine. Nothing was too tight, nothing was too loose. It was just as he had planned and not as he had planned at all. He could have said, The war is wrong. He could have said, The President lied. It was more complex than that. It was better to say nothing and stand there and not see the cordoning off of the sidewalk and the leveling of the revolvers (revolvers? guns? pistols? automatic weapons?—he had experience with none of them) and the heated glaring of all the personnel so freshly descended upon him. He was going to be in a lot of trouble, he was in a lot of trouble. If he said anything—I'm not going to hurt anyone, I don't have a bomb—they could mishear him or not believe him. They might shoot him to save the baby, but the baby was right over his heart. A stroke of genius, the baby.

They were shouting things at him. He stared blankly at nothing. He could imagine what his mother would say. He could imagine how his brother might defend him. He could hear the exasperation of his one sister and the indifference of his other sister. At least his in-laws would probably be pleased. Hadn't his mother-in-law been screaming and throwing tomatoes right before she had gone into labor with his wife? He allowed a smirk to play on his lips. Perhaps it was the President's own smirk. Anything he said could be used against him. Anything he said could be misinterpreted. Anything he said would be reductive.

A military dog sniffed at him with disinterest. A long wand approached and swept him.

He was a pacifist, a peacenik, a protestor, a professor.

"You're in a heap of shit," someone said.

"Evans," someone else said.

"Is this a hostage situation?" said a third soldier—or a cop. You couldn't tell who was talking. There were too goddamn many of them.

He's my son, Walter wanted to say proudly. But he knew it was better not to talk. Now that he had acted, there was no need for talk. He was done talking, yet he had never talked. The fact that Sam was his son would mean nothing to these people. It occurred to him he should have made a sign. What would the sign have said? Stop the war. Too basic. It had all been said by everyone else. He felt himself slipping into nihilism. Not a good sign. There were no good signs now. Why had he done this?

"Daddy," Sam said. And from him wafted an instantly recognizable odor. "Want a fresh one."

Maybe the baby had not been such a good idea after all.

"He's clean," a smiling officer said. It wasn't even dark yet. It should have been nightfall, but it wasn't. He hadn't lasted ten minutes on this fence.

"You'll get one soon," Walter whispered to the baby.

"Now!" the baby whined. "Need one now."

I have made a very bad decision, Walter thought. It was like precipitating a car accident—the one last maneuver you shouldn't have taken—yet apparently so much worse than that. What had he meant to accomplish here? Across the street a few bright lights flicked on.

He could say, It's about the war. He could say, Bring our men and women home. He could say, Stop the lies. It had all been said. Was there no more eloquence?

"Daddy," his baby cried.

Was there really nothing to be done?

"Please," Sam said. "I want a fresh one."

"That's a good sentence, Sam," Walter murmured. "A really good sentence."

Hands were upon him. They'd moved in. "Give me the baby, pal."

"I can't," Walter said.

"Damn, he's locked in good."

They just wanted to sweep him away.

"You have the right—"

"Not now, you dumbass. Just get him off the fence, for christ's sake."

"Daddy," Sam whimpered. "Please, Daddy."

"That's real nice, what you've done to your son there."

Walter tried to look past him. They were so in his face all he could see was skin and shadow.

With something like shears they snipped at his parka. It fell at his feet. The baby shivered.

"What about a blow torch?"

"Locksmith?"

"It's a combo."

"I bet you don't know the combo, do you?"

"That's correct," Walter said, trying to warm Sam with his breath and wincing at how professorial he sounded.

"Mr. Miller?" His wallet was held to his face. "And this would be..."

"Sam," Walter said.

"Isn't that just perfect," someone said.

"Cold," Sam said.

"Fucking bolt cutters."

"Language!"

"Get those damn media people."

"We got 'em. We got 'em."

"No one's ever gonna see your face, Walter."

Walter just breathed with the baby. Behind him they commenced pounding and sawing at the lock and the chain.

"We could take him with part of the fence."

"Don't be so damn absurd."

Someone tucked a military blanket into Walter and the baby.

"Kid needs a diaper."

"No kidding."

Walter's teeth vibrated with whatever they were doing. The baby shivered and chattered.

"You guys getting anywhere?"

"Nope."

"We could tent him."

"Now there's an idea."

"Then we could...uh...proceed in...uh...privacy."

There was general laughter.

"Now don't you believe everything you read, Walter."

Somehow a yawn escaped him.

"You bored, Walter?"

"I can guarantee you Walter is not bored. Walter is scared."

A wall of canvas sprung up in front of him, around him.

"Welcome to Camp Fence, Walter."

"You boys knock it off." A guy in a tie stood eye to eye with him. "I'm Agent Wright, Professor Miller. You have committed a crime on Federal property in the District of Columbia. Without a doubt you will be arraigned on several charges. Is there anything you wish to say?"

"The baby," Walter said.

"Oh the baby," Agent Wright said. He stroked his moustache. Walter hadn't thought facial hair was allowed. "Your wife is on the way down with your other two kids. And your mother-in-law should be here shortly. With any luck the baby will never see our custody."

"That's great," Walter said.

"Great?" Wright said. "Are we off our meds today, Walter? Or perhaps trying something new?"

Walter gave up a laugh. He wouldn't mind something new right now.

"You are aware, Walter, that this was all begun on our soil? You are aware that we didn't choose this conflict, that it chose us?

You are aware that not five miles from here innocent people perished in a fireball?"

Behind him, at the fence, they continued hammering and cursing at the padlock and exposed chain link. His whole head reverberated with the pounding.

"I'm not reading your rights until I know exactly what I am arresting you for," Wright said. Then he read him his rights anyway. "Have you figured out what you want to say?"

"God no," Walter said.

"No one will ever hear it anyway." Wright glanced beyond Walter. "Any progress?"

"Hell no."

"Excuse me?"

"Hell no, sir."

"I was Navy," Wright said. "I fought in the first war."

"Thank you," Walter said.

"You're most welcome." Wright shoved his hands into his pockets. The baby was eerily quiet. "That is one scared kid."

Walter nodded.

"You realize how much simpler it would be without him?"

"Nothing is simple anymore," Walter said.

"You remember that when you registered back in seventy-nine you wrote C.O. on the little card?"

"Well—"

Wright pressed his nose practically up against Walter's cheek. "Wasn't that enough, Walter? Don't you know how much you're costing us here? Right now something dangerous could be happening somewhere, and you've gone and tied up twenty or fifty of our guys. That to me is the real crime, Walter."

That was not the whole point, but a good point, Walter thought.

"You think Sam here is ever going to forget any of this?"

"I hope not," Walter said.

"And what do you think Tracy's parents will have to say about this?"

"Nothing good," Walter admitted, trying to hide his shock at how quickly they already knew everything.

"Our intelligence is sometimes outstanding," Wright said, noting the surprise in Walter's eyes, "but of course that isn't always the story." A muscle swam in his face, close to his ear piece. "Your mother-in-law's here." He grinned at Walter. "Don't worry. We're not letting her in."

"Thank you," Walter said. His mother-in-law was okay and he was grateful she was here to take the baby, but he didn't need to see her.

"I don't have a lawyer," Walter said. "Not really, anyway."

"Not a problem," Agent Wright said.

"Just some guy back in Pennsylvania who did the closing and our wills."

"But this wasn't spontaneous, was it, Walter?"

"I guess not," Walter said.

"Bingo!" one of the soldiers said, and the chains loosened around his groin.

Wright tugged gently at Sam, who began shrieking. "Get the mother-in-law," he barked.

She was brought in by two guys with white MP helmets. Walter could now see it was dark outside. For a moment bright lights splashed into the tall narrow tent.

"Grace,' Walter said.

"Oh Walter," Grace said. She reached and Wright handed her the baby. "I—"

The MPs shuttled her from the tent.

"Visitors come later," Wright said.

They snaked the chain from his waist and chest. He was gripped very firmly and far more heavily than all that metal had.

"Drape him," Wright said, and they hooded him with a sheet of his parka. When he tried to move his hands they were already cuffed. "Time for a ride."

Walter heard Wright throw open the tent, and the light pierced what was left of his coat. People began calling at him, jeering him, interrogating him with half-phrases and nouns.

"Why now?" a woman shouted.

"Look over here," a man ordered.

"Faggot!"

"Asshole!"

"They're loving you up," Wright said, as his hand cupped the top of Walter's head and ducked him into the back seat of a car. "Now scoot over so we can ride properly."

The fabric fell from his head as he banged against the far window. Lights flashed and he kept his eyes shut. They started out Pennsylvania in what seemed like a three-car parade. The window was wet. When had it started raining?

"Just what were you hoping to accomplish back there?" Wright asked, looking at his watch as if no answer would make any difference to him.

"I'm not sure," Walter said. "It was just a gesture."

"The best you could come up with?" Wright sighed. "Moral conscience needs more imagination than that."

"The march wasn't any better," Walter tried.

"Too many goddamn channels, is what it is." Wright gave Walter an apparently friendly elbow. "You can avoid seeing anything you want to avoid seeing, and usually you don't even know it's there." He nodded his head backward. "You'll probably end up on YouTube, for goodness sake."

"That wasn't the point," Walter said.

"But here is the point, Walter. This could have been the living room-bedroom-kitchen war, what with all those embedded personnel and all those televisions everyone has. But with seven hundred channels it's like the war's not happening. Just like we're living lives that aren't happening," Wright said.

Walter stayed silent.

"You don't take meds, do you?" Wright said.

"I drink," Walter said.

"He drinks!" Wright cheerfully acknowledged the driver up front for the first time. "Think we can slap you with a D and D? And can't we add an ex post facto DUI?"

"Not today," Walter said.

"All this courage and you're sober? You should have been a soldier, Walter."

The car swung down a steep grade and entered an underground lot.

"Well, we're almost home, Professor Miller. I meant to ask you:

You get good evals, Walter? I mean, if I looked you up on Rate Your Professor, what would I find?"

Walter just looked at him. The car squealed to a stop.

"I see our time is about up," Wright said, launching himself from the car and swinging back to pull Walter with him. Walter straightened himself under yellow light outside an all-window white-walled office. "I could say good luck to you, but I wouldn't mean it."

He led him into the basement office where three gentlemen stood waiting, apparently just for him. "These guys will take you through the rest of the night, and perhaps in the morning everything will be significantly clearer. Travis?"

Travis took him and Wright quickly stepped into an obedient elevator. "Lots of paperwork," he sighed, as the door closed on him.

"This way, Professor Miller." Travis opened a door and he was led ever downward along a sloping windowless extremely well-lit corridor. Travis was so young he had that kind of acne, and his nose was glistening from a cold that he mopped at with a handkerchief in his free hand. Walter could have asked where they were going, but it wouldn't have made any difference, and Travis didn't appear nearly as talkative as Wright. The corridor seemed to go on and on.

"Your mother-in-law get your son all right?" Travis finally said.

"I believe so," Walter said.

"That's a good thing."

"It is. It is."

"You wouldn't want your son to be stuck in here with us. We really don't have the facilities."

"It was poor planning on my part," Walter agreed. He wished he could recall the excitement he felt when he first thought of the scheme, first envisioned himself chained to the gate, but back then he saw himself singlehandedly blockading the whole White House. Back then he saw it as an act. It was only an infinitesimal gesture. He'd known that, these last days, but he hadn't admitted it. He might as well have taken a dip into a pool of invisible ink and then given a speech in sign language. That's what the guys had meant when they'd said no one would see him. He'd made himself disappear.

"Here we are," Travis said, opening another door.

Inside were the requisite photographic equipment and observation rooms and a half dozen people milling about and no one bothering to look up. He was almost entirely irrelevant.

"Have a seat," Travis said, and sat him on a cold metal-framed chair.

Travis sat a desk opposite and looked at a computer screen. He nodded behind Walter. "We'll get you into a room as soon as one opens."

"Sure," Walter said. So this kind of stuff happened all the time. Of course it happened all the time. And it was all swept under some giant textile of competent security and indifferent public reaction.

"Do you need a sip of water or anything?"

"No thank you."

In the silence he tried to hear what was going on behind him, above him, anywhere. He heard nothing. He wanted to ask some questions but he wasn't sure he'd like the answers—if any would be given. It was better to wait and not know. He thought there might be more hope in that. In an odd way, he still had a lot of faith in his country and he didn't think he had done anything truly terrible. He might be ignored but he doubted he'd be imprisoned, at least not for long. His whole point was he wasn't a threat. Now anybody could see that.

He sat there so long and became either so relaxed or so exhausted that he fell asleep. When he woke he was sitting in a different chair in a small room.

"You know where you are, Walter?" a new man said.

"Vaguely," Walter said. He wanted to rub his eyes of dust but he was still cuffed.

"Do you think you've been depressed lately? Do you have feelings of inadequacy? Any trouble sleeping?"

"All of the above," Walter said.

"Have you entertained thoughts of killing yourself?"

"God no."

"Why not?"

"The kids," he said. "And for the most part I like what I do and where I live and who I live with."

"Then why'd you throw it all away?"

"It was a statement." Walter shrugged. "A not very effective one, apparently."

"What are your thoughts about the President?"

"I try not to think about him."

"The Vice President?"

"I *don't* think about him." Although over Christmas he'd driven down to see where the Vice President lived. They had barricades that looked like monster snowplows, and men on bikes perched along the fence, smirking into walkie-talkies latched to their shoulders.

"Sure you don't." A scrap of glossy paper was slid across the desk to him. He felt ill before he even looked. It was a photograph of him staring intently as he drove past—they both knew what he was driving past. "You wouldn't believe our database," the agent said.

"So I'm not allowed to drive past the Naval Observatory?"

"Not looking like that. Not considering that you've done what you've done. You know what this shows, Walter? A pattern of behavior. A pattern of behavior that is of great interest to a lot of people."

"But I didn't *do* anything."

"You trespassed on Federal property. You breached Presidential security. You held a two-year-old child hostage. That's a lot, Walter."

"I want a lawyer," Walter said.

"This is a different kind of thing, professor. You should know that."

"What do I have to do?" Walter stared at him. "What do you want?"

"We want what's good for the country," the agent said. "What do *you* want, Walter?"

It was like dealing with an unhappy child and trying to figure out what would appease him.

"You know why laws exist, Walter?"

He hated that the agent always used his name. And of course he didn't know the name of this guy at all.

"To protect you, Walter."

"I know," Walter said.

"Why do you think you broke these laws that were meant to protect you, Walter?"

"Because I'm an idiot," Walter said.

The agent looked at him. Now Walter felt sufficiently awake to take in his handsome blandness, his non-descript, unremarkable features. The kind of face you wouldn't recognize again because it looked like everyone else's. His suit was navy blue, his shirt white and crisp, his tie red and blue stripes.

"Are you crazy, Walter? That's one question everyone is asking. Do you hear voices? Do you have a martyr complex? Do you feel people pay you too much attention or no attention at all?"

"I did something foolish and futile and inconsiderate. That's all."

"What were you thinking about when you drove by the Vice President's?"

"I don't know," Walter said. He suddenly was hit by a headache. It bloomed above his right eye and instantly stretched in a tight band around the inside of his head. "Is it still today? The rule is..." he tried to think through the pain. "The rule is seventy-two hours."

"In cases like this, there's a school of thought that thinks there might be no such rule."

"Have I been drugged? I've got a terrible headache."

"Goodness no."

"Sleep deprived?"

"Actually, you did sleep," the agent pointed out.

"Starved?"

"You haven't been here that long, Walter. How long do you think you've been here?" The agent looked at the window. "You'll get something to eat soon."

"What do I need to say to get out of here?"

"Come on, Walter. You committed a crime. Or two. Or three. It doesn't work that way."

"I hate the Vice President," Walter heard himself say.

"Okay."

"That's not against the law."

"It's a free country," the agent agreed.

"I don't own a single weapon."

"You own baking soda. You own vinegar. You own detergent. You own several tool kits. You have two cars. A garage full of newspapers and flammable liquids. A basement with four jars of turpentine. A stockpile of bottled water and canned food—"

"—We were told to!" Walter said.

"9/11," the agent said.

"9/11," Walter eagerly agreed. "My wife bought that stuff."

"What do you think of 9/11, Walter? Do you think it was our fault?"

"My first reaction," Walter admitted, "was that they wanted us to experience what life in their country every day was like."

"And?"

"And after the plane hit the Pentagon I realized it could be seen as an act of war."

"You agreed with Afghanistan."

"I agreed with Afghanistan. I have a student there."

"—Mitchell Phillips."

"Mitchell Phillips. He's all for it. But what happened to the football player was disgraceful."

"So you're not for Afghanistan any more?"

"I don't know. I'm probably for killing Bin Laden."

"You want to kill him yourself."

"I've never killed anybody," Walter said.

"What's the closest you've ever come to doing somebody real harm?"

Walter shut his eyes and tried to get past the headache. "Drunk driving," he finally said.

"Drunk driving?"

"The driving that I've done while drunk could have been considered or could have resulted in real harm."

"And that stuff with your wife."

"That stuff with my wife is between me and my wife and wasn't even when we were married," Walter said hotly. "And the fact that we got married shows it wasn't even anything."

"Everybody's got stuff with their wife," the agent said encouragingly.

"I didn't say that."

"And everybody's got stuff with the President."

"Come on," Walter said.

"And everybody chains themselves to the White House fence with their two-year-old. My goodness, Walter, you could have smothered that kid."

"Please," Walter said.

"You consider Sam a patriotic name?"

"It was my father's name."

"Why don't you think your father liked you?"

"I don't know." Walter looked at the floor. It was the whitest linoleum he had ever seen. There weren't even decorative specks for depth perception or why ever they had them. "He never understood what I was doing, and I was a pain in the ass as a kid. Essentially I don't think I ended up being worth the trouble. You wind up not connecting with the kid who gave you the most aggravation, and there's going to be some unexpressed hostility. How's that?"

"That's very good," the agent said drily. "Where do you think you really are, Walter?"

"At the bottom of some federal facility in Washington, D.C., where I'm not going to see the light of day anytime soon."

"Walter." The agent looked at the window and smiled. "Walter, Walter, Walter." He laughed and gently slapped Walter on the back as he lifted him to his feet. "You didn't see anything on the floor, did you, Walter?"

"Like what," Walter said.

The agent opened the door into a bare-floored room with just a few green desks staffed by military-looking people that looked out onto deep blue water as far as Walter could see. Instantly he felt the heat and noted the lazily whirring overhead fan.

"Guantanamo Bay," Walter said.

"It's a shorter flight than you think," the agent said.

## II.

Walter stood there dazedly. For a moment he couldn't see anything. Hysterical blindness, he thought. Then, gradually, he could make out a series of structures—barracks and prisons, he assumed—painted in a military khaki.

"I guess this is the end of the line," he said sadly.

"Do you think you're a danger to anyone, Walter?" The agent held him lightly by the arm. "Do you think you might be a danger to yourself? What do you think makes people act?"

"They can't speak. They can't articulate. They aren't heard or they feel they aren't heard. Then there's nothing left to do but act."

"You never said anything, Walter. I mean, of course you muttered things to your colleagues and even your wife—"

"*Even* my wife?"

"You don't tell her everything," the agent said.

"Telling somebody everything is never a good idea."

"But if somebody told her..."

"*If* somebody told her," Walter said slowly, feeling more ill with each word, "then she wouldn't care if I came back."

"I don't think anybody would care if you came back, Walter."

"I deserve this," Walter said.

"It's just a chip," the agent said. "Just a chip."

"You know how hurtful total honesty can be? I don't want to know everything about her. I don't want to know everything about anybody."

"That's a very sane attitude," the agent agreed. "Tell me about that piece, 'Why Haven't We Marched Yet.'"

"Obviously, I never had to finish it."

"It might have been a good piece."

"But I never had to finish it. They marched. It was pathetic."

All this time nobody even looked up from their desks at him.

"I want you on this wall," Walter muttered. "I need you on this wall."

"Easy, Walter." The agent turned him firmly around. "Shall we go back inside."

Again they sat across a bare table.

"Does your brother's importance diminish you, Walter?" the agent asked.

"I don't think so," Walter said wearily. The whole thing was like being stripped naked and then feeling like they kept stripping you beyond that, like they could see inside your balls and all the way up your rectum. "Probably," Walter said.

"You're feeling it," the agent said, each word working to make obvious that the pronoun was all-encompassing.

"I'm feeling it," Walter said.

"That's important," the agent said.

Walter tried to think about something concrete—his children, his work, his wife—but it was all slipping away. Soon it would be as if his life had never happened. It was liberating and terrifying at the same time.

"What about your sister? You know, Evelyn."

"Evie," Walter said, and for an instant he could see her photograph atop his dresser. She was wearing something red, sitting next to her husband. It was well after the diagnosis, but it didn't look like it was after anything. She looked stunning. "I failed her."

"Everybody was going to fail her," the agent said. "That's the way those things play out."

"Whatever," Walter said, and now he could see himself taking his sister for a colonic, taking his sister for an MRI, taking his sister for chemotherapy, taking his sister for a drive, and in the gigantic cannister taking his sister's ashes home. "How many people have died here since 9/11?"

"Tracy," the agent said.

"Tracy didn't die here," Walter said.

"Of course not," the agent said. "I was just thinking about her since we were talking about death."

"She loaded airplanes."

"You basically begged her not to go."

"I thought she really didn't want to go. I thought if someone was forceful with her that she would act on that impulse."

"You offered her money."

"I did."

"I think that's illegal."

"You could see she was marked," Walter said. He tried to wipe his hair from his eyes as if to see her better, tried to wipe sweat from his head as if to think more clearly—had they turned off the air conditioner—but he was still handcuffed. Oddly, he felt hunger. "You could see she was going to get killed quickly, and she did."

"Everything is about luck and timing," the agent said. "If you hadn't been approached at the fence, you might not have done what you did."

"That's obvious," Walter said.

"It was almost a gesture of self-defense."

"It was," Walter agreed too eagerly.

"There are a lot of ways we could support a lot of different scenarios," the agent said. "That's life right now."

There was a knock on the door. The agent muttered something. Walter thought it was *too philosophical* but maybe that was what he wanted it to be.

"Time for chow," the agent said.

The door opened. Walter tried to glimpse the sea again. Seeing the sea would help him, he thought. From his angle, all he could see were walls.

The agent nodded at a tray. Walter saw something resembling chicken tenders and fries. A straw gleamed from a carton of nonfat milk. The agent patted him on the shoulder.

"The only thing Henry eats," he said. "Enjoy."

Left alone Walter stared at the plate. They hadn't bothered to uncuff him. Carefully he bent his head and mouthed a piece of chicken. It was hot but not too hot. He raised his head and chewed. His throat felt unprepared to swallow. He moved the piece of chicken around in his mouth and kept chewing. When he thought there was room in there he bent to the straw and sipped. The milk was cold, and it began to open his throat. Through the straw he gulped. Finally he was able to swallow the chicken. The milk was almost gone. He felt sleepy and full.

If he dozed, when he woke, would he be in Abu Gharib?

He descended in a slow swoon, and in his dreams saw nothing. In sleep he searched for the non-dream. Where was Claire, where were his children, where were the house with the roof that needed to be replaced and the garage door that could no longer close and the basement that took on water from under the center of the floor and all the other million little things that irked him and he had thought were driving him crazy, pulling him down further from any capacity to act? Where was the mailman who often left them someone else's mail and the stationwagon that sucked up a grand just to fix an oil leak and the backyard that had killed off all the grass and the damn puppy that had just gotten her period and leaked blood all over the kitchen and dining room and the two cats who needed dental work which he was in no way going to pay for and the big screen HD LCD TV he had bought for a football season that had turned into a disaster and the fireplace that seemed to not like anything burnt in it and still they lit their Duraflames and afterwards the basement smelled like a bomb had gone off and even the cats waddled up stricken and teary? From wherever he was now or was going to be when he woke or they woke him he tried to reach back and grab hold but it was like reaching after something that dissolved just as it came into focus, as if it were an image mirrored in a pool of water or generated from the hot asphalt of a desert road. How many days had he been gone?

Whoever woke him was someone else and he was on a cot and for a moment he thought his hands were free but when he went to move them, each laying on its respective side of the bed as if neither knew the other, he found they were strapped securely to the frame of the bed. He checked his ankles. Still liberated.

"Walter," the person said.

He made himself look and saw sunglasses and a deep tan, a desert camouflage shirt not tagged with any name, a five o'clock shadow around the lips and coating the chin.

"Yes," Walter said.

"Do you know where you are?"

"Guantanamo Bay?" Walter tried.

The soldier laughed and Walter stared at the ceiling, too tired to raise his head and look around. "That must have been some dream," he said.

It wasn't a dream, Walter knew. "Yeah," he said.

"You're in a secure facility on the eastern seaboard of the United States."

"Right," Walter said. "Which state again?"

"It is my job to orient you into the transitional incarcerated population," the soldier said.

"I'm here temporarily?" Walter said.

"That's right, sir. Three square meals, one hour of yard time, shower every other day, brief stints of labor."

"North Carolina?" Walter guessed. He raised his head, and saw with disappointment three walls and a series of bars where the fourth wall could have been. "Delaware?"

"Panic won't get you anywhere," the soldier said.

"I'm not as far from home as I thought," Walter tried to reassure himself.

"No sir," the soldier agreed.

In his chest he felt an absolute emptiness, as if everything in his system had been used up, pumped from him, exhausted.

"All this for chaining myself to the White House fence," he said.

"You violated three Federal statutes, two District statutes, and a temporary statute, sir."

Walter let his head sink into the pillow. "Oh," he said.

"It's time to get up, sir." Swiftly the soldier unlocked the wrist restraints. "You are free to sit on the side of the bed."

Free to sit on the side of the bed. That had a definite and clear limit. Just sit on the side of the bed. Very carefully, he swung his legs down and pushed himself up and sat on the side of the bed.

"I am so tired," he said.

"You've been interrogated in accordance with the guidelines set out by the Geneva Convention, sir."

"You guys have been starving me," Walter said.

"On the contrary, sir." He pointed to a small dot on the back of Walter's hand. "You refused sustenance, and we had to feed you through a tube."

That didn't make any sense, but he wished he hadn't said anything.

"Are you good to stand, sir?"

"No." Walter shook his head, and even that slight gesture nauseated him. "I'm not good to stand."

"One more minute then," the soldier said.

In the silence Walter thought, where am I really? He bit his lip. He felt as if he'd been boiled down to nothing.

"Sir?" the soldier said. He began to lift him by his arm.

"Okay, okay." He recognized his daughter's impatient plantive tones in his voice, or was it the other way around and had she taken on his? He hoped there was as little of him in her as possible.

He rose in a brilliant orange jump suit and synthetic slippers. His legs felt as if they hadn't been used in weeks, and he imagined them as bony stalks under the bright color. He imagined he must have lost at least another ten pounds. He no doubt weighed less than when he graduated from college twenty-three years ago. He had other observations, but he and the soldier were moving now, the floor seeming to shift under him like a conveyor belt. They passed five empty cells and were buzzed through several thick and heavy doors until they stood in a small yard overseen by a piece of sky bit off by barbed fencing that ran along the top of tall cinderblock walls. In one corner, under the shade of the wall, was a rusting stationary exercise bike, in another corner a stunted basketball backboard and netless rim under which sat—as if out of a still life—a bald, practically brown ball.

"How long will I be here?" Walter asked.

"One hour a day, sir."

He breathed in deeply. The air seemed dry and wrung of any scent; the sky was very blue. He thought it still had to be February. He wondered if he had missed Valentine's Day.

The soldier motioned him back inside.

"What's the date?" Walter said.

"Your meals are served in your cell," the soldier said, leading him through the several doors. "Your labor is executed in your cell." Past the five empty cells they walked, each without any apparent inmate. "Tomorrow is your shower day."

He was locked into his cell and sat on his cot listening to

the soldier's retreating footsteps. The place was like an aquarium filled only with water—you couldn't see anything when you were inside it and yet you moved against some kind of resistance and you had no depth perception until you hit a wall. Perhaps he was in northern Florida or South Carolina. Alabama and Arkansas were not on the 'seaboard,' but he could be anywhere. There was no mirror and he felt his face for growth. It seemed about three days' worth, but they could have shaved him. He took off his slippers and looked at his toenails. He examined his fingernails. He felt the length of his hair, but at forty-four that didn't grow so much as recede. What other clocks were there? If you took away time and setting, what was left? Weren't those the two variables that determined everything? There was only himself left. That wasn't at all pleasant to consider. He looked around the spotless cell. A stainless steel toilet without a real seat, a stainless steel sink with only a cold-water tap. The cot he sat on. He stood and went to the bars. He could see only the wall and off to either side of his cell a few feet of corridor. He pressed his ear between the bars. At first he heard nothing, then after a while a humming came to him. A very low droning tone. He looked up and above the outside left corner of his cell he saw one of those mirrors that sometimes appeared at the end of tangled driveways to gauge oncoming traffic. Of course someone could see him. He looked closely at the mirror. Still not close enough, but he was sure he could see something. He pulled the cot over and stood on it. In the mirror was a little boxed image. A television! On the television was an orange-jumpsuited man. Of course it was him. But it wasn't him at all—the man was blindfolded and kneeling, he saw as he got ever closer to the mirror. Around him were masked and hooded men pointing rifles and guns at the blindfolded man's head. Now he knew what he was looking at. He stepped down from the cot and tugged it over to its original place. These guys had thought of everything. He rested his head in his hands and tried to think of how lucky he was.

# AT THE VETERANS HOSPITAL

★ ★ ★

*Joseph Mills*

She says she wonders what has happened to The Book of Life and The Book of The Dead now that everything's gone digital. It's hard to imagine God swiping a Kindle, or St. Peter, that maître-d' at the Gates, looking up arrivals on his iPad. But why, he asks, do these seem any stranger than vellum, or parchment, or paper? We have always been told this world is virtual, a simulation of another. At this she starts to cry, and when he places a hand on her new leg, she pushes it off, saying, *This is not real.* Her tone is hard to read, and he doesn't know if she means the limb, the crying, the empathy, the room, the world. *Maybe not*, he says, *but it's what we have.*

# Sacramentum

★ ★ ★

*James R. Duncan*

Thank you for your service," the young woman said. Flat and polite, like 'how do you do' or 'nice weather.' Cordial, Tom thought.

Tom sat in his wheelchair where they had placed him, clenching his silver pen like he sometimes did for hours upon hours. The mumbling nurse with the off-yellow teeth had introduced the reporter. The nurse had then turned and left without another word, her heels squeaking into a distant murmur of voices. Fluorescent lights sizzled overhead.

Tom watched the reporter sit in a metal chair in his hospital room, nothing between she and Tom except ten feet of cold white tiles. The young woman's folding chair squeaked, her black heels clicked, and her moist brown eyes fluttered over Tom's face to the floor. Maybe Susan, or Suzanne? Her beautiful young legs now crossed, and Tom saw there was a tiny green shamrock tattoo on the left ankle. She was probably about the same age as Bree. And trying to be cordial.

It was during their senior year that Bree had bestowed the virtues of cordiality to Tom, normally while stopping his hand from moving either too far up, or down, the approved zone around her stomach. Always, of course, with warm wet reassurances into Tom's ears of a future with no such rules.

Promises.

Tom's left ear and eye were now gone along with much of his hair on that side. In their place was a coating of burnt skin that looked like cooled lava. A tuft or two of hair still mockingly poked from the ruined skin for some reason. Part of his right jaw was gone, and a couple of his teeth showed through in patches where anyone could see all kinds of awful things you were not supposed to, moving and straining inside. His left arm was missing, and his army uniform on that side was pinned to it in a crisp fold. He wore no shoes or socks at the end of his dark green pants, and his bare feet rested pink-pale, somewhat shriveled, between the two tiny wheels on the front of his chair. When he tried to stand, which hadn't happened much since returning state-side, Tom would often lurch to the right.

Since entering the room, the reporter had looked at Tom once, then not again. It was cordial not to stare.

The reporter's blue blouse was crisp at the collar, and her nails a slicing red. Her lips seemed to turn naturally down at the sides like Bree's, and her hair was long and dark, too. So straight and slick it might have been mistaken for black plastic, had it not frayed at the shoulders, tendrils clinging to the blouse. Tom had often imagined falling asleep in hair like that, a clean fresh smell and coolness, he was sure. Peace. Sometimes he still dreamed about it, but dreamed of the other things, too. Of smoke and orange flash and gasoline stench, screams so loud it felt as if his eardrums would burst. But when he thrashed awake, all his dreams now led to the same place.

"It's called The Heart of Heroism," the reporter finally said, of course with her head down, powering off her phone. "It runs sometime this summer, Corporal." Her voice was predictably reassuring, like the cool babble of a mall waterfall.

In his good right hand Tom clutched that thick metal writing pen, his knuckles white and a vein bulging. The pen was strong, a gift from his mother for graduation, and he needed to crush against it. His muscles, the ones that were not damaged, seemed to always simmer now with a desire for grabbing, hitting, tearing, biting.

The reporter stared down at her feet for a moment longer as if there was something more there than just hospital floor. Eventually, she put her phone in her leather bag and began rummaging through its contents. And Tom knew that pause, that moment she had stared blankly down, was where she would have normally made eye contact. With a normal person. Sometimes, when the nurses put Tom's silver pen away, he would instead grasp the metal armrest of the chair, and the entire chair would tremble with tiny metal squeaks.

The reporter's chest rose and fell as she dug through the bag— a sliver of pale skin panting beneath the blue lapels with the slightest hint of moisture in the cleavage, like rotting fruit. The young woman wrestled out a baby-blue notebook and two pencils, dropping one back, and then her eyes went to the fluorescent lights above. Not to Tom. Not just yet. The big clock on the wall with the black numbers ticked once, then twice, and then again and again, while she examined those lights. And that made Tom smile. Or at least, the side of his lips that could still move, twitched.

"I'm ready when you are, Corporal." Her eyes, those perfect brown eyes, jolted down onto Tom's face, and she swallowed hard. She smiled. Or at least, one side of her lips twitched.

"I have a tattoo," Tom said, straining to shift himself a millimeter in his chair. "Want to guess what it says?"

She looked away. Tom had taken to calling what he sat in his pussy chair, and he twisted a bit in it, trying to relieve where the pressure built in his hips and thighs. The machines in the room whirred and clacked softly as if in a sterile reverence for him, like even they, too, wished to assist but not disturb him. Never disturb him. And it was that sterile-ness, that ever-same white-walled help, forever enveloping him these days, which had caused Tom to blurt out the phrase "pussy chair" one morning to the nurse with the off-yellow teeth. He had actually meant it as a joke, more about himself than anything else. But the nurse's reaction, a wrinkled up nose in politely muted dissatisfaction, had made Tom repeat it each morning since.

"It's a phrase," Tom said. He could feel the spittle slinking from the damaged side of his mouth. He sucked hard, and pounded his fist into his thigh. "My tattoo is a phrase."

Tom wanted to break things. Tom had to break things.

Her eyes widened, and she looked away, over at his bed of rumpled sheets. The faint outline of an awful stain on its white surface, and her shoulders rose tightly as she breathed. She shook her head barely, the weak smile again at no one, and then tried to glance at him as she tapped the face of her thin gold watch. "Can you…can you just go ahead and tell me what happened, Corporal?" Another buzz from the overhead lights, and her eyes gratefully shot to the ceiling.

Tom shifted in his chair again, his uniform creaking. One of the many medals over his heart jabbed sharp in his chest. The pen had "*boundless potential*" inscribed in cursive, and he jabbed its hard tip just a bit into his thigh. Tom's orders were to talk to her, so he inhaled deep, a slight whistle of air through the torn side, and began. He began to explain as truly as he could exactly what had happened to him. What had made him such a goddamn hero.

Fuck cordiality.

Tom's father's love had been as intense as it was confusing, Tom told her, all howling winds and scalding sun. Like Jupiter himself, hurling magnanimous lightening bolts down to a wandering-in-the-dark mankind. Bigger than existence. Bigger than all Tom knew. Big as myth.

One of Tom's first lasting memories was from an afternoon listening to his father's beer drenched tales of the sun god Apollo. He must have been eight, or maybe nine? His father's voice boomed loud and wet in the bar and the table between them trembled. The college student sitting in the booth beside Tom's father, a girl with brown freckles beneath her green eyes, giggled, and punched his dad playfully in the arm. From his side of the table, Tom watched the sun melt low and red in the hazed sky outside the bar's steamed window. Students could be seen with backpacks crossing the dead leaves, hunched against the chill.

Tom told the reporter that a group of students had all clustered around them earlier that afternoon inside the bar with eager ears, as if Tom's father were a great oracle. They had even acted like Tom was special, too. In between the stories, they had looked at Tom with that same reverence, given him red and green and blue colored candies, and argued over what Tom wanted like he was someone destined for greatness. Like the gods of his father's myths.

Soon, there was just the one female student left, and she and his father leaned into each other often.

His father was a Professor of Latin, Greek and Roman Mythology at the local community college, but dreamed of becoming a world famous author. He loved nothing more than to speak words of a dead language, to revel in the splendor of eternal deeds. While Tom's mother worked, Tom would spend many of his days with his father. Sometimes in class, but more often in the dank confines of that slender tavern with the dense, square tables carved with student's names. Things smelled tight and sticky within the bar, and the low afternoon light glowed through the windows but altogether died to blackness before reaching back to where the music softly thumped.

"Apollo…," his father had barked across the table from Tom that afternoon, the girl putting green shavings into a wisp of waxy paper. "Apollo was the greatest of all the gods because he was the god of light and music and art. Of truth!" The girl rolled the green shavings up in the paper with a long lick and a wink at Tom, and Tom wondered what his mother was cooking them for dinner. "Music," his father bellowed, slapping a meaty palm down on the table to send the girl's beer sloshing over her rim as she giggled. "Beauty! We need music and art, passion and love, just as Apollo would command us." The girl put the special cigarette into Tom's father's lips gently. "Glorious Apollo rips the sun across the sky each day, Tom, in a chariot of winged horses, saving lowly man from the darkness once more." Smoke soon billowed around Tom's father's wide face, blue veins on the sides of his nose showing. He leaned over to wiggle his greying eyebrows at the girl, "and, he killed a great and dangerous python, too." He pretended to bite her. She giggled again. "You will be as great as Apollo, Tom, I promise," his father belched, "we both will be."

When the afternoon was over, Apollo's chariot nearly already drowned in the soaking dusk, Tom's father whispered things in the girl's ear and Tom waited by the door. She looked down, smiled, and glanced at least once over at Tom before squeezing his father's hand. Then she pulled her hoodie up over her head, orange curls of long hair poking out, and left by the back door. Tom's father strolled toward the door, so light and bouncy the fat of his stomach giggled beneath his shirt.

Tom and his father then drove home, playing the "go-home games" where they both chewed many pieces of mint gum and made up stories of what they had done that day to tell Tom's mother. Stories, Tom's father instructed him, that will make her smile. "Because we love her, Tom," his father explained, "and it is good to make her smile."

Tom's mother was a thin, tight woman, who provided proper doses of vegetables, proper doses of bible verse, and proper doses of hugs and kisses. Smiles when warranted. "That is excellent, Tom," his mother said while she set the place mats around the lopsided white table that night. "How long were you in the library?" His mother had wide brown eyes, and long brown hair, and she always smelled of something wonderful which Tom knew as home. Vanilla. "How long did you and the destined author do such productive things?"

"All afternoon," Tom answered. "And we read, and we studied Latin and Dad taught me about the god Apollo, and—"

"That's just excellent, Tom," she replied, crinkling her deep brown eyes and placing a soft, cool palm to Tom's lips to quiet him. "So, so, excellent." Then she kissed him on the forehead. "Everything is going to be just fine, Tom, just fine. You remember that."

Thinking back on it, Tom must have remembered that particular afternoon and night so vividly because when he woke up the next morning she was already gone. Tom had gone to his parent's bedroom after the sun came up to find the door ajar. His father's large bulk still rose and fell with gravel snores, but his mother's side of the bed was empty. Her dresser drawers were open and empty. The bathroom door was empty of the soft white robe Tom loved to snuggle against while being read to. And on the mirror, written very neat and clean in bright crimson lipstick was just one word, '*sinner.*' She, Tom would find out three days later, had gone to live with a man named George.

"But…," the reporter whispered, her eyes flitting to Tom's face for just a moment like a butterfly trying to land, then on to something of interest on the bare white wall behind him. "I don't mean to be rude, Corporal, but… um, about over there? About Afghanistan—"

"I'll give you a hint," Tom said.

Her nose wrinkled a bit, her gaze drifting into the air as her head cutely tilted to the side like a puppy hearing a high pitch.

He set the glistening metal pen on his right thigh and used his one good hand and feet to start grinding the wheelchair forward. The right front wheel, the tiny one that wobbled, squeaked, and the reporter's back straightened. She glared down at the wheel, and Tom stopped after about six inches, his breathing shallow. He picked back up the pen.

"A… a hint, Corporal?"

"Yeah," Tom said, "my tattoo. A hint about what my tattoo says."

The reporter sighed ever so slightly, turning her face toward the door. The door was partially ajar, and passing in the hall were the sounds of padded feet and female voices. Just behind where the reporter sat was the wall, with a portable metal stand. On the stand was a plastic tray and a white paper cup of orange juice. Tom never drank the orange juice, and everyday it sat there until warm.

"The article," the reporter said with a slow smile to the door, "is supposed to be about your heroism, Corporal."

"Oh…," Tom's voice rasped. "Heroism." His feet pawed weakly at the cold white tile again, but this time he didn't let go of the sharp metal pen. His chair inched closer to her perfect hair and perfect lips, closer to those deep, soft brown eyes. Closer to the lie which must be broken. "Heroism?"

Her eyes flashed hard into his face for a moment, her lips stern, her dark brows tight until his chair stopped.

"Yes," she said. And her eyes went down, flipping through the pages of her notebook.

Tom cleared his throat. Then he started telling her about nights in the Korpesh Valley at Firebase Youngblood. The firebase wasn't much, a large slab outcropping over the Papijal River, but Tom and Jonsey and Attison and Sleestack manned it for ten-day stretches at a time. The four of them made up Bravo team of Combat Company's First Platoon's Weapon's Squad and that pretty much meant they sat, fought, slept, ate, argued, shit, and laughed up on that goddamn rock day after day after day, waiting to shoot anybody who looked Taliban trying to cross the log footbridge below. For a long time no one ever came.

The firebase was only a haphazard rectangle of C-wire and sandbag walls with a tarp covered lean-to with two walls of plywood to cut the wind. The whole base only there to give plunging fire on the river two hundred yards below and keep some occasional eyes toward the southwest quadrant of the valley. No internet, no phone, no completed brick and mortar or even an established burn-shitter. But regardless of discomfort, somebody was always on lookout to the half-hewn log bridge below while the rest of them took turns laying against sandbags and talking about chicks. Everyone though keeping one ear for the crack of a twig, the chambering of an old bolt action rifle on the wind, or the thwack thwack thwack of 7.62's suddenly slapping the wall.

It was either hot as hell or cold as hell in the valley, and when it got cold Hill 1106 in the distance got dusted with snow. As the temperature dropped the Papijal would slow from a foam churning tributary of the Pesh to a gurgling stream of slick black rocks, Holly trees crawling its vertical sides. Terrain in the valley was always up or always down, so never an easy place to patrol. If you did leave the wire to patrol, you would have to grab a tree or hug a boulder to rest, scrabble rock forever sliding away beneath your boots. Unless, that is, you wanted to walk on a flat dirt road in the open and get smoked. So they didn't leave the wire if they didn't have to, and in those kind of circumstances, you got to know each other real well.

Attison was the lady's man of the group, Tom explained. He would tell all sorts of wild tales Tom couldn't repeat to the reporter. About his days as a bartender in Ybor City prior to enlisting. Stories involving three-somes and four-somes and some stuff that could only be described as Roman orgies. Attison would smile his wide

Latino wolf grin as he cleaned his M4, convincing them that getting laid wasn't the hard thing in Ybor, getting them out of your bed the next day before your girlfriend's hot sister came over was.

Jonsey, however, had only ever been with two chicks, both of them fat and one of them with a mild form of epilepsy, which caused laughter for a month straight. He often said he needed to get back to the states in order to marry the one with epilepsy before some other ugly Jody bastard scooped her up. Jonsey was the Texas wild man of the group, half-Samoan, half-horse with back hair dense as a gorilla but already going bald on his head. 'Infidel' was tattooed on Jonsey's chest, and he wore only boxers and a Halloween mask of George W. Bush to as many firefights as weather would permit.

Hands down, the two of them, Tom said, Attison and Jonsey, were the best guys to have by your side if you needed to shithammer the enemy. Never even a stutter at having your back in a firefight, and Tom loved them like brothers. But Sleestack, it turned out, was a real dirtbag.

Sleestack was shifty from day one. It was common knowledge he was born from a lizard humping a rock. An ugly Nebraskan rock. And he lied about all the girls he had been with without anyone buying his beady eyes for a second. He never seemed to completely buy into carrying his own weight, and was always complaining and cutting corners. It wasn't like he was a fat guy, or a weak guy, or sick or something that couldn't be helped, either. He just always seemed to want to game the system. He even got caught once trying to steal Attison's watch, and Jonsey almost beat him to a MEDEVAC, but that still didn't knock the shifty out of him. Whenever packages arrived from home, if you weren't watching, Sleestack would sneak in and rat-fuck the whole bunch, taking all the good shit for himself and leaving everyone else shells and wrappers. He once borrowed Jonsey's squad automatic weapon and went cyclic on some chattering monkeys. He fired so many goddamn rounds at the monkeys, Tom exclaimed, 900 a minute, that it melted the fucking barrel of the SAW. Over goddamn monkeys. Jonsey was so pissed he couldn't look at him for a week.

Tom watched as the reporter began tapping her left black shoe, soft but quick. She cleared her throat, staring down at one of her nails, and began to scratch at it with another. Red dust drifted toward the floor, and her pencil lay on the blank page of her notebook.

"The night I finally opened up about being a virgin," Tom said. "That was the same night we got hit pretty bad."

And at this, the reporter stopped digging at her nail, stopped the tapping of her foot. She straightened the notebook in her lap, and picked up her pencil.

"The night was black and quiet, cold and clear," Tom said, "and there were so many stars glittering in the sky that in spots they looked alive, dense and shimmering like a goddamn school of silver bait fish churning or something."

As the reporter began to scratch notes, Tom set the pen down on his thigh again. He pushed the chair forward with his hand. The feminine muscles in her slender neck strained beneath her skin as he talked and she worked. So smooth. So porceline. So perfect. He pulled the chair forward with his feet. So slow. So quiet.

He told her about Jonsey trying to convince Tom to get his first tattoo, to let him do it with a piece of sterilized c-wire like a prison tat. Everyone laughed, smoke churning from their mouths into the chilled air, and then Attison and Jonsey both sincerely said they would do it too—brotherhood—if Tom could just figure out what he wanted. Sleestack, of course, said he wanted no part of it, but that was typical. It was then when Tom fessed up about never having done it, and how Bree and him made a promise to save themselves for each other. They would get married as soon as he got back. He pulled out a photo of her from his ACU and explained how he and Bree were going to do things right, not get everything fucked up, not have a broken home but a big family where none of the kids would ever have nightmares. Everyone was really respectful, and nobody made smart-ass comments, not even Sleestack at that, and they all just sat there nodding and listening. Really cool.

But then the wheel on Tom's chair squeaked, and the reporter's writing stopped. Her head stayed downcast, but Tom could see her eyebrows rise.

"That was when the first tracer rounds came in," Tom said, and she started writing again. He started creeping his chair forward again.

Tom told her that for a split second everyone was just amazed how beautiful it was, almost like a silent shower of sparks from a welding torch, but far straighter and faster and with no noise. At least for a second, and then the noise came behind it, cracking, thumping, dust and flint flying in all directions. An RPG whistling overhead, and everything was an orange flash and jarring madness. Tom told her they rarely, if ever, got hit at Youngblood because it was almost the highest spot in several clicks which meant that nobody could get easy position on them. Also, because there simply wasn't as much traffic in their end of the valley. But that night, for a while, they got lit up. And everyone, except for Sleestack of course, did their jobs well.

The reporter had scooched forward in her seat a bit, scribbling notes faster and faster. Tom crawled his chair closer, and closer.

Attison grabbed his .50 cal, Tom said, and dove behind a barricade and blasted back. Jonsey jumped up to run for his weapon, almost fell down because of his flip flops, but then had the sense to kick them off and get cover behind a sandbag wall when he started tearing into them with the M240. Tom did the best he could with his M4 and some 203 rounds, his ears ringing the whole time from the initial rocket propelled grenade blast, while Sleestack lay in the dirt with his head covered, grunting. Sleestack wasn't injured, you see, just had his eyes caked with dirt.

Eventually, once Attison could see where the fire was coming from, he was able to crawl over and make a TIC call, requesting gunmetal to clear the ridge. Two Apache helicopters came chopping in quick, and used their chain guns to rip the tree line apart. The sound of breaking branches and burning wood would smolder for hours.

That night, Tom said, was actually like a big, beautiful, perfect game. A game that gave everything purpose and meaning, and made things matter. You could do things well and bravely and do your job and see that things mattered, and made sense. No one got hurt and maybe none of the enemy even got hurt for all he knew, but afterward everyone got to sit around and the MRE's actually tasted good for once, earned, and everyone laughed excitedly and talked for hours and hours about how close each of them had come to taking a bullet here or a blast there. Even Sleestack admitted he froze, and everyone forgave him because no one was dead, and it was all okay. Because up ahead there was a beautiful promise of PCS-ing home where they would all be destined to win in life. That firefight, Tom explained, had been exactly what he imagined before he enlisted. That night, Tom told her, things all made sense for the first time since he was six years old.

"But? Wait... no one was injured," she asked, her pencil stopped, and so Tom's chair stopped. "I mean...that wasn't the night you received your... um, I mean—"

"Nah. The next day, we all got the tattoos." Tom smiled, and snatched the pen up in his hand again. There were only about five feet left between him and her now. "Are you ready to guess what it is? Mine? It's on my arm."

"I'm sorry, Corporal, I'm confused." Her voice trailed off with a sigh as she looked down, trying to unwrap a piece of gum. "It's just that... I've only got a certain amount of time to be here, you see, and—"

"You can't guess?" Tom asked.

"No," she exhaled, and popped the gum into her mouth. "I only have time to know about you becoming a hero."

So Tom nodded, took a deep breath, and started pushing his chair forward again, telling her that ten years after his mother had left, Tom's father had changed. Decayed. He had left his post as a professor to write a novel after their divorce, to fulfill his greatness, he had said. But things did not work out. Ghosts began to haunt his father's head. He would spend hours upon hours, day after day typing away, only to break down at night and cry over dozens and dozens of ripped and torn pages, empty bottles cluttering the floor. Tom's father began to scream and rant after a while, day and night. He spoke to no one except to Tom for days, for weeks. Worst of all were the nights Tom would have to take the gun out of his father's hand. It was always worse in the night.

Throughout school, the black gleaming muzzle of that .38 became a huge dark anvil hanging over Tom's life, but never dropped. A recurring nightmare chasing Tom from boyhood into being a man. Of a shadowy figure sitting in a chair, moaning and crying, the moans growing louder and louder until eventually Tom would realize the creature was calling out for him to save it. To help it. Tom would move towards the figure, but always, always hear a deafening, awful gun blast in his mind before he could get there. Then he would rip awake. Those nights he would go check on his father, and with each step down the hall toward the living room where his father slept in a chair, Tom's breath would come in shallow slivers wondering. Wondering, if tonight were the night he would find his father dead.

"Promise me, Tom," his father said once, with the gleaming .38 in his hand, his breath burning with whiskey, the barrel resting against his temple. "Promise me." Tears spilling down his cheeks and wind rattling the living room window.

"Promise, Dad?" Tom asked. "Promise what?"

"Promise me, Tom...," his father said, his finger tightening on the trigger. "Promise me your life will not turn out like mine."

"Don't be silly, dad," Tom began, outstretching his hand as tears slipped from his own eyes, "you're life isn't that—"

"Promise me!"

"Okay, Dad. I promise...," Tom smiled. "I promise."

And at Tom's smile his dad smiled, too. And Tom gently lifted the gun from his father's hand.

He set it out of reach on the coffee table, the gun so awful and dense, so charged with wild violence, and his father collapsed on his arms. He sobbed into them as Tom petted his father's head until exhausted into sleep. Tom stayed up until dawn, thinking how someday he and Bree would have a normal family and take care of his father, because his father was a good man. Or maybe, Tom also thought as he was getting ready for school, how he should just run away. Because it was breaking him apart inside.

The reporter's back stiffened. Her eyes stared hard at his chest, but her lips seeming to ever so slightly tremble. There was not much space left between them now.

"Corporal, please, could you just—"

"I like your tattoo," Tom mentioned. His hand griped the pen so hard that an indentation was forming on his knuckle from its sharp metal clasp. "Mine probably doesn't look as good. Not now."

The reporter stood, and straightened her skirt. She walked behind the metal chair, between it and the tray on the stand. She clasped her hands behind her back, and stared away from Tom at the bank of machines by his bed.

"I'm sorry, but how would I know what your tattoo is, Corporal?" she asked. Tom could tell she was trying to sound stern, but still polite. "Can you just tell me honestly how you became a hero? Honestly?"

"Honestly?" Tom asked, his voice wavering. He looked up toward the lights and clutched the silver pen even harder. "Honestly?"

And Tom began to talk quickly. To tell her about the way Sleestack annoyingly rubbed his legs together like a cricket while he was asleep, the noise of his shuffling sleeping bag driving everyone nuts all night until he got barely shot in the ass by a sniper and choppered out to get it patched up. But then no one could sleep for days without it. And how Jonsey spent weeks nursing a starving, mange ridden kitten back to health and just when it could scamper again it got run over by a Humvee. How, for a while, they made monthly bets on how many Afghani insurgents would get killed when the big bombs came down, until they came across the little girl's body on patrol one time and they never made bets again. And how Attison once almost stabbed a guy over a hostess cupcake, for real, a fucking hostess cupcake. And how some nights it would be so quiet in the valley except for the wind creaking all the trees that they would think they heard moans like Jonsey said bigfoots made. How Tom tried to do a card trick one night for hours and hours because he was just so shitty at it that no one could stop laughing. And how he no longer had nightmares over there after a while, and he didn't want to know what that meant, until Bree sent him a letter with a locket of her dark hair and said she was pregnant. And how then the dark anvil returned to hang over his every day again.

The corner of the young woman's eyes darted to Tom, and she starting pacing with her head down, back and forth in tight steps behind the metal chair. Her steps quick, congested in the area between the chair and plastic tray.

"Corporal Walker, I'm sorry. It's just that I have an article to write. I have—"

Saliva began flinging from Tom's busted mouth as he angled the chair over a couple of feet, in the path between her and the door, blurting out that he didn't realize how bad his injuries were at first. He had forgotten what had happened. It wasn't until he was on the transport plane back to the States, when he saw the look of horror flash across even the nurses who had obviously seen a lot and had been trained not to be shocked. How he had eventually demanded a mirror from one of the doctor's and made them pull back some of the bandages on the way here. When he saw his own face he had simply thought, it couldn't be real, could it? God couldn't hate him, could He?

And Tom clanged into the metal chair between them, the reporter lurched back, knocked against the plastic tray on a stand behind her. The orange juice tipped over, splattering to the floor.

"Jesus," she exclaimed, spinning back to the metal chair, throwing her hands on the back like she were clutching a shield between herself and Tom, glaring at his feet. At the door. At his feet.

Tom stammered that they had said his legs would eventually heal with a lot of work, that he would be able to get out of the wheelchair someday, but obviously his right arm would be gone forever. Tom told her how that had terrified him, because he didn't know how he would salute, shake hands, or hell, even jerk off anymore and how he had cried for hours and hours until he exhausted himself to sleep. How he wished Attison and Jonsey would still be alive and that Sleestack was home, and that his father would not have been crushed so long ago like he was, and that Bree had not turned out to be a vile lying cunt, but she had, and that somehow, things could still work out for everyone. But the strangest thing was every time he still woke up, Tom said, he continually got the mirror to check that it was all just an awful dream, and it never was.

"You've got to have a guess? You must have a guess? Because it will be fun, it will be normal, and fun… and… and I don't understand—"

"I don't know what your fucking tattoo is, Corporal."

Tom pushed up from his chair, rising to a lopsided stand, the pen tight in his hand, gripping it like a dagger to thrust deep into all the cordial bullshit of the lying world.

"I'm sorry," she stammered, trying to back up, but with nowhere to go. "I'm truly sorry."

He took a small, awkward step toward her.

When they had wheeled him out of the back of the transport plane, his father had run across the tarmac to him. No matter how much they had been trained, no one seemed to know how to act, except Tom's father. There was the nurse who pretended like everything was wonderful and completely normal and talked about Tom and his father going to get ice cream or some ridiculous shit. There was the other nurse that couldn't say anything and ran off. There was the soldier who gave Tom's shoulder a sorry-you-lost squeeze and then walked sadly back toward the plane, and then the doctor who simply immersed himself in numbers, names of medicines, and scientific terms. Tom, too, had no idea how to act, no idea what to say as his father ran toward him. Ever since he had awoke, his mind seemed to lurch between gratefulness and horror, disbelief, rage, fear and awe. And looking at his father, he wondered if there was anything he could say that would be right.

Tom almost stumbled as he limped around the chair. She turned against the wall. "I'm sorry," she said, her chest rising and falling, rising and falling. She again stepped back, this time knocking the tray completely to the ground. "I…I…" Tom squeezed the pen with all his strength, its metal clasp digging further into the knuckle on his finger, the pain so good, so true, and wished he could shatter himself into a thousand pieces if he couldn't figure out the answer. Moisture rimmed the edges of her eyes, and her chin began to tremble.

Tom's father had dropped to his knees on the tarmac at the base of Tom's wheelchair and buried his balding head into his son's legs. Tom thought how his father had seemed more shrunken, more withered than he had imagined him from just a little over a year earlier. "What happened, Tommy," his father sobbed into Tom's legs. "Oh God…What happened…" Tom tried to comfort him again. He raised his one good hand in the air, and went to place it on the back of his father's crying head, but something stopped him. He set it back down in his own lap. Tom felt like he should be crying, like he wished to cry, but that everything in him was dry and silent. That there were absolutely no words that could be said that would be honest and true anymore. "Oh, what happened, Tommy, what happened?" His father wailed and wailed, and for a long time Tom sat, simply watching him, wondering why he had always been so sad.

Tom took another tiny, wobbly step toward her, and was now so close he could feel her heat, could smell her hair. Vanilla, just as he had imagined.

"I kept my promise, Dad," was eventually all Tom could think to say to his father. "Don't be sad, I kept my promise."

Tom began to raise his hand with the pen.

"I'm sorry," she said, over and over again, putting her blue sleeve arms before her face, covering her eyes. "I'm sorry. I'm sorry."

"Pussyhound," Tom said. He laughed, and opened the hand of his outstretched arm, the pen laying in his open palm. "That's what my tattoo said. Pussyhound in bad green cursive so you could hardly read it." He tried to smile. "We all thought it was a funny joke, because I had been saving myself for Bree. But now I think it is actually funnier that it was on my other arm. The one that got blown off. Because the last time I saw it, a hungry Afghani mutt had picked it up with his teeth and ran off with it into a grove of holly trees. Ironic huh? A hound stealing my arm with Pussyhound written on it."

The reporter stared down at the pen in his open hand.

"Would you like to have dinner with me," Tom asked. "Like a date?" He offered the pen closer to her. "I don't have a cell phone right now, but if you write your number down I will call you."

The reporter swallowed and let her head drop forward, long dark hair covering her face, and exhaled deep. She stayed like that for a second, and Tom was not sure why, except that people had been getting sad for no reason around him all his life. Maybe it was just tiring, he thought, for them to keep up with all of their lies, to keep trying to be cordial.

"I'm no good at this. I don't know... I... I... don't understand how to be. I'm sorry if I scared you, but I'm no good at this and I just want to know... want to know what is true? Will you please have dinner with me?"

Tom watched a single drop of something fall from her downcast face to splash tiny on her shoe. She sniffled and sighed again.

"No," she calmly said, brushing the dark hair behind one ear. And then she stepped around him and his outstretched arm, and back to her bag.

Tom's eyes moistened. All he had ever wanted was to be enough of a hero to put things right, to be worthy of falling asleep in hair like that. His arm was still partially raised, drifting after her with the palm open, the blood speckled pen resting on it.

The young woman replaced her notebook in the bag and then took a tissue from it. She wiped both her eyes, then put the bag over her shoulder. She breathed deep, and took two steps toward the door. At the door she turned, though, and stood tall before him for one brief moment and looked him in the face without flinching. Looked him in his goddamn awful face without any excuses, without any bullshit, she looked at him.

"Thank you," she said again, and this time, Tom saw, she meant it. As there was nothing cordial about it. In fact, it seemed there might have been a little hate in those hard brown eyes. "Thank you for your service."

Much later that night, when all the voices had settled in the hospital wing, only the soft whir and clack of the machines in

Tom's room, he looked at the empty metal folding chair. He looked for a long time at that metal chair which held absolutely nothing and no one, nothing except perfectly vacant space. Nothing, Tom looked at, except boundless potential.

"You are welcome," he said.

# MONSTER

★ ★ ★

*Jim Walke*

The glass jar sat on the grocery store counter next to the register, the picture of the two of them at the hospital taped to the side. Liza froze with her hands locked around the handle of her cart. Kyle's eyes had sunk into his new face, leaving those familiar brown irises at the bottom of small pits, skin drawn tight—pebbled like football leather—the lines between the grafts glowing faintly against the too-dark surface. One side of Kyle's nose had melted and opened and slid down to hang like a flap over the edge of his ragged mouth. He had his arm around Liza in the picture.

Inside the container a pile of mixed coins reached halfway to the top. A few soft bills lay twisted through the layers. Liza saw a paper straw wrapper and a handful of bottle caps. Hand-lettered wording framed the picture, marching around the curve and out of sight:

> Local VETERAN needs you
> Severe burns from roadside
> Engaged. Rehabilitation
> Of his sacrifice. PLEASE

The IGA smelled of old vegetables and the rubber mats that lined the floors. The woman behind the counter had been a few years ahead of her in school—Kayla or Carla. She'd put on weight, and now covered her double-chin with a base too dark for the pale spring sun outside.

"Who put this here?" Liza asked.

Carla shrugged. "The church, maybe?" Her nails tapped against the keys, ringing up the groceries.

"I didn't ask . . ." Liza said, "We don't—"

The woman in line behind her had crept her cart to within inches, as if she could slowly push Liza out of the way. Other people were scattered across the front of the store. Liza felt the weight of their stares.

*Look at the girl, the loyal one who didn't break off the engagement.* Her hands shook as she paid. The jar sat within a few inches, begging. Give money to the burned man so they wouldn't have to look at him. She'd seen their eyes slide away from Kyle. Only children stared, filled themselves full of the sight like little ticks that would drink it in unto bursting, until they were yanked away by thick mothers. Liza had an urge to drop money into the jar for herself, for the bride-to-be who seemed like a girl she had known years ago.

The rain had stopped and the blacktop glistened. As she drove home she could still see the jar sitting next to the plastic dog soliciting spare change for the animal shelter, beside the Lions Club candy display where you were supposed to put in a quarter for every sucker you took. Liza pulled onto the lawn of her parents' brick ranch house, featureless and bland like the others in the subdivision where she'd grown up.

She left the groceries on the counter and headed downstairs. The phone began to ring again, one of a thousand calls: florists or caterers, officiants or someone in town with another perfect job for Kyle, the reporter again, asking if she would go through with it. The shades in the basement were drawn, the available light filtered to slots and rectangles of gray. She wondered what her friends thought of her fiancé living in her family's finished basement, or what the ladies at the Lutheran church said. They didn't know that she saw him less, now, in every way possible, than when he'd lived across town in the creaking rented house that had flooded every spring.

At the bottom of the stairs she paused to allow her eyes to adjust to the dim light. He stood behind the loveseat, his shape recognizable even in the dark. He stroked the quilt cast over the back, the same one he'd arranged on the carpet each time they quietly made love in this room throughout high school, with her parents asleep upstairs. Since his last treatment—the silicone injections that had hardened his palms and made them shiny— he'd enjoyed touching different textures to see what sensations passed through the numbness. Liza meant to ask her mother for the quilt as a wedding present.

"Are you ready to go?" she asked.

They had an appointment. She'd been trying not to think about it. This job offer had come like all the others, a friend of a colleague of her father's, something like that. People had seen the story. Complete strangers sent wedding gifts—baguette pans and pasta rollers, nothing she'd asked for—and they sent far too much advice. Notes, drawings, wretched poetry accompanied by dried, crumbling flowers. At least two people had sent hand-knit snowmobile masks. Liza had stopped opening the packages a month ago.

His broad shoulders were tight, raised up toward his ears as though he was about to be scolded or struck.

"The Ford property," she said.

Kyle stopped stroking the fabric.

Henry Ford's northern retreat, thousands of acres of forest he'd purchased out of spite when the nearby Huron Mountain Club denied him entry back in the '20s because of his anti-Semitism.

"The new owner wants a caretaker," Liza said. "There are supposed to be two or three private lakes in there."

A place in the woods for Kyle to hide—that was the offer— ignoring their plans of college, moving away. Her drafting table sat unused under a dust cloth. She hadn't touched it since he'd returned.

"Do you want to go?" Liza asked. Her chest hurt.

He nodded. He shaved his head to keep the hairs in the back from outlining the dead and fake areas on the front of his skull. Three more reconstructions were planned, the maximum allowed by the VA. The doctors were working from his graduation photo, slicing away the dead, adding, shaping him back into a mask of what he'd been. Liza wondered if she would recall later what he'd looked like during these stages between.

She wanted to go to him, take his hand, but Kyle didn't like to be touched by her now. Not before the wedding, he said, as if a ceremony and some lighted candles at the church would make a difference.

He breathed through the left corner of his mouth, a complicated technique that they'd trained him in at the VA hospital to bypass his ruptured septum. The thickened skin that hung down over his mouth swayed as he panted.

"We could," he said, "go look."

"You sure?" she asked. He'd not wanted to leave the house in daylight since the half-hearted parade, when the people in town had clapped until their palms were red, their eyes fixed on the flag.

"I want to get out," he said.

Liza put the windows down as she drove the highway out of town, along the shore of Lake Superior. The road dipped and curled through dunes before cutting back into the forest and away from the water, following the easiest path northwest. Cottages flashed past at a declining rate, so similar in shape that she wondered how their owners found the right home. At times he was fine with riding in the car.

He claimed not to remember what had happened. Blazing sunshine on patrol one moment, and the next he was in Germany with a bandaged face and all of his friends dead. Liza felt the same way about his 'accident,' as his mother insisted on calling it. Liza had had a life here with her boyfriend, a plan together, and then he was molded into a new shape like a candle taken from the form too soon. She'd blocked out his departure and return, leaving room in her mind only for the photo of him before and the daily reminder of after.

The highway split once twenty miles from town, then twice more, turning to hard-packed clay and gravel. She almost missed the turn-off where the underbrush had crawled up around the shaped concrete pillars as if they were continuations of the forest. The metal gate stood open. The car bumped and lunged over the two-track, taking several minutes to cover the mile of private drive. Kyle twisted to place both hands on the door. The trees fell back from the road at the edge of a small lake, perhaps forty acres of water lying in an arc around a peninsula. The house coiled along the sandstone outcrop like a python, ells stretching along each elevation before dropping to the next. Liza saw Prairie Style in it, but the finishes were wrong—the cedar shingles covered in moss, a railed veranda perfect for a line of rocking chairs.

When she was twelve Liza had found a book about Frank Lloyd Wright's architecture in the library, and after one brief look had slipped it into her backpack and snuck out the door. She'd read it a hundred times, tracing the designs that seemed to grow from the landscape, imagining what it would be like to live inside the architect's mind. She still had the book at home, hidden away in the same dusty spot where she kept Kyle's class ring and her birth control pills.

He seemed to study the forest, his breathing calm.

Liza followed the lane around the near end of the lake, past a crumbling two-story boathouse and then a neat cabin set back in the pines, facing the water and the main house. The road ended in a circle of gravel with brush sprouting through it, in front of a stable large enough for a half-dozen cars or twice that many horses. When she'd killed the engine they sat and listened. The water sloughed at the shore behind them. A red-winged blackbird called from his sideways perch on a cattail. Kyle fumbled at the seatbelt with his good hand and then hauled himself out of the car. Liza followed. He seemed transfixed by the white pines. They stood twice as tall as the jack pines and Norways that hugged the ground across the rest of the Upper Peninsula. These trees held their branches farther off the ground, forming a ceiling sixty feet up that framed rather than blocked the sunlight. She tried to remember if he'd been to the woods since his release.

He dropped his gaze from the canopy. Liza felt a breeze. Kyle's face had relaxed, the parts which were him and not him moving together for once so that she could see what he might look like when he grew old. He turned to walk along the edge of the forest past the house, his face raised as if scenting the air, arms swinging.

Liza thought that she should knock. He said something.

"What?" she asked.

"Do you think he'll want to walk the property today? Are you awake, Li?"

Kyle. Just normal Kyle asking her a regular question. Not the grunting and silence in the half-dark that she'd endured for three months. Liza's heart sounded too loud. She shouldn't be able to hear it in her ears. Her lips didn't seem to want to work. She nodded, but he had already returned to his contemplation of the forest and walked away from her.

Liza hurried onto the porch, under the shadow of the projecting eave. She knocked twice on the oversized wooden door, almost black with age, before seeing the twist bell in the middle of the portal. She reached for it, but then took one more look in Kyle's direction. He'd disappeared past the edge of the house, and she went after him without hesitating. If the owner was here he should have heard her knock.

A thin trail cut through the duff on the forest floor. Liza would have thought it a deer path if not for the cracked, greening statuary every few yards: a huge frog, then two stags locked in combat, a nymph or dryad holding a ewer aloft to pour over her nude form.

The trail opened on a small beach, or the remains of one. The sand brought in decades ago lay pushed almost to the water's edge by chokecherry and runners of wild strawberry. It continued beneath the water line and spread out under the clear surface in a fan like a sand dollar viewed through a prism. Swept circles marked fish nests where bluegill hovered over their eggs. Kyle stood knee deep in the lake, the hood of his sweatshirt pushed back from his shaven head. The fish seemed unconcerned by his presence, and for a moment the only movement of the scene was the twitch of their translucent pectoral fins to hold position. He stared, not at the reflection of himself reaching out in a slanted line from his soaked jeans, but above the pines to the rounding slopes of the Huron Mountains.

Liza glanced back over her shoulder. A screen of poplar and birch hid the house from view.

"How far do you think the property goes, Li?"

"I don't know." Her heartbeat had settled into its new, fast rhythm. Perhaps it was an old rhythm that she barely remembered. The breeze was still on her, reaching under her clothes and touching her skin. Her fingers went to the buttons of her shirt. She watched his reflection. It could be any version of him: the before, the first Kyle she'd ever seen, her future husband, the father of a little boy, someday, who would be unscarred. She undid the top button, then the next. The skin that her fingertips brushed seemed to belong to someone with a different life. She rushed. One of the clouds might drift in front of the sun, the reflection vanish.

"Kyle?" Her voice shook. "Kyle."

"Yes."

"Please look at me."

He turned slowly.

"Liza—" he said.

She held out a hand to him. Hurry.

He took a step, and the bluegill disappeared in flicks of silver. The water streamed off his legs as he emerged. Kyle stepped carefully to avoid the pile of her clothes. It was all she could do not to gasp as droplets fell on her bare legs. His arms went around her waist.

"What brought this on?" he asked. The left side of his mouth, the good side, tried to curl up into a grin.

Liza kissed his left cheek, where she knew that he had sensation. His neck. She tucked herself into his warmth, felt his arms tighten across her back.

"You're here," she said.

He traced one hand down her spine, making small circles. Liza pressed into his crotch and felt him respond through the layer of denim. She reached up to touch his face. The right side, the burn, rough under her palm. He pulled back, but she tried to maintain contact with her Kyle.

He took hold of her wrist and removed her hand from his face.

"Don't," he said. The light had changed in his eyes, switched to the basement look. He took a step back, and turned to the hills again.

Liza stood naked, cold now. A stream entered the shore of the lake a few yards away. It cut into the bluff in the direction of the heights. He looked back at her, and the spark was there again. A flicker as if he'd touched a battery.

"I'm sorry," he said.

"Go," she said.

His gaze went to the forest and came back to her.

"You sure?"

"I want you to. Don't be gone long. I'll write a note for the owner and we'll find another time to meet."

He looked back once before entering the trees, his pace increasing. His last stride into the mouth of the ravine was the bound of a deer.

Liza stooped to retrieve her balled jeans. She brushed sand from her underwear before pulling them on. When she knelt for her shoes, Liza leaned forward and put a hand in the water. Frigid. Her fingers were numb in seconds. How could he have stood so still in it? She should have gone out to him rather than making him emerge. Anything to preserve that light.

When she straightened she saw one window of the house through a frame of branches. The birches had not yet leafed out completely, and in only this spot someone in the house could see down to the beach. The window was dark. She stood still. Her camisole hung in her hand. The feel of Kyle's hand on her spine ran through her.

Liza finished dressing, facing the blank glass. Showing off for an empty house. She thought of the strippers at the bar over in Hurley where Kyle's cousins would drag him tomorrow. Would they be able to hold their smiles when they saw the melted face of the bachelor? They'd make him sit on a chair center stage, his hands trapped underneath him, and they'd feel the difference when they rubbed their breasts over one blushing cheek, and then the dead one.

The sound of a sneeze came from the direction of the trail. Liza tucked her shirt into her jeans.

"Hello?" she said.

A black Labrador waddled into sight and let out another sneeze. Its muzzle was graying, the lumps of its spine standing out under a thinning coat.

Liza let the dog sniff her hands. It seemed mildly disappointed that she had nothing to eat, but still allowed her to scratch behind its ears and rub the wrinkles of its loose neck before heading back the way it had come. Liza followed the animal into the shade under the trees, passing the statues on the trail back to the house.

"Did you make a friend, Doll?"

The sound of the man's voice brought her up short. He stood at the edge of the porch, leaning against a pillar with arms folded. He waited for her to approach, and extended his hand.

"Andrew Toth."

He was slender, and no taller than she, with white-blonde hair. Older . . . thirties. He wore a thin gray sweater that looked like cashmere with tailored chinos.

"Liza McAfee. Pleased to meet you, Mr. Toth," she said.

"Delighted. Call me Andrew."

Liza rushed on. "I'm sorry about wandering off. We didn't mean . . . Kyle wanted to—"

He held up one hand to stop her. "Not a problem. You were curious about the place. I think that's a good sign." Andrew looked to the pines soaring overhead. "Never logged. One of only three stands in the Upper Peninsula spared by the people who got rich cutting the rest of them down. Come."

He turned and entered, Doll at his heels, without looking back. She followed him into the dim interior of the house, past a grand staircase and down a low-ceilinged hallway, the dog's nails clicking on the inlaid floor, to what must have been a library. It held scent memories of dust and old paper, but rather than books an arrangement of sleek architectural models covered the shelves. A single massive desk, dark as blood, stood dead center.

Andrew touched the surface of the wood with the tips of his fingers.

"Too big to remove," he said. "They added the walls around

it." He scanned the room. "Look at this placement. Anyone coming through that door was confronted by this beast." He shook his head. "Of course, if you sat at the desk, you had a great view of the fireplace instead of that." Andrew indicated the windows that ran the length of one wall, overlooking the lake. "Do you think that your husband might help me move it when he returns?"

"I don't—Won't it scratch the floor?" Liza didn't know if she could budge it, but moved to the other end of the desk. "I can help you." She felt herself babbling. "He's my fiancé."

Andrew watched her, his head tilted slightly, waiting to see if she was done.

"For six more days," she said.

"Congratulations," he said, "and the floors will be re-finished in the autumn." He rapped the desk with his knuckle. Andrew took a grip on the edge. "Come on, then, if you'd like to give it a try."

Liza leaned her weight into it, and the heavy desk slid an inch. Between the two of them, mostly Andrew, who was stronger than he looked, they moved it from its central spot to in front of the windows.

She straightened, panting, and felt a trickle of sweat run between her breasts.

"Now that is a view," Andrew said.

The glass framed the end of the lake and the beach, but the spot where she'd stood was out of sight around the curve of the shore.

He retrieved a highball glass from the mantelpiece, and indicated the bottle and spare tumbler that stood there for her. Liza shook her head. She wanted to ask when he'd arrived. The ice in his glass was almost completely melted.

She turned to the model closest to her on the shelves.

"The Palmer House," he said.

"Ann Arbor," she replied automatically.

"You're a Wright fan?" Andrew seemed surprised.

She wanted to snap back that they had books up here, even the internet now. Liza took a breath and traced the low triangular prow of the model's roof without touching it. "From the first time I saw a picture of one. His lines . . . improve upon what's there."

"Exactly. Which is impossible."

Liza nodded. "This house, your house, looks like one of his. Almost."

Andrew's eyes were dark. "You think so? Other people have said the same, but Wright denied any connection." He re-filled his glass. "I think that there may be something to that. Can't you see it? Henry Ford and Frank, two of the largest egos in history, clashing over the details, and Wright huffing off and destroying the evidence that he'd been involved. I can, which is why I added this place to my collection."

Her eyes jumped from design to design: Kentuck Knob—the house down the road from Fallingwater—the bridge cottage on Lake Michigan, at least two of the Oak Park houses, and others that had to be in the west. It took her a moment to realize that Andrew meant more than the models. She felt dizzy.

"So," he said, "your fiancé was in the military."

"Army Ranger." There was no place for her to sit down, aside from the desktop.

"He should have the necessary skills to keep poachers and trespassers away. Yes?"

Liza tried to get a grip on her thoughts. The image of Kyle in his uniform when he'd returned home on leave after graduating from the Ranger school in Georgia kept appearing in her mind, the strong jaw and long eyelashes under the black beret.

"Kyle won't hurt anyone for you," she said. Now she wanted the drink he'd offered.

"Of course not. I simply want to be able to walk in my woods without worrying about being shot."

"He'll be back soon. He wanted to scout the property before considering the job." As if they had a raft of offers like this.

Andrew spun his glass slowly between his palms. He looked up at her. "You know him better than anyone. Do you think he can do it?"

She felt a blush coming on, and willed it back down by thinking about putting her hand into the freezing water of the lake.

"Yes." The word seemed to open a drain in her head, and she felt the pressure ease. She'd committed to something, or at least admitted to it. Kyle would be wonderful at this.

"Will he do it?"

Kyle's eyes, alive inside their walls. "He will."

"I'll need to meet him." Andrew cocked his head and studied her. "And what do you want to do?"

Liza touched the small panes of leaded glass in the window over the desk.

"I don't know yet." She wanted to live here in this house.

After a pause, his words came out faster, clipped. "Two thousand a month. The use of the cabin located on the drive. An open charge account at that horrible little grocery store in town."

"The IGA?" The dark wood everywhere she looked made the room feel close and airless.

"Yes. Not much of a selection, but I suppose beggars can't be choosers in a town this size." Andrew extended his hand to shake. Liza looked at his other hand. No ring. "Oh, and I'll need you to be my assistant when I'm here, once a month. Nothing too strenuous. Scheduling, email if I can ever get decent service out here, research. I promise you that it will look good on your résumé. Perhaps you can help me find the proof that this is a Wright design. We can discover what it looked like before it was ruined."

This house swallowed noise. She couldn't hear the wind in the pines or the water. They could be anywhere.

"We'll talk it over and let you know tonight," Liza said. "Kyle should be waiting for me at the car."

He bowed slightly. She couldn't tell if he was mocking her. Andrew walked her to the door, and then stood watching from the veranda as she continued on to the car. As she passed the stable, Kyle appeared silently from the woods, breathing hard. His sweatshirt was gone. Mud streaked his bare torso. The months of inactivity had pared him down but the movement of the hard muscle that remained still made a knot catch in her chest. A stain at the corner of his mouth looked like blood. She tried to get him into the car before Andrew could get a clear look.

Liza took the drive too fast, purposefully keeping her eyes on the lane and not looking at the cabin which would be theirs if they took the offer. Kyle touched her thigh, his hand tentative and gentle.

"Are we going straight home?" he asked.

She couldn't look at him, either. The rear wheels slid in the gravel and then caught as she took a hard curve.

"One quick stop," she said.

He sighed. "You should have seen it, Li. It's like another world in there. I found a waterfall. I didn't want to come back."

She nodded. They reached the end of the lane, and she headed for the highway.

"Is everything all right?" he asked.

Liza patted his hand. "It will be."

He was quiet for the rest of the drive, lost in the memory of his run. She kept hearing the voice of the nurse at the hospital, the lumpish woman who had taken the picture. She'd asked a hundred questions about the wedding and how many children and where they would live. "I cannot believe they are still getting married," she'd said. Not to them, but to another nurse outside the door, where she'd thought Liza couldn't hear.

The picture had been in the paper: the two of them hemmed in by the frame and announcement. Kyle had tried to break off the engagement in the hospital, but she wouldn't let him. Liza knew he was still the same man under there, the one that had promised her any life she wanted. Kyle had only sunk a little deeper, and she could help him back up.

She pulled into the parking lot of the IGA and left the engine running. Kyle didn't ask any questions. The door, usually hard to open, flew back as she pushed through and headed for the register. Carla paused in her cashiering. The counter was filled with groceries. Liza didn't see whose cart she shoved aside. Her vision had narrowed to a point. The jar held more money than before, full to within an inch of the rim. It was heavy in her grasp, and warm, as though other hands had been holding it before Liza.

She heard the door open behind her, but could not make herself turn to see if Kyle had followed her in. The coins shifted and slid inside the jar. Now that she held it, she had no idea what she'd intended to do. Put the money into the plastic dog for the animal shelter. Pour it out into the lake, the change flipping and shining as it trailed down to the sand bottom. Liza imagined raising it overhead right here and smashing it to the concrete floor. Coins and shards of thick glass would ring off the surface and skip in every direction. They'd hit her legs and the shopping cart. A jagged triangle might rise toward her face and lodge in her skin. Someone would scream, maybe her.

The picture would lie in the wreckage on the floor at her feet, Kyle looking up at her. She would stoop and pick him up by the edges and raise him out of this mess. Any moment now she would do it.

# ANTIDOTE

*Paul Stroebel*

*"War don't ennoble men, it turns 'em into dogs."*
—James Jones

I've lived in two worlds—at least two worlds. The difference between them is nothing you can feel or explain right away. You board a plane to some known destination, some place on the map, a location you can point to with your finger, and you land. And at first everything looks about the same. You breathe the air and it feels the same. You sweat and your sweat smells the same. Even your thinking seems the same—at least at first. But somehow it's also different, and after a while the world makes you different. But you don't know this at first.

Words can't explain it. It's as if this new world scrambles every thought, and all you have are vivid pictures: I remember Nixon getting shot and the bullet that traversed him shoulder to hip. I remember Jimbo being blown up by Pakistanis because I lost a compass. I remember Kislow with a bullet clear through his helmet—and how he only lost his foot. And Evans, who asphyxiated on his vomit two weeks after coming home. And Captain Castoro, with his face covered in diesel and burning. And Dayton dying before he met his baby. And Beezley, shooting himself in the face after his separation from the military. And then there are the things I can't see, but just know. I don't know about all the wives who left their deployed husbands, and all the husbands who cheated on their faithful wives. And I remember the way time passed in that year I spent away.

When I came home I took all the memories that I couldn't yet understand and I put them on a shelf in my mind. And they just sat there like forgotten souvenirs, a letter from that other world that says, *hey you were here, but just 'cause you left don't really mean you're gone. You ain't home yet. And you ain't ever going home.* And you read that letter in your secret place, knowing the truth of what it says. Then you put it back on the shelf with rest of your baggage. Until one day, you go to that shelf, to find something small and insignificant, but what you need is stuck to the rest of it. So you tug and pull till all this shit falls out.

Sometimes you take them out, these souvenirs, and hold them up, hoping you can find someone who knows exactly where you've been.

We were on patrol. Oil was belching out of the ground. Big tarry pits like a cancerous oasis. The Commander, he's talking to some Imam about how to fix the busted pipes and stop the flow of tar. I'm sitting on the truck with our Lieutenant, the LT. We're just watching these little kids pouring out of the desert. Waves of kids, hollow-eyed with bloated bellies and flies drinking from their empty eyes.

We try to read their faces. Which ones are scowling? Which ones would kill us if they could.

"These kids hate us, sir," I say.

"Of course they do. We just killed their parents, and two days later we're offering them economic advice. They know we don't care anything about them," says the LT.

About four feet from the driver's door, a group of ten kids is all bunched up and squatting on the sand-covered pavement. After our driver, Larson, handed them cigarettes instead of food or money until they stopped begging. So now they are all sucking solemnly on unlit cigarettes. One small girl is playing with a small oil soaked puppy. Back home it might have been a golden retriever, or some *normal* kind of dog, but here it looks like an alien creature.

"It's bad enough we're dumping raw oil in their lawns, Larson. Let's not give their kids cancer, too," the LT says.

"Sir, I don't think they have any concept of a lawn here," I tell him.

"Besides sir, these kids already hate us," Larson says. He lights a cigarette with a M.R.E. matchbook. Then he ignites the entire booklet and the sulfur is a welcome change. He tosses the flaming bundle at the puppy.

The children don't even flinch. They watch the small thing with interest as it ignites.

The LT is livid. "What the hell, Larson!" He rushes to the small black thing and hesitates.

The children seem to feed off his intensity.

"Tell him to stomp it out," I say to Larson.

Larson begins hopping from foot to foot, yelling, "Stomp it out, sir! Stomp it out!"

The small thing is black, and slowly becomes blacker. Finally it is still.

Later, on the drive back to base, the LT seems broken.

"Sir, are you okay?" Larson asks.

"I'm fine. I'm just thinking," he says.

"We were going to have to shoot it anyway," Larson says.

"And that's fine, I get that. But why set a puppy, covered in oil, on fire?"

"Okay, that might have been fucked up, sir," admits Larson.

"Not really, sir," I say. They seem surprised that I am even listening. "Have you ever tried to set a puppy on fire that isn't covered in oil? Now that would be fucked up."

So we laugh together, and the LT feels better, and this is the kind of thing that happens in that other world.

# THE EDGE OF WATER

★ ★ ★

*Kevin C. Jones*

That November after Iraq, after all the surgeries on my leg, after I could get around with crutches instead of a wheelchair, after the bruising was only a memory and the concussion toned down to a few, minor headaches that only bothered me in bright sunlight or movie theatres, I found myself in California again. I was having a beer with my best friend, Greg, and his new wife, Chelsea. Greg was the creative director of a PR firm. He'd told me the name once, but I couldn't remember. He seemed to jump companies every other week and all of their names sounded the same to me. The bar was his idea. He said that I needed to get out more and that he wasn't going to allow me to spend my entire convalescent leave in my hotel bedroom with the shades drawn. He was talking about his new hobby, real estate.

"You should look into getting something, Paul," he said. "The market is totally stacked for buyers right now."

"Right, stacked." I stared down at his wedding ring. It looked like he'd won the Superbowl.

"I know you don't have a lot of cash," he said. "But I can put you in contact with some people. Pull a few strings, get you a good deal."

"I'm still stationed in Hawaii, why would I want something here?"

"Investment. Besides, you aren't going to be there that much longer, right?"

"I don't know," I said, sipping on my drink. Greg loved dark beer so we'd met at a British pub downtown. They didn't have anything Mexican so when the bartender asked what I wanted I told him "Anything that isn't the color of mud." What I got was something that looked and tasted like overpriced Budweiser.

Greg kept trying not to look at my leg, at the brace I'm only allowed to take off in the shower. He was trying to be casual about it, but when you're deliberately trying to not look at something it's just that much more obvious. Chelsea wasn't much better. With her slick, page boy haircut and designer clothes she looked like someone out of a silent movie: Dorothy Parker in Prada. She kept staring at me and I wondered if she was going to say something. I wore a beanie to keep my head warm but you could still see the shrapnel scars on my neck. When I'd had enough I deliberately looked directly into her eyes, smiling as she quickly dropped her gaze down to my arms resting on the table between us.

"That's an interesting tattoo," she said, looking at the inside of my left forearm. Exposed from where I'd pushed up the sleeves of my thermal shirt was the black silhouette of a winged skull with crossed tridents behind it, the words *Aut Vincere, Aut Mori* in Latin below, USMC in Old English script above.

*Victory or Death.*

Greg looked out of the window, watched rain spatter against panes, run into gutters.

"He's got a bunch," he said.

"Really?" Chelsea looked at me with new interest. Diamonds hung in her ears like stars.

"One or two," I said.

"One or two?" Greg laughed. "Christ, what have you got, really, fifteen or sixteen now?"

"One less than I used to. The surgeons took care of the one on my leg."

Chelsea looked down at her Amaretto Sour, back up at me. She had brown eyes with long, thick lashes that made me think of someone else.

My team was coming back from patrol. There were five of us in the Humvee: Ortiz was driving, Alexander, Weatherford, and Simone were in the back seat. I rode shotgun. It was surreal, the drive. We had just spent three days in the ass end of the city looking for insurgents. Sixteen hour patrols, trying to scrounge up any source of intel we could find, any sign of were the bad guys might be. Kicking in doors when people wouldn't open them for us, staring into the faces of children and old men. People we terrified with our helmets and goggles and rifles. Now, here we were, after all that, stuck in traffic.

"Just like L.A., right, Sergeant?" Ortiz said. "Just like home."

"If this is what L.A. is like it's no wonder y'all can't fucking drive," Weatherford said, reaching over the seat with his huge, dark hands and smacking Ortiz on the helmet.

I turned around and looked at him. "I've been to D.C., Weatherford," I said. "It's no fucking picnic either."

"Too true, too true," he said. "But I'll sure as shit take the Beltway over this bullshit here any day of the fucking week." He reached into his IBA and pulled out a cigarette.

"Let me get one of those," I said. He looked at me.

"Thought you didn't smoke."

"I don't. Mission's over, we're in one piece, I feel like relaxing a bit. That okay with you, Lance Corporal?" I was fucking with him by pulling rank. When there weren't any officers around I never made anyone call me sergeant. They were my friends, my team. Ortiz was the only one who addressed people by their rank, a habit he hadn't broken yet, born of his time in Boot Camp and the School of Infantry the year before. More than once I'd told him if he didn't relax I'd shoot him myself.

Weatherford handed me a smoke, then his lighter. "It's your lungs, man," he said. "But I will collect later."

"Deal."

Alexander said, "Don't talk about being in one piece. You'll jinx us."

Weatherford snorted a laugh. "Fuck that superstitious bullshit."

"Whatever, dog," Ortiz looked over the steering wheel at the crowds and traffic all around us. "It's bad luck to talk about how good things are when we're not back at the FOB yet. It's…what do they call it?…tempting fate."

I took a deep drag off of my cigarette, coughed once, exhaled.

"See," Weatherford said. "I knew you didn't smoke. That's a waste of a good cigarette right there."

"Fuck you," I said. "I'll buy you more when we get back."

"Damn straight."

We drove another few blocks and traffic slowed to a crawl. There was some kind of accident up ahead of us. People shouting, waiving their arms. Some guy in a polo shirt and shitty slacks stood with a cell phone up to his ear. I finished half of my smoke, rolled down the window, and tossed it out into the street. We stopped at the edge of the intersection and that's when I saw the woman.

"Head's up," I said.

"She walked out of a nearby building and made her way towards us. Everyone in the Humvee turned to watch. She looked left and right, nervous, taking small, hesitant steps across the pavement.

"Sergeant…" Simone's voice from directly behind me. I could hear him adjusting in his seat to bring his weapon around and point it at the woman.

"Wait," I said. "Just a second. She's alone. Something's up."

I'd never seen a woman travel without a male escort in Iraq the entire time I'd been there. I had my own rifle turned outboard, the barrel pointing out of the window as she approached me. Plastic bags blew across the street like tumbleweeds. I kept the muzzle aimed at her chest.

Her body was hidden behind the black folds of her burka and all I could see were her eyes, dark brown against the pale mocha skin of her face. They were beautiful, with long, dark lashes and an intensity, an energy, I'd never seen before or since.

"This is insane," Alexander said. "She must need some kind of serious help or something if she's coming to talk to us in public like this."

"She must need food," I said. "Or water. She must have kids."

"Sergeant?" Ortiz motioned at the road ahead of us. The traffic had cleared. It was okay to go now. "We can tell Civil Affairs or whoever when we get back to the FOB. This is their kind of shit, not ours."

The woman continued towards us, walking into the street now.

"Just a sec, Ortiz," I said, reaching down to get a bottle of water and some rations from my pack. "COIN. Hearts and minds, remember? Let me give her something and we'll go."

Then she detonated.

"Well," Chelsea said. "You look pretty good, considering."

"Considering what?" I said.

"You know." She nodded towards my crutches, the brace on my right leg. I could sense her discomfort, wondered what she'd tell Greg in their car on the ride home. "Greg told me it was bad. You were lucky, I guess."

"Yeah, I'm lucky." I said. "My leg? The docs at the combat hospital told me that it's always going to look this way." The skin was covered with long, erratic scars still prominent despite hours of skin grafts. "You're right, Chelsea, I'm lucky. Lucky that I was ducking down behind the door of the Humvee when the blast went off. Lucky I only got "light shrapnel" over the entire right side of my body. Lucky I wasn't looking directly at the explosion, like Ortiz, who lost his eyes, or Simone, who'd taken his helmet off right before we stopped and was killed instantly."

Chelsea looked down at the floor. Greg leaned across the table towards me.

"Dude," he said, in a low whisper. "Relax. People are staring."

I looked around and noticed that the bar had grown quiet. I took a large drink of my beer and felt my fists unclench, my heart beating in my temples. Chelsea looked at me, said something, but I couldn't make it out. For a moment, everything became muffled, like I was underwater, and I wondered if it was the swelling in my brain coming back. The doctors told me to stay away from alcohol, but that was over a month ago, and I was only on my first beer.

"What?" I said to Chelsea in what I hoped was a quieter voice. Around the room people drank and laughed and shimmered in my vision. After a moment sounds became clear again.

"I said, 'I'm sorry.'"

I finished my beer, stared at the empty glass, wondered if I should order another. Greg beat me to it. "Two more," he said, flagging down a waitress as she walked by.

"It's okay," I said to Chelsea. "It's just…"

"What?" Greg leaned in close, almost whispering. "It's just what?"

"I ordered them to stop," I said. "Ortiz, my driver, he hadn't even been in the Corps for a fucking year yet." I looked around the room, noticed a woman with long, straight hair the color of snow sitting at the bar across from our table. I watched as she drank a glass of white wine, waiting, hoping for her to make eye contact with me, but she never did. It doesn't matter; I wouldn't have known what to say to her. I remembered the blast, the way Ortiz's eye sockets looked like they were packed with jelly, the sounds of screams that took me a long time to realize were my own. "Simone's wife had a baby while we were over there. A girl." I looked at Greg. "He never got to hold her, to meet her. All because I ordered them to stop."

"You didn't know."

"I should have," I said. "It's not like it was the first time I'd been there."

Back in my room at the Naval Hospital in Hawaii, a Purple Heart still sat in its box, unopened, on my nightstand.

"You need to think about the future," Greg said. "About what you're going to do next when all of this is over with."

"I can't think that far ahead."

"Start." He took another sip of his beer. "You talk to your dad lately?"

"He sends me an email every now and again," I said. "You know my dad; he blames the president for what happened to me."

"He may have a point," Chelsea said.

I looked at Greg. "You know we've never been that close."

"Yeah, well, I read somewhere that traumatic injury can change that." He laughed. "Didn't you used to go to the beach together?"

"Yeah, when I was a little kid. Jesus, I'd forgotten about that. When my parents were still married, we used to rent a cabin near Bodega Bay at the end of summer each year. What made you think of that?"

The last Labor Day weekend we spent together as a family, before everything imploded, my father rented a cabin on the beach for us. It was so cold there, and I wondered how that was possible when it was still summer. On the last day he took me down past the sand dunes and we walked along the shore, my feet numb and pink in the icy water. We went into the surf together and I held onto his leg as the waves crashed into us. I was small, just a kid, and I was afraid that the current would carry me out to sea. I don't think my dad realized that, just by being there, he was saving my life. That just by letting me hold onto him, at the edge of the water, he was keeping me from washing away with the tide. It's the last good memory I have of my father, and I can't even see his face in it. Just the waves washing over us, my arms wrapped around his leg, and the sea stretching on forever to the end of the world.

"We just spent a weekend up there about a month ago," Greg said. "I remembered you used to talk about it."

"It's been years."

"Call him. Let him know how you're doing." He dropped a bone colored business card onto the table in front of me. "And call this guy. I'm telling you, he'll hook you up with a good deal on a house."

"I'll think about it."

"Hey." Greg leaned across the table and squeezed my arm. "There are other things you can do with your life, that's all I'm trying to say."

Even with all of the physical therapy I'd been doing, the doctors told me it could be months, maybe years, before I ever ran again, but that my military career was probably over. I'd never really thought about reenlisting, but hearing that I couldn't made me realize that I wasn't sure what I was going to do.

It didn't feel right, me sitting there, enjoying a cold beer in a bar while people I knew were still overseas. Still patrolling at night, kicking in doors, looking for bad guys. Today, four civilian contractors were found on the side of the road next to their burned SUV, shot in the head, execution style, left to bloat and rot in the afternoon sun. Last week a truck full of Mississippi National Guardsmen were killed when their convoy drove past a car rigged with explosives.

The week before that, an Air Force jet got the wrong coordinates and dropped a bomb on someone's apartment, killing an entire family. They sent a Civil Affairs team to apologize on behalf of the United States, but there wasn't anyone left to talk to.

We stay for a few more beers and then Greg takes me back to my hotel. The next day I fly to Hawaii where the Naval Hospital releases me back to my unit. To the Rear Detachment. Everyone else is still over there. Still fighting.

During the next few months in Hawaii, where the entire world was a shock of green and blue and high, wet heat that made my uniform stick to my skin, Command makes me see the chaplain once a week. I nodded a lot. I told him I was fine. I said that I looked forward to my leg fully healing so that I could get on with my life. I said that, even though the doctors finally figured out that my leg would fully heal, I knew my time in the Marine Corps was coming to an end.

"So, what are you not telling me, son?" The chaplain said. "What are you still afraid of?"

"Nothing," I said. "It already happened."

"You ever talk to anyone else about this? About what happened?"

"No, sir," I said. "I'm okay, really. I'm fine."

Today, at the barracks, in my room, there are a dozen emails on my computer. All of them from my father. All of them unopened. There are letters from Simone's wife. Pictures of his daughter. A description of the funeral I couldn't attend because I was still in the hospital. This morning, someone in Admin told me that Ortiz is doing better. He's living with his mother in Baldwin Park, trying to learn Braille so that he can go to college. He turned twenty last month.

I open one of the emails from my father and it's a photo of me and him when I was a kid. We're standing on the beach. I'm all elbows and knees with a red pail and shovel in my hand, my father next to me with his arm around my shoulder.

I pick up the phone. I try to dial but I can't. My hands are shaking.

# MEN OF PRINCIPLE

★ ★ ★

*Jon Chopan*

I found the guy I was looking for at Six Pockets. I was with my two buddies Lesh and Jeff. The night before, Emma, the woman I loved, had told me about a guy who raped her years ago. I was sure I knew him, though by the time I started looking I'd forgotten his name and was, with foggy recollection, searching for a face. I had been back from the war for three months, now. The celebration was over, most of the questions about combat had been asked and all of my stories had been told, and I was, just then, becoming accustomed to home life, the drinking, seeing a woman with some regularity, a shit job at the meat-packing plant. In many ways, I was a civilian. But I had not forgotten things about the war, a desire for swift justice, for example. How sometimes, when a guy from our division was hurt or killed, be it by sniper fire or an IED, we'd walk the streets and harass civilians. Or, if we were in a remote location, how we'd stand, circling an empty mosque, and fire round after round until the building was nothing but pockmarked cement. In this way, what we sought was often the quick and necessary relief men feel when they feel loss. It seemed to me then that I was just a young man and could not access a language for my pain and so released it through force. But it occurs to me now that this is too often something that affects all men. From a young age they are taught that to feel anything is to be weak.

That night we started at the Mirage. I was looking for the guy everywhere. I wanted to find him because of what Emma had told me. I thought I could, through an act of violence, even the score. I had told my friends I was looking for him, but not why, told them I was sure I'd seen the guy a week or two before, maybe at the

Mirage, maybe at Six Pockets. I wanted to find him and I wanted their help, because as memory served he was a big guy, the type of guy who would require strength I didn't have.

When we arrived at the strip club I was too distracted to "participate in the festivities," as Lesh called them. Every time the front door swung open a gust of the cold January air punched into the room, and I turned, trying to make out the face, which appeared illuminated in the contrast between the light of the outside and the dark of the inside. The Mirage was a strange kind of place. On the edge of the working-class neighborhoods of Lake Avenue, and set in the middle of the Kodak industrial park, its clientele was an odd mix of blue- and white-collar men. This, somehow, made the place feel even more remote, even more artificial than the average strip club. How they catered to both sets of regulars, domestic beer and strange imports none of us drank, the skinny college girls who danced every other set, and then the "full-figured girls," as Jeff said. All I knew, when I was there, was that I never wanted anything in my real life to feel as fake as the inside of that place. In part, this was why I drank so recklessly, but also, because I could not calm my nerves, tapped my foot rapidly and out of pace with the music just to keep myself in my seat. I had, to that point, sounded two false alarms. My friends were growing tired of me.

"Look at these fucking broads," Lesh said.

We sat close to the stage, drinking Genny Light and eating twenty-five cent wings. Jeff stood up during every song and tipped each girl a dollar.

"The fuck you doing that for?" Lesh asked Jeff when he sat down again.

"What?"

"You don't have to tip all of them for every goddamned song," Lesh said. "You're setting an awfully high standard for the rest of us. You're making the ugly ones think it's all right they're ugly."

The girl on stage stopped dancing and shot Lesh a glance. He was a scrawny guy, wiry arms and legs, with stubble on his face at all times. It was hard to decide at any given moment, because of the look of him, whether he'd had a particularly good or a particularly bad day.

"I didn't mean you, honey, you're fine." He licked wing sauce off his fingers, pulled money from his wallet.

"Somebody's gotta make up for this guy," Jeff said, pointing to me, because I didn't get near the stage, did everything in my power, even on a normal night, to divert my attention, staring into the bottom of a beer, watching whatever game was on the televisions tucked in the far corners.

Just then the door swung open and another man walked in. I turned and stared.

"Remind me why you're looking for this guy?" Jeff said.

"Long story," I said. "Just have to sort something out."

Jeff finished off a wing. He washed it down with half a beer. "Relax," he said. "You're starting to creep me out. We're bound to run into him sooner or later." I refilled my glass, looked up at the stage where Lesh was talking to the girl he'd offended.

We had come to the Mirage, in part, because of my search, but more importantly we'd come because this was one of Lesh's spots, one of the places on Friday and Saturday nights where he sold cocaine. He brought Jeff and me along as a kind of protection. He didn't believe in guns, but felt strongly about a show of force. Jeff was six-foot-four, a bulky two-hundred-and-eighty pounds. He walked with the long slow strides of a caveman, his arms hung by his sides as if he were carrying clubs in each hand. He was all the force one coke dealer needed, or at least, that's what I thought. But Lesh said he liked using my credentials. "United States Marine," he said. "Pretty badass."

The song ended and Jeff moved to get up. He liked the next girl, was bound, at some point, to get a lap dance from her.

"I just want to find this guy and settle it," I said.

"Enjoy the show," he said. "I'm trying to, but you're making it awfully fucking hard."

I laughed.

"What?" he said, reaching into his pockets for his wad of singles.

"That was a pun," I said.

Jeff finished off the other half of his beer.

"See," he said. "Your head's in the wrong place."

★ ★ ★

Because Lesh dealt coke we had what could be called special privileges. During a lull the DJ waved us over. My friends rose in unison. Our time to move, make the deal and head out for a few more, before ending the night at Six Pockets where Lesh held court, met with regulars, often disappeared into the backroom with the owner or one of the bartenders.

Just then the door opened again and I turned to look. The place was getting packed because some college football team was playing a big bowl game and it was cold and no one wanted to drive home in this weather.

"Jesus," Lesh said. "This shit again."

I stayed in my seat. I wanted to make sure it wasn't him. It was getting dark out so it was harder to make out the faces. I could see snow falling in the background, coming down in sheets that looked like laundry twisting in the breeze on a clothesline.

"You coming, or what?" Jeff asked.

"Yeah," I said, standing up.

Jeff smiled. We were headed into the dressing room, which was his favorite part. "Jesus man, you really know how to ruin a good time," he said. We walked, Lesh in front, me in the middle, Jeff in back. When we got to the curtain the DJ parted it. "Gentlemen," he said. We stopped a few steps in so Lesh could make nice with the owner.

"Paradise," Jeff said.

The backroom at the Mirage looked like a locker room, each girl with her own stall, some with makeup strewn about, others with wigs hanging in tangled piles. Behind them, in a corner, was a set of beds where the girls would lie, resting between sets, catching up on sleep they had not gotten between their day jobs and this. All of them seemed more beautiful than they had on stage. They wore bathrobes, smelled of too-sweet perfume, let their hair fall around their shoulders and down their backs.

The girls moved around us with the pace and force of fish trapped in a net. A woman just like them came over to us, started talking to Lesh. She was tall, with dark hair, and she looked too pretty, somehow, to be here. By the way she spoke I imagined her as someone older, like the mother of all the girls there. But she couldn't, by the look of her, have been. She reminded me of Emma. Something about how out of place she seemed, something about the confidence she exuded. It was what had drawn me to Emma, made me believe that she could save me from the world I had come from, was surrounded by at that very moment.

This woman, she looked over Lesh's shoulder at me. "What's wrong with that one?" she said. Lesh turned toward me.

"The smaller one?" he said.

"Yes."

He smiled, turning back to her. "Just shy is all."

Before long the whole thing was over and my friends were sitting in a circle with some of the girls, a pile of coke in the middle of them, enjoying a few lines before we moved on to our next stop. I sat by myself, thinking about what I would do if I found the guy I was looking for, trying to decide what I'd say to him. The woman who reminded me of Emma walked up to me then, smiling, put her hand out.

"Can I do something for you?" she said.

I felt very sad just then. Somehow everything felt cheaper. My head was cloudy from all the beer I'd drank.

"No thanks," I said, my arms folded across my chest.

She untied the belt on her robe.

"What's the problem?" she said, her hands on her hips.

She looked very young then, younger than I'd guessed before. It was because she was so thin, too thin really, with her long hair framing her, and her eyes a blue something like Lake Ontario.

"Not you," I said. "I'm with someone."

She leaned in then, her robe falling away. She put her mouth on mine, ran her tongue over my lips. I closed my eyes. The music from the front room hit its peak, the men whistling and cheering for the girl who was dancing. I kept spinning. I inhaled deep gusts of perfume. I was so overcome with grief I thought it might suffocate me. And then, she stood, pulled her robe tight, winked at me.

"I love men of principle," she said.

★ ★ ★

On the way to Six Pockets we made a pit stop. By then I was pretty drunk and needed the break. We drove through the city, across town, toward the low rises and split-level houses of the projects. In the summer months these neighborhoods would be swarming with people, with life, but in January they looked abandoned, picked over, with a few lights on here and there. The roads were slick and lightly dusted in a fine snow that kept falling, but mostly just swirled in tornado-like cyclones, stirred by the winter wind. The building we stopped in front of, a three-story brick apartment complex, looked ready to sink into the earth beneath it. It was dark with the exception of the flickers of candlelit shadows moving behind the static of snow.

As we climbed the stairs to the third floor I felt a sensation I'd felt when I was in Iraq, going to a specific target to inspect a house, a feeling that this was not a place where good things happened. The door to the apartment looked worse off than any of the others, the screen hanging from the bottom hinge, slumped over, open, resting against the rail. Lesh walked right in.

Over his shoulder I could see that the room was lit with giant candles resting on sheets of tinfoil, probably purchased in bulk at the public market. The room was heated by a single space heater and I could see my breath in the air. I heard the faint cries of an infant somewhere in the next room.

Once inside I plopped myself into a worn out Barcalounger, ready, I was certain, to sleep and dream forever. Jeff sat on the couch next to the man we'd come to see and Lesh stood over a plastic table, the kind people might use for picnics or weekly card games. He opened a bag and laid out a line. A woman stood in the doorway between this room and the next.

"Your buddy all right?" the man said, pointing over to me.

"Yeah," Lesh said. "He's a Marine; he's just being all inconspicuous and shit."

The man laughed. I flashed them a thumbs up. Jeff sat with his hands in his pockets, watching the woman as she paced.

"Hey, you want a line?" the man asked, motioning toward me.

I shifted my weight, slid down the chair a bit so my head was the only thing touching the back. "No thanks," I said. "Not my cup of tea." In this room I felt thirsty. I could taste some kind of cruelty that both intrigued and repulsed me, the trace of a perfume that could destroy everything.

"I see," he said. He walked over to the table and blew a line. "A regular G.I. Joe," he said. "A real boy scout." He laughed. I smiled.

Before I knew what was happening Lesh had him pinned to the floor, his hand around his throat. "What'd you say, you idiot, what'd you say to my friend?"

The baby was crying in the next room. The woman made a move towards Lesh, but he held his hand up, palm open. "You're gonna make it worse," he said. She stood, frozen. I sat upright, awake again. She glanced at Jeff, then at me. She looked like a child who knew a beating was coming, wanted us to do something to stop it. She knew her husband, or boyfriend, whatever he was, was in trouble, but she didn't know how to save him and neither did we.

The room was quiet except for the sound of the child. I wondered if it was a boy or a girl. I wondered how old it was. The man put his hands around Lesh's. I could see he was having a hard time breathing. I could see he was trying to say something.

"Apologize," Lesh said. "Apologize for what you said."

The baby kept crying. And I, just then, felt like we, all of us in that room, in that part of the city, that we were living hollowed-out lives, like bone with no marrow.

On the way to Six Pockets I told them, repeated Emma's story exactly as she had told it to me. And in an instant I could see their faces change, the way it often happens when men are given a real purpose, a mission to believe in. It was as though, suddenly, nothing we'd done that night had ever even happened, like we'd, the three of us, been born again to bring justice to an unjust world.

As soon as we walked through the door I spotted him. A song by Jimi Hendrix was playing, a tune I knew but couldn't place. I elbowed Lesh. "That's the guy," I said. "That's him."

We walked over to the bar. Lesh made small talk with the bartender, ordered all of us drinks. "That's him," he said, elbowing Jeff, pointing right at him.

Six Pockets was only half full, mainly regulars, the drunks on the bar side, the pool leagues finishing up on the other. I couldn't stop looking at the guy, waiting for something to happen, for a chance to arise. He stood by the jukebox with a group of people, his pool team. They were saying their goodbyes, readying to leave.

"He's a goddamn monster," Lesh said. "He's bigger than Jeff, for Christ's sake."

"You aren't scared, are you?" Jeff asked, laughing, taking a drink.

The man moved to the bar, his team leaving, sat down and ordered.

I felt, because of all that had happened that night, like I had spent my whole life looking for him and now that he was alone I wanted to get him outside right away, I wanted to confront him and get it over with.

Lesh finished off his drink. "No. I'm just saying he's big is all."

"Well," Jeff said. "What do you want to do?"

"I'll get him outside," Lesh said. "He's bought shit from me before."

"Then what?" Jeff asked.

I sat on the stool next to Lesh. Jeff stood behind us. Another Hendrix song came on and people were leaving in small groups, it was settling into a nice slow night, just regulars and the few stragglers from the pool league.

"Then," Lesh said, "follow me out. We'll go from there."

When we got outside Lesh was talking to him. They were smoking and laughing. The patio was empty, except for the four of us, our arms drawn in toward our bodies, fighting off the cold. Jeff handed me a Marlboro and we stood, the three of us facing the guy, blowing smoke at him.

"My buddy here, Tully," Lesh said. "He says he knows you," the laughter leaving his voice.

The man looked right at me then. Our eyes locked and I could see him searching for me in his memory. Lesh sat down in one of the plastic lawn chairs, put his arms behind his head. Jeff spat on the ground at his feet. The man looked away for a second as a car left the lot, flicked his cigarette into the snow.

"I'm afraid I can't place you," he said, reaching out his hand.

I pulled my cigarette to my mouth, drew in a deep breath. "Well, I know you," I said, exhaling puffs of smoke as I spoke. "I've heard about you."

"Okay," he said.

"I know what you did," I said.

The man pulled his hand back then. "I'm not sure I know what you're talking about," he said. He took a step back. For the first time it dawned on him that we had not come as friends.

He looked at Lesh. "Is this a joke?" he said.

Lesh smiled. "No," he said. "No joke."

"What's up then, what's the problem?"

When I heard him say that, something in me snapped. I guess all along I imagined he'd fess up to it, start bawling like some kid who'd got caught stealing, and before it even came to violence, I dreamed this man falling to his knees and begging our forgiveness. His ignorance made all the anger and disgust I had for him rise up into my throat.

Before I could do anything Lesh got up and punched him in the Adams apple. The man fell to his knees, the weight of him falling popped one of his kneecaps free of the socket. Lesh grabbed the lawn chair he'd been sitting on and smashed it over the guy's back, the whole thing splintering into pieces. Lesh stood there with only the arms of it left in his grip.

"That's the fucking problem," Lesh said, tossing the arms aside.

No one said anything after that. All I could hear was that man sucking for air. I brought my knee to his face, could feel his nose bend and snap, as he rolled, slowly, like a dog going down to play dead. There was no stopping the beating that followed. We set to kicking him, Jeff stepping back so Lesh and I could work on him uninhibited. We kept at it like we were trying to kick in a door. And with each kick I felt, again and again, a sense of righteousness pulse through me, something like I'd never felt before.

During the war nothing felt this pure, this right. When we moved into cities, when we engaged with the enemy, it always felt played out, like no one really knew who was good and who was bad or why we were even there. The people we fought against hid in plainclothes amongst the population. Who could blame them, in a sense, because otherwise they had no chance. But then, too, it seemed like a cowardly thing to do. It meant so many people who should not have been killed were. Fighting a war like that had a way of muddying the line between the good guys and the bad guys. It had a way of making things happen that could not be clearly or easily divided into right or wrong. You did, sometimes against your better judgment, anything you could to feel safe, to feel like you'd make it through the war and get home. And because of that, I needed a righteous cause, needed a clearly defined enemy and a valid reason to destroy him.

We were winded after a while. The snow had stopped falling and the ground had started to freeze. I stood, doubled over, sucking in air that burned my lungs. Lesh lit a cigarette.

"Jesus," Jeff said. "Look at that fucking mess."

In front of us, the man lay curled in the fetal position, writhing, not knowing which parts of him hurt the most. "Shut up," Lesh said, flicking ashes on him. "You're giving me a headache."

I started coughing, violently. My muscles were already getting sore. I picked up my beer and finished what was left.

"Carry him to the bathroom," Lesh said, pointing to Jeff.

"What for?" he asked. "I think you pretty well ruined his night as it is."

I caught my breath, held the empty bottle in my hand. Lesh looked over at me. "Bring that," he said, pointing to the bottle. "We're going to finish this off."

I held the bottle in my hand. The lights in the bathroom reminded me of the lighting at a police station. I thought of myself, if only for a second, as a cop beating the information out of a suspect. I wanted to say all the cheesy things I thought a TV detective might say, make him confess, make him beg for his life, but I was tired just then, was sick from the whole thing and ready to go back to the bar and drink another beer. I was angry because what we'd done hadn't fixed anything for Emma, and I knew now, if I ever told her what I'd done, that she'd leave me, that she wouldn't find any good in it. I just wanted the guy to disappear.

"You're a piece of shit," I said. "A real piece of shit."

Lesh spat on him. Jeff stood with his back against the door, holding it shut so no one could come in. "Let's get this over with," Lesh said, bending down to get a closer look at the guy. Someone knocked on the door. "Fuck off," Jeff said.

I looked down at the man for a few seconds, sitting there in his own blood, his own piss. I felt sorry for him, but that only made me hate him more. After a minute, I raised the bottle up over my head.

"You've got the wrong guy," he said, spitting out strings of blood. It was something in the sound of his voice, how desperate it was. I knew that he was telling the truth. I knew that he was not the one.

But I said, "I don't care." Said, "You're going to pay."

# SEVEN IN THE MORNING

★ ★ ★

*Max Ruback*

Sergeant still brings you his leash, secured in his mouth. He waits by your bedside, tail wagging. He only senses something wrong, a whimper when he glances at the prosthetic legs leaning against the wheelchair. A car bomb at dusk in Iraq. This first week home and you refuse to leave the house. It is seven in the morning and your mother walks into your bedroom and smiles, nothing said, grabs the leash and leads Sergeant outside for his morning walk. Good boy, she says. Good boy.

# THE CITY OF SCREAMS

★ ★ ★

*Court Merrigan*

1.

The Afghan villagers outside Combat Post Khawji Qasar had never seen an American Indian before. Fascinated by Jackdaw, the old men and children ignored the blacks and whites in his platoon to hover over Jackdaw as he spaded out an irrigation ditch blown up by the Taliban, close enough he could smell their breath, rank with garlic and pukka tea. He called the interpreter over to ask what was going on.

The interpreter said, "They say you look Mongolian. Are you Mongolian?"

"No, man. I'm Lakota."

"You see that city up there?" asked the interpreter, pointing to the ruins that topped the hill on the far side of the combat post, commanding a view of the ragged green valley and the pass clefted between the white peaks ducking and dancing in a serried procession of clouds. "Genghis Khan swarmed over the pass and killed every man and child in that city and gave the women to his soldiers to rape. Then he burned the city. It is called the City of Screams."

"That was like a thousand years ago."

"Your time is not the time of the villagers. To them this happened only yesterday. Genghis Khan was Mongolian, you see."

"And they think I am, too?"

"As I said. You very much look like one."

"Hey, JD," said the sergeant, "this ditch ain't going to dig itself."

"Roger, sergeant," said Jackdaw, leaning back into his shovel.

"Well, I didn't have any goddamn thing to do with it. You tell them, all right? Tell them."

The interpreter shook his head sadly. "I am afraid they will not believe me."

Sure enough, when Jackdaw went on patrol, the air grew thick with gesticulation in his direction as the men considered him huddled in doorways leaking smoke from cooking fires. Young boys with toy guns fashioned from scrap metal took aim at him from hard-packed lanes where brackish sewage dribbled into the dust. Women drew their veils and fled, leaving empty buckets at the village well.

Jackdaw got to thinking about the rez back home. Tried to envision those distant days of starvation and defeat, gut-shot old men, violated women, bayoneted babies. Atrocities carried out in the name of the same flag that flapped over Combat Post Khawji Qasar, by the same Army where he was a grunt. No, you couldn't blame those Afghans for their long grudge.

The question was, why didn't he have one?

When a full-bird colonel came on a command inspection, Jackdaw was on guard duty in a tower. He ran his fingers down the rifle pondering a little revenge and was suffused with sudden strange happiness.

"What the hell's wrong with you?" said his fellow in the tower.

"Nothing," said Jackdaw.

"Then wipe that shit-eating grin off your face."

Later, Jackdaw sat in the reeking honey bucket, laptop hot on his thighs, blonde taking it up the ass onscreen. Pictured himself as a Mongolian warrior hoisting that blonde into the saddle, impaling her on his cock at full gallop, yellow hair bunched in his fists, laughing at her screams. He walloped himself so hard his dick chafed and bled.

Soon after, a suicide bomber pulverized Jackdaw's platoon as they humped sacks of cement to a new school building. The heavy sack of cement on Jackdaw's back kept him alive but his legs got splattered with shrapnel. He almost bled out before a medic applied a tourniquet, watching a goat munch on a candy bar wrapper in the rubble as tracers flew overhead and mortars blossomed on the hillsides above the City of Screams.

2.

Jackdaw slid down the ragged brick wall of White Buffalo Liquor clutching a bottle of vodka, flecks of fresh vomit on his lips, scar-rippled legs throbbing. His shirt was ripped halfway up his arm and crusted with blood from a fall several days old. No one listened to his slurry demands for justice. Just another drunk Indian. When he hit the ground, he blacked out.

Lamar War Bonnet crawled over on hands and knees and pried the bottle from his fingers. He had a long pull, waved to a couple youngsters dropping cases of malt liquor in a pickup to haul back to the reservation. Then Lamar War Bonnet toppled to his side on the cracked asphalt and choked to death on his own vomit.

As Jackdaw woke, the cashier from the White Buffalo stepped around the group gathered around the corpse.

"I told you," said the cashier. "There isn't nothing more I can do. I done called the authorities."

The group let the cashier pass, muttering. Lamar War Bonnet laid there with slack blue lips leaching red bile, trousers stained with shit. Jackdaw pushed aside legs to retrieve his vodka. He sat cross-legged next to Lamar holding the empty bottle until a Highway Patrolman pulled up in a blur of pulsating lights.

"Stand aside, stand aside," the smokey said, curled his lips at the reek of vomit and shit. "Christ on a crutch. Hey. Hey you."

The smokey was talking to Jackdaw. Jackdaw slowly raised his head.

"What?" Jackdaw said.

"Move on. Get away from that body."

Jackdaw looked up at him stupidly. "I'm sitting here."

"Move along, I said."

Jackdaw struggled to his feet, legs pounding with fire, head awash with whirligigs, and stumbled away. It had been nearly a year since Afghanistan, time spent mostly drunk and often as not here in Rattlecreek, home to three liquor stores and one abandoned church, a town which existed for one reason: to peddle poison to his people. The reservation was dry and no whites lived within forty miles of Rattlecreek. Yet here it stood. The liquor stores addled his people into collaborating with their own conquerors, reducing them to drunken serfs in their own homeland.

Time he quit with the goddamned talking.

He staggered to the front of the White Buffalo and ripped off his torn shirt sleeve and stuffed it in the empty vodka bottle. Pulled out his zippo with the 71$^{st}$ Engineers emblem etched on it and lit the rag. He wanted to make a Molotov. He saw insurgents do this in Afghanistan.

"Hey!" yelled the smokey, and trotted over. "You there. Stop that!"

The smokey knocked the bottle out of Jackdaw's hand with a nightstick. It shattered on the asphalt and Jackdaw staggered and fell. Yelling onlookers closed in. Fracas ensued, pepper spray misted the air, the smokey shouted into his shoulder mic for backup.

By the time the lawmen pulled out of town, seven residents of the Roubidoux Reservation were on their way to lock-up and three lawmen required stitches. A coroner's van hauled Lamar away. Jackdaw crawled out of a ditch and into Lamar's yellow 1985 Datsun pickup. He raked up the keys from the floor mat and drove back to the reservation.

Lamar War Bonnet was conveyed in the back of a pickup to the Catholic church house in a hand-built plywood and pine casket. The casket was too large to fit in the church's narrow entrance. Someone suggested turning the casket rightways up but then it was too tall. So the mourners left the casket upright, facing inside, so Lamar could be listen in and be sprinkled with holy water by the priest.

During the service several flasks made the rounds and the pallbearers dropped Lamar three times getting him back to the pickup. As the procession snaked out of the churchyard, beer cans glinted in every cab.

Jackdaw didn't go. He was partially sober and he hadn't talked in a week. He stood in the deserted churchyard, looking at Lamar's yellow Datsun still parked there.

Alma War Bonnet, Lamar's niece, came out of the church house when the last of the dust from the procession blew away.

"Hi, JD," she said.

"Hi," said Jackdaw. "Listen. I'm through with it."

"With what?"

"With this," he said, and stomped his empty beer can, nearly lurching over with the effort. "Watch."

He stuck fingers down his throat and vomited a thin bile of beer and vodka and peanut butter. Wiped his mouth and felt a little less drunk.

"That's it," he said. "I'm done with that shit forever."

"Come on," said Alma.

She took him by the hand to the Datsun. Drove to a copse of trees down by a creek where they fucked, axles screeching, as dry clods of dirt lumped onto Lamar War Bonnet's casket in the bone orchard.

Slow and gimpy on his bum legs, Jackdaw hiked back into the hills where the wildflowers exploded in breeze-shaken patches, passing under shelves of limestone with banks of pine clinging ragged to their sides, tangled root skeins cracking the rock.

He stayed in the hills a month, living on spring water and the canned beans and spam Alma humped back to him, until he was sure he lived with no lust for the bottle he'd succumb to. Started doing pushups again and soon got back to three hundred a day. Alma did two hundred.

They ran side-by-side down the dirt roads of the rez, as far as Jackdaw's twitchy legs held out, drawing guffaws and catcalls from government-issue trailers where the stacks of empty bottles reach the window eaves. Feeling good for the first time since he got blown up, Jackdaw fucked Alma with abandon. After, he twirled her blonde hair in his fingers.

Alma dyed her hair when she was out in Illinois, playing basketball at a community college. She lasted a semester and a half, until she tore her ACL and dropped all her classes. The black roots were slowly edging out the blonde ends. Jackdaw cussed these roots kindly.

They were in the room Alma shared with her stepsister in her stepmother's trailer. Her step-sister was six. The wall by her bed was covered in Disney princesses printed out from the Internet at school.

Jackdaw said, "I mean it." He ripped Belle down.

"I know," said Alma.

"I don't give a fuck. Do you?"

"No."

Jackdaw's come still squishing inside her, Alma felt a twinge of what women in the City of Screams knew, ravished by fur-clad warriors still spattered with the blood of their fathers and brothers. In the next room Alma's stepmother guffawed to the canned TV laughter.

"Then you're with me," said Jackdaw.

"Yes," said Alma.

"They're going to sing songs about us. I learned one thing from them Afghans. If we don't pull this off, someone after us else will."

### 3.

Jackdaw climbs out of Lamar's Datsun. The bed rattles with packing crates full of beer-bottle Molotov's. Alma totes a 9mm pistol and an MP-5 submachine gun. Jackdaw is strapped with two 9mms and an M4. He cashed out a VA disability payment and the last of his combat pay to get a hold of the weapons, buying them in the back room of a flea market from an arms dealer more used to dealing with neo-militias than a nervous, hobbled Indian.

"We're about to tear this motherfucker up," says Jackdaw, "and you want me to get all painted."

"Shut up," says Alma. "You're doing it."

She leads him through the sagging doorway of a jackshack at the tail end of a weed-blown two-tracker. Jackdaw steps over raccoon and deer scat and looks around. Two empty rooms, slats showing through jagged cracks in the wall, pebbles of plaster scattered on the warped floorboards. Jackdaw eases himself to a squat and picks up a pebble, thumbs powder from the edges.

No one's here," he says. He'd expected some wrinkled elder.

"You noticed," says Alma.

"Who's going to do it, then?"

"Me."

"You? What do you know about painting?"

"Only those assholes who go fancy dancing know how. So I got out a book."

"From the library?"

"Yep. Directions and pictures and everything. Look."

Alma pulls out a thick volume from her backpack, revealing a slice of brown back. She props the book against a wall and sets canisters of grease paint alongside it. Opens to a chapter entitled "The Art of Lakota War." Helpful pages have been dog-eared and attacked with magic marker.

"I'll do you, you do me," says Alma.

Jackdaw hurls three Molotov's at the glass façade of High Plains Spirits as Alma shoulders open the door to Ace Liquor. Then he shambles into the White Buffalo carrying a crate of four Molotov's. Drops the crate, fires the M4into the ceiling twice, then slings the rifle over his shoulder.

"Get the fuck out of here!" he shouts to customers staring from the aisles and the clerk gaping from behind bulletproof glass, the clerk who watched Lamar die.

Everyone scrambles for the exit but a quaking fat woman. Plastic whisky bottles tumble from the shelves and skitter across the peeling linoleum floor. Jackdaw grabs the woman's meaty arm and yanks her towards the exit. Grabs a Molotov and lights it.

"Jackdaw?" the woman says. "Jackdaw Le Fourche, what are you doing?"

"Get the fuck out," Jackdaw says.

Jackdaw throws the Molotov. Then another and another and another. He trips on the bottles in the aisle and catches his balance on a shelf. Warm forties of beer shatter on the floor.

Tendrils of blue flame curl into the cheap particleboard as smoke wallows into the rafters. Jackdaw ducks outside coughing. Alma is at the Datsun, grabbing more Molotov's. The clerk stands in the road, watching flames lick his car's windshield. Jackdaw unslings the M4. Switches the safety, shoulders the rifle.

"Hey, what the hell?" the clerk says. "Hey!"

A three-shot burst and the clerk is road kill.

★ ★ ★

Smoke from Rattlecreek smears the sky as Jackdaw sits on the vestibule of the shuttered Episcopalian church, rifle across his lap, waiting. Ashes whorl around the banisters of the vestibule. Alma puts her head on his shoulder. A line of people begin to creep back into town, taking pictures with their phones, as the liquor stores collapse in on themselves. Jackdaw is hoping for a lady cop. A blonde one. He looks at Alma.

"You didn't really believe we could get away, did you?" he says.

"No," says Alma. "Not from the start."

"Me neither. I tell you this much. They ain't taking me out of here alive."

"Me either."

Finally they hear a keening siren. Over the far ridge comes a fire truck. Alma hops off Jackdaw's lap. The onlookers flee, taking video as they go.

A Volunteer Fire Department truck howls past the church, screeching to a halt in front of the clerk's body. The volunteer firemen, ranchers and railroaders in real life, jump to the street. Not one is a blonde or a woman.

Jackdaw and Alma squeeze off their whole magazines as the radio shrieks with requests for backup. Just beyond the horizon where the smoke vanishes a long string of sirens are helling for Rattlecreek.

# Came a Flood

★ ★ ★

*Paul Crenshaw*

To divert a stream, Heckle said, you would need a lot of rocks. Jeckle looked at her sister. She was pretty sure Heckle had just learned the word divert. Maybe that was why Heckle had come up with the idea in the first place, which Jeckle thought was a stupid idea since her sister had thought of it. If she had thought of diverting the river so that it ran through their house she would have liked the idea though, she had to admit that, but she wasn't going to let Heckle know.

And a lot of shovels, Jeckle said. She raised an eyebrow to show Heckle how much work it would take.

They stood watching the water roll past. It was raining, and the rain on the leaves of the trees sounded like September. Heckle and Jeckle wore yellow slickers. Jeckle thought they made them yellow so you could see them from far away. But no one was watching. Behind them, the rain fell like a curtain. They could see their house at the edge of the rain, and the other houses to either side.

Jeckle said, Normal people don't do things like this.

We're not normal anymore, Heckle told her.

Jeckle hated it when Heckle was more right than she was.

The river wasn't a river, but they liked to call it that. It ran behind their house, behind all the houses on their street. On the other side of the stream stood a thin stretch of trees they called the forest, but it wasn't a forest anymore than the river was a river. From the stream bank you could see through the thin trees to the back of the shopping center where the dumpsters were, where at night high-shouldered cats howled at one another like ghosts.

They were howling now. Heckle and Jeckle sat in their bedroom with the lights off, looking out the window at the small rain falling through the streetlight in their back yard. They didn't know why there was a streetlight in their back yard.

Heckle said, Look. She held out the notepad she'd been scribbling on.

Jeckle could see what looked like a stream drawn on it, and rocks, and arrows pointing toward the square box that passed for a house. In a window of the house were two faces.

We cut a channel here, Heckle said, pointing at the paper. All the way to the house. We dig it out and line it with rocks. And, when we are ready, we break the last little bit and let the stream run this way.

Into the house, Jeckle said.

Right into the house.

Ok, she said. But why?


They were eleven. Heckle was seventeen minutes older than Jeckle. Heckle had brownish-blond hair and Jeckle had blondish-brown hair. Both their eyes were blue, but Heckle's eyes were more blue than Jeckle's, she claimed. They both liked April and didn't like September. They both liked spaghetti but not linguine. They both liked encyclopedias more than dictionaries.

Why not a moat? Jeckle said.

Heckle rolled her eyes. Sometimes it was hard being the oldest, she thought.

We're not trying to keep people out, she said.

What are we trying to do then?


Here, Heckle said. She handed Jeckle encyclopedia E. Look up excavator, she said.

They sat cross-legged on the floor. Above them rose a tall shelf, all encyclopedias, different years, different covers, complete sets. They had a computer downstairs but they didn't use it often. It made too much noise, their father said. Their father didn't like noise. When they were upstairs they crept around. When they went outside, they never let the door slam.

Jeckle couldn't find excavator. She wasn't sure she knew how to spell it, but she couldn't tell Heckle that. So she tried to look up digger but it wasn't there. She looked up archaeology but she was pretty sure that wasn't what Heckle had in mind.

Downstairs they heard a door close. They looked at each other. They crept down the stairs and quietly opened the door at the bottom of the stairs and quietly looked out. Their father stood in the light of the refrigerator, peering in. He had not shaved in a very long time and his hair looked like a mad scientist in an old film.

Or werewolf, Heckle whispered, and Jeckle nodded. They closed the door quietly and quietly crept back up the stairs.

At last count, they had seventeen sets of encyclopedias. They had kids' versions and regular versions and special editions. They lined the walls of their upstairs bedroom, in shelves their father made when they first moved in to the house.

Their mother brings them a new set of encyclopedias every time she comes home. But she comes home less and less. She sells encyclopedias, and people don't want them anymore so she has to stay gone longer. Sometimes she is gone for days at a time. She calls at night and says I love you, and I miss you, and Is your father all right?

Heckle and Jeckle won't throw the old ones away. They like the oldest ones, the ones that still refer to the Cold War in the present tense, the ones that list Jimmy Carter as the current president. In those encyclopedias, the Russians were fighting in Afghanistan. Their father was their age then. He had not yet been to Afghanistan. He had not yet returned to walk around the house unshaven, his hair wild, a look in his eyes like he was still over there.

After archaeology, Jeckle looked up earth. But she only got a distant picture, from outer space. It was too far away to make out their town, their house, the stream, their room. Too far away to find their mother, wherever she was now. When she called and asked to speak to their father they stood outside his door and listened to his muffled voice. From under the door came a smell like mushrooms growing among pine needles in a wet rain. Sometimes they lifted the kitchen extension very quietly and listened. Their mother said I love you and I miss you and Are the girls all right? But their father just breathed into the phone until their mother said when she'd be home next.

Jeckle put archaeology back on the shelf. I'm tired of this, she said.

Heckle marked her place with a finger. She took her time doing it, too, which Jeckle knew was on purpose.

We have to look up how to do this, she said.

Ok, Jeckle said. But I still don't understand why.

Just look up these words, Heckle said. She held up her notepad: Strahler Number, erosion response, backhoe, post-traumatic stress disorder.

Besides the encyclopedias, they used the phone book the most. They looked up pizza delivery and grocery delivery and plumbing services. Once, they looked up marriage counselor. Another time they looked up Veterans of Foreign Wars, but when they called the number they hung up before anyone could answer.

I didn't know what to say, Heckle explained.

You could have said. . .Jeckle started, but she had no idea either.

Heckle thought Afghanistan looked like drawings of the stomach they found in the encyclopedia under Digestive System. Jeckle thought it looked like a manta ray, the kind that could sting you hard enough to kill. Both of them thought it was a long word, difficult to spell, a place that was difficult to find on a map.

In the shed they found a shovel and a pickaxe and their father's boots. The leather was dried and cracked. They both remembered when he used to polish them every morning. He would sit on the front porch before first light and watch the darkness stalk around everything. Their mother would come downstairs sleepily and sit with him while he polished his boots, and some mornings they woke and came downstairs and they all sat in the darkness with the smell of boot polish rising into the coming morning. Their father smelled like shaving cream. His face was smooth when he kissed them.

Be careful, Daddy, they would say.

I will, he would answer.

They put the shovels aside and took down his boots. In the footlocker they found his rags and polish. Heckle took one boot and Jeckle took the other. They spit on the toes of the boots and made little circles until they could see their faces in the leather.

This is going to be loud, Jeckle said.

They both looked at the house. They knew about noise, ever since their father had come back. He did not like noise, not doors slamming or cars backfiring or TV shows in which gunshots went off.

Start with the shovel, Heckle said. The ground was wet and the shovel slid in easily. Heckle lifted the pickaxe. She wondered how loud it would be, but when she swung the pickaxe it tore into the wet ground without a sound, as quiet as the house had been since their father came back.

Heckle had blisters. Jeckle's back hurt. They worked all morning and now a small trench grew from the stream to their back porch. It wasn't wide enough or long enough or anywhere near big enough, but Heckle liked what she saw. She rubbed her blisters softly with her forefinger.

Well, she said.

Well what?

We got started. It was late afternoon. The house had been quiet all day. Once they heard the doorbell and they ran to the side of the house, but it was only one of the neighbors. Sometimes they came by and dropped food off. They spoke carefully to Heckle and Jeckle's father. They said things like: I was just checking up on you, and I bet you're glad to be back, and Do all the women wear those things that cover their faces?

Jeckle sighed at all the work that was left. She kissed her blisters so Heckle would see. They watched the neighbor leave. When their mother was home she met the neighbors at the door. She took what food they offered but did not let them in. She said, Thanks for coming by and I'll tell him and He doesn't really want to see anyone right now.

Tomorrow, Heckle said.

From the window, Jeckle thought their trench looked like the trenches in World War I, which her encyclopedias called the Great War, not because it was actually great but because so many countries had been involved. They read about mustard gas and machine guns and trench foot and triage and barbed wire. They read about airplanes and tanks and a devastated countryside, but in Jeckle's mind that war had only lasted four years. She knew from her old encyclopedias that the Russians had been in Afghanistan for nine years and they knew from the Internet that America had been there for ten years now.

They both hated Afghanistan. Heckle hated the vast distances she had tried to calculate when her father was gone. Jeckle hated that he was only able to call every few weeks. She hated the way he sounded so far away. She could barely hear him. He said, I love you, and I miss you terribly. He sounded used up, like his voice was disappearing and would soon be gone.

Most days when he first came back he stayed in his room with the door closed. Their mother stood smoking in the kitchen, looking out in the back yard where the stream ran through. Heckle and Jeckle wondered why, if he had missed them so much, he stayed in his room as if he didn't want to be around them.

It was raining again. The stream ran fast and full, sweeping leaves and sticks along, the water no longer clear, turned now the color of old coffee. The rain ran off their yellow slickers in sheaves. Their hair stuck to their forehead.

By lunch the trench was past their knees in places. The rain kept getting into it and the mud squelched beneath their feet and it was cold as it seeped through their shoes.

When they ate tomato soup standing at the sliding glass door that looked out onto the back yard the trench looked like a long gash where some cataclysm had come climbing out of the earth. To Jeckle it still looked like the trenches in World War I. In her encyclopedias there were pictures of men sitting hollow-eyed in the trenches, smoking and staring off into what she assumed was some place that was not here.

There was only one listing under excavating equipment. Heckle dialed, since she was older. She put a handkerchief over her mouth and spoke gruffly.

She said, Yes, a backhoe.

She said, How much is the charge for that? and Do you take credit cards?

She said, Yes, tomorrow.

Heckle thought Afghanistan was the color of old socks. Jeckle thought it was the color of weak tea. Both of them thought it sounded like wind through the bare branches of trees in November, or the way rain sounded early in the morning, before the sun was fully awake, when the house was quiet but for a man with a long beard wandering from room to room, picking up things and holding them in his hands as if they had no meaning.

They weren't a praying family. Sometimes their mother used to say Oh God Oh God Oh God as the bed squeaked late at night, but that was it, until Heckle suggested they ask for guidance.

How do we do it? Jeckle said.

Get down on your knees. Now close your eyes. Pretend it's raining.

Why raining?

They throw water on your head.

They knelt with their eyes closed, pretending it was raining. Jeckle's knees hurt but she didn't move. She thought maybe that was part of it. After a long time, Heckle said, Well?

Well what?

Did anything happen?

My knees hurt.

Mine do, too. Maybe we didn't do it right.

Heckle stood. Come on, she said.

They went silently out the front door and down the block. The creek ran behind their houses where it always had. The school was shuttered on Sunday. In the distance somewhere it was raining.

They stopped outside the Catholic church at the corner. They could hear voices inside, an organ vibrating the windows.

Are you supposed to sing? Jeckle said.

I don't know. We could try.

They listened for a long time, standing on the sidewalk.

I like the word cathedral, Jeckle said.

It is a big word, Heckle agreed.

Jeckle nodded, but she thought it was bigger than just a word. When their father returned people held signs that said God Bless America, but Jeckle didn't see how God could have that much time on his hands. Heckle thought that if God really wanted to bless America He wouldn't have started the war in the first place.

In the morning they heard the beeping truck and ran outside. The man raised an eyebrow as he looked at them. He said, I can't let you two sign for this.

Their father stood in the window. His hair was wild and his beard seemed to move of its own will. He looked down on them with a blank expression in his eyes as the rain fell from the gray sky in streaks down the gray window.

It's for our father, Heckle said.

He needs to come sign for it.

Jeckle bit her lip. Then she said, He can't write. She leaned closer. He forgot how in Afghanistan, and he's very embarrassed about it. She turned her blue eyes upward. Please?

They waited until the man drove off. Then they climbed into the cab of the backhoe. There were lots of levers. Heckle turned the key and the backhoe came on, rumbling like thunder. She wondered if it was too loud, but then she remembered that her father liked thunder. It's real, he said once. He had not yet gone quiet, and their mother was still here. She lay on the couch with her head in his lap. His fingers played with her hair. Heckle and Jeckle were supposed to be in bed but they wanted to keep seeing their father so they snuck downstairs. He had just come back and he seemed like some strange exotic creature, a llama, or an emu.

I know it sounds like bombs in the distance, but it's not. It just means rain. I can handle rain.

Out the window lightning flashed, throwing Heckle and Jeckle's shadows on the wall. Their father turned his head. Come here, he said. Their mother raised up and they climbed up in his lap and together they all listened to the thunder.

When their mother came home her car was still weighted down with encyclopedias. She sat in the driveway in the rain. After a time she got out. Heckle and Jeckle met her at the front door. She wore brown slacks and a sweater and her hair was pulled back in a pony tail and Jeckle thought she was the prettiest woman in the world. She wondered why her father could not see that, and she wondered if his eyes were disappearing like his voice.

Is he still in there? their mother said.

She knocked on the door. After a minute she went in and they could hear her soft voice.

When she came to tuck them in she smelled like flowers. Her hair was down and she was humming to herself. She said, Sweet dreams and Don't let the bedbugs bite and Don't be afraid of the thunder.

At the door she turned around. Why is there a backhoe in our yard? she said.

Jeckle went in the house while Heckle worked the levers on the backhoe. At the door, Jeckle watched the backhoe buckle and jump. The engine died. She furrowed her eyebrows at Heckle but Heckle waved at her to go on in, and then a minute later the backhoe started around the side of the house and Heckle was smiling. She stuck her tongue out at Jeckle.

Inside, her father was standing in the kitchen. His hair touched his shoulders now. He had never worn it long. His beard looked like the homeless men under the overpass. His eyes were no longer blue, but had faded almost to gray.

Why is there a backhoe in our yard? their father said. Jeckle could barely hear him. She wondered if his hair and beard would grow to cover all of him, if his eyes and voice would fade away to nothing.

She smiled and went to hug him. He felt like concrete, unyielding. He smelled like cut grass. It's the neighbors, she said into his stomach. Plumbing. Or something. Out the back window, the backhoe turned the corner of the house.

After he had been home a few weeks and they knew something had happened to him and they all began to worry, Heckle and Jeckle took the receiver end of their old baby monitor—their mother would throw nothing away—and hid it in their father's room. Some nights they heard him mumbling to himself about mountains and missiles and drones hovering overhead, children in cities with limbs missing from landmines. Some nights he prayed to some distant god whose name they could not understand. They looked up all the gods in the encyclopedia, but none of them were right. After a few weeks he stopped saying anything. They snuck into his room to see if the batteries were dead, but everything was working.

Under cover of heavy rain, Heckle got to work. The arm of the backhoe buckled and snapped but after a while she figured out where everything went. Jeckle stood in the cab with her, watching the house. The windows were grey with rain. They remembered their father saying it never rained in Kabul in the summer. They read that the average summer rainfall was less than 5 millimeters. That the heat went up and up and up and the soldiers stood in open doorways cursing the sun or ducking their heads when rounds went off in the streets.

They read on the Internet that the war in Afghanistan was the longest war the United States had ever fought. It had lasted longer than both the World Wars and Vietnam and Korea and Desert Storm. It was older than their mother's favorite sweater, older than the newest encyclopedias she carried, older than the worry lines on her forehead. It was older than their father's beard, the boots he had hidden in the shed, the letters he had written to their mother from halfway around the world. It was almost older than they were.

Their mother had left that morning. They did not know when she would be back. The trench had turned into a ditch. Then a channel. The rain gathered in it. The stream rose all night and threatened to spill into their channel now. The wheels of the backhoe shredded the grass. The engine rumbled like thunder. Somewhere inside, their father was listening to the rain.

At first everything was fine. They hung balloons from the trees and made signs with magic marker that said Welcome Home Daddy. He stood in the front yard in his boots and uniform and hugged them hard enough to stretch their ribs. He was trying fiercely not to cry. When they went inside he ran his hands over everything. He kept hugging them. Their mother started back to work. She made short forays into surrounding counties. She said, We need the money, but she was back every night and the sounds coming up from the bedroom made them giggle. Then their father quit showering. He said, I feel like I'm still there. Their mother took his face in her hands. You're not, she said. He was staring out the window at the stream. He said, We were lost in the mountains. Scoot was driving, so to me it just felt like we hit a big rock. But then Scoot was screaming and we went off the road and there was shrapnel ricocheting around the cab. When I woke up I didn't know where I was. He looked at her. It's not even the explosions. You can get used to that. It's dislocation. I didn't know where I was, and I still don't.

Everyone else did, though, Jeckle thought. They could smell him anywhere in the house. He stopped shaving. His voice disappeared. Their mother stayed gone longer. She sat at the kitchen table with bills spread everywhere, running her hands through her hair. Heckle and Jeckle sat on the stairs and watched her. One night their father

came in. He stood behind her for a very long time. I don't know
what to do, he said. They could barely hear him.

They had left a strip of earth less than a foot wide between the
stream and the channel. The channel ran all the way to the back
door now. They had lined it with rocks. The backhoe grumbled
where it was parked. Heckle wore goggles and earplugs. Jeckle
watched the stream rush past.
    What now? she said.
    Now we let it go.
    And then what?
    Heckle leaned closer to hear. What?
    I said, What happens next?

Their mother turned to face him. Heckle and Jeckle saw she was
crying. On the table the papers weren't bills, but letters he'd written.
I don't know what to do either, she said. I need you back from that
fucking war, but I don't know where you are. I don't know how to
reach you. I keep hoping you'll be here when I come home, but it's
not you, so I stay gone longer. It's driving the girls crazy. Have you
thought about them?
    In Kandahar half the children are missing limbs, he said.
    What? she said.
    His voice sounded like rain that meant to stay. Little girls, he
said, no older than ours. They go out to play and come back missing
a leg. There's been war there for thirty years, thirty years worth of
landmines. You see holes everywhere. Things like that get inside
you, dig holes of their own. They eat at you until you feel hollow.
Yeah, he said. I have thought of them. I think of them all the time.

Heckle's hands were shaking. She looked at Jeckle and Jeckle
nodded and then she raised the bucket and lowered it into the
earth and scraped away the divider they had left and the stream
came rushing in. She kept swinging the arm until the divider was
down and the stream filled the channel. Then she lowered the
bucket and stood up in the cab of the backhoe. Jeckle was standing

too, both of them watching the stream fill the new channel. It splashed against the rocks and wallowed into the bed and rolled for the back door, then Heckle and Jeckle were out and running, Jeckle opening the back door so the water could come in. She propped it open and they ran around the house and opened the front door and a moment later the water came flowing out onto the sidewalk in the front yard. They ran back around to the side of the house and climbed in the lowest window and got up on the kitchen table and sat watching the stream run through the house.

In a moment their father's door opened. His hair touched his shoulders now, and his beard covered most of his face. His eyes were sunken inside his head. He stood watching the water rushing through the house. He moved as if in a dream. He had his uniform on, his boots polished. Their mother came in the front door, the water parting around her ankles, wetting her slacks. She stopped with her mouth open and watched their father standing in the middle of the stream. He reached down and touched the stream with his fingers. He cupped his hands and splashed water on his face. He took a step and knelt in the stream. Then he leaned forward and began scooping water with both hands, throwing the handfuls over his head.

I wish something would come along and wash this feeling from me, he said. Their mother knelt, her arms wrapped around his waist, her head pressed tight against his stomach as if listening to whatever it was inside of him that was making him this way. His hair was still short then, his face shaved clean. Heckle and Jeckle came down the stairs. Their father held his arms out.

What can we do? they said, but he didn't answer, just stood staring out the window at the stream rushing along.

# I Demand to Know When You're Coming Home

### ★ ★ ★

*Robert Wallace*

My father is a dead soldier in Iraq. Here in Fayetteville, North Carolina, where I live with my sister and mother, we wait for his return. Several months before he is killed we drive down to Jacksonville to hang a banner on the fence along Freedom Way Drive. In the bright sunshine, we attach the painter's cloth with cut strings of clothesline. WELCOME HOME, DADDY, the banner says, in all-capital letters. LOVE, STEPHEN, LITTLE JEN & BIG JEN.

I do not know what adults think of loss, but this is what I know: grief changes. Grief isn't static.

My father used to take me to the ocean to fish. We'd leave early in the morning, long before sunrise. My father would pack a thermos of sugared coffee, and we'd stop at Bojangles, thirty minutes from the beach, just outside of Wilmington, and buy a bag of biscuits. The yeasty smell of warm biscuits would fill the cab of my father's truck and the heady smell would stay with us all the way to the water. We'd eat from the bag of biscuits all morning and fish until it got too hot to be outdoors, or until the sun shone straight above us like some inescapable fiery ball. Then we'd collect our catch and head straight to a fish place in downtown Wilmington, along the Cape Fear River, called Sammy's Fish Shop. My father would order a plate of popcorn shrimp, and while we waited for our plates, I'd stuff myself with hush puppies slathered with Crock's margarine scooped from tiny cups. Afterwards, we'd sit on a bench on the boardwalk and watch the ships and boats slowly float by while raucous crowds of seagulls hovered above tall masts and overloaded tankers.

Now, when I think about those times, it feels like they happened to another boy in some parallel universe, almost as if I wasn't there at all. You see, I can't grasp the idea that in the not too distant past I was with him—my father—and now I can never be with him again. Ever. Tell me. Someone. Please! How does that work?

In dreams, there is no loss without happiness first. In real life, this consolation means nothing.

My grandmother tells a story about a day in my father's childhood, when he and his own father were in the fields picking tobacco. My father was a young boy, only nine, and he had to use the bathroom. Rather than walk the longer distance to the outhouse, he headed to the woods, carrying with him a small roll of toilet paper. My father and his dad went home for the noon meal. At the table, my father kept squirming in his chair, and my grandmother asked if he had ants in his pants. Turns out he had run out of toilet paper when he was in the woods, and he had used some nearby leaves. The plant was poison ivy, and my father's buttocks swelled up so severely that my grandmother applied salve to it for weeks.

My father tells his own story. He went ice fishing with his grandfather on a cold afternoon in Michigan. They drove out onto the lake and walked about twenty yards from the car. He watched his grandfather cut a two-foot diameter circle into the ice and then with a sharp instrument pluck the ten-inch thick round out of the frozen water. He marveled at the existence of an entire lake frozen underneath one continuous ice cube. This was a big deal to a boy who grew up with his family in the coastal plains of North Carolina.

Out on that lake, so many years ago now, a car went down, was sucked under the water like a predator taking a hapless victim. He was there that day, my father said. He and his grandfather sat perched on two padded stools, fishing silently. His grandfather puffed on his pipe, sending rings of sweet smelling tobacco smoke in the air, and sometimes he pretended too, to be smoking like his grandfather, cocking his head back and blowing warm air into the cold. His grandfather would smile at his miming grandson.

There was a Father and his son. They were fishing not more than two hundred yards away. In the cold quiet their voices carried over to where they sat. But their voices were not loud. There was stillness about their voices. The car of this man and son was not far from where they sat fishing contentedly, a lot closer than where their own car was. My father said he would always remember the sound that cracked ice makes. It's like the sound of lightening splitting the air. The ice cut a swath around the car, like a moat, and it balanced there a moment, then fell into the water and was sucked below. The man and boy looked over at them; their frosty breaths visible even from where they sat. Simultaneously, they hung their heads.

Like something concrete and irrefutable, my father's grandfather said: "They had parked over a pressure ridge."

Out of nowhere, out of the blue, my mother says to me one day: "We are alive so little and dead so long."

Only months before my father is shipped off, I complain about going to the postbox to get the mail. "Let me tell you a story," my father says. "During the depression my grandfather walked five miles in the dark to work. Once there, he plowed behind a mule all day, at least ten miles in all. Then he walked the five miles back home. It was dark when he would arrive and Artie—your grandfather—was already fast asleep in bed. He'd do that six days in a row—he was lucky to get the work—and it wasn't until Sunday that he would see your grandfather awake."

Another day my mother says to me: "The suddenness of it all. That's what gets me."

"Look at this," my mother says to me one night. It is late, and I'm tired. I want to go to sleep, but my mother won't let me. She's afraid to be alone at night. Often my sister sleeps with her.

My mother hands me a photo of my father. She has shown me the picture many times before, but each time acts like it is the first time. I look at the picture of my father when he is sixteen. He wears black shoes with white socks, long cut-off shorts that reach below the knees, and a short-sleeve shirt, the tails hanging out. He has the same grin, younger of course, but more prominent in a way, less hidden by adult age. He has dark eyes, deep blue in color; they smile, but behind the smile is a certain knowing, almost clairvoyant. His hands appear smallish, thin, and boyish, not the hands I remember at all.

In this picture my father is holding his hands in the air. They're hugging each other above his head. He is sitting on the seat of his bicycle; the edge of the orange, banana shape protrudes between his legs like something grotesquely large, comical. A baseball mitt looped over the handlebars dangles from the wrist strap. He is wearing black-framed glasses too large for his face. His head is covered in brown curls, like a prince or cherub from a renaissance painting.

"I could put my hand in your father's," my mother says, "and it would disappear." She takes my hand in hers. "Your father could do finger pushups." My mother turns my hand over. "He used to say the most profound things. At first they made little sense to me, but if I gave it some thought, I would realize, later, how thought-provoking it was. Right after you were born, he said, 'there are times when small things appear to be more than foreground, like a lone ship in the ocean, a bird in the sky.' He was all the time saying things like that."

Years later, I could imagine my mother taking my hand and saying she could feel my heart beat. "When your father held my hand," she'd say, "he sensed the pressure of my blood shifting."

This is a story of my own making. We must shift around in time. Time, space, they're not human concepts; they belong to the physical world. "This is why humans will not be the last survivors," my father once told me. "Ants," he said, "would one day rule the world. Though the cockroach will put up a good fight."

My father wanted to go back to school when he returned from Iraq. He wanted to study archeology. He said he wanted to go on digs in faraway lands, use little tools and brushes to scrape away ancient soil and rock. He liked to go to the Goodwill store and buy used National Geographic magazines. Sometimes he'd appear in my doorway, a magazine in his hand, a faraway look in his eyes.

"Did you know they found a new mummy in Egypt?" he'd ask.

"No."

"Yes. In a place called Oranistan. Near a dried lake-bed. Six-thousand years old. He'd smack his lips, as if he'd been eating pretzels heavy with salt. "Can you imagine?" he'd say.

"Nope," I'd say.

"They've probably only found less than twenty percent of all the mummies in Egypt."

"Oh."

He'd stand there, leaning against the doorway, flipping the pages of his magazine.

By the time he knew he was going to be shipped off, two more mummies had been discovered. I imagined him keeping a thermometer-like tab with the mercury slowly creeping to one-hundred percent.

Sometimes I'd catch him asleep in the recliner, an open magazine laying face down in his lap, his closed eyes twitching, a pinkie-finger tapping the arm, and I'd wonder where he was.

Now, when I think of him flying back to us, in his casket draped with an American flag, I think it would have been better to have left him in Iraq so that his body cannot rot. I do not want to see his body. The thought of it frightens me.

Here in Fayetteville, day and night, I think about my future. Our future. My mother worries about money. She says we may move back to Chapel Hill, near her mother and father. She says she can't raise us alone. She's got to have help, she says.

During the night, while my mother and sister are asleep, I wander the house from room to room. I run the water in the kitchen faucet to see if it still works. I pull the blinds and look at the street lights, push up the windows and listen to insects humming and screeching, watch their insane gathering around street lamps like some kind of death wish.

In my father's study, I turn on the desk lamp, sit in the desk chair, and turn it from side to side. My father's study smells like menthol, as if he has just been here right after shaving. If I want I can make myself touch his smooth cheeks, but it gives me such an ache.

I walk up to his bookcases, pull a volume off a shelf, flip the pages and stop on page sixty-seven of *The Confessions of St. Augustine*. I count the number of times the word God is on both pages. I flip the pages some more and stop on page one hundred twenty-nine, count the word God. I do the same, over and over again, page after page, until the word becomes a kind of mantra that I repeat until I can't remove God from my brain.

As if that would make a difference.

I pull a volume of Sartre off the shelf, a man my father once told me who didn't believe in God. I read several paragraphs until I become frustrated by the circular language, the repetition of certain words, so that words themselves become meaningless. You see, what I don't understand, under all the layers about belief and truth: what is fact and what is fiction? Because the truth is I don't think anyone knows. We know the body dies and that we bury only the body. Or we cremate it. No human has come back and given proof that there is some essential part of us, and it goes on. Other than the thoughts we have of that person, which seem to me are simply our own remembrances, and nothing else. What real knowledge do we have? Is it all conjecture? Speculation? Or wishful thinking?

My imagination: he flinches awake. Wincing, he realizes it is still dark. What rouses him? Is there someone outside his tent? Friend? Foe? He hears voices but can't make out the words. The heavy muffled sound of boots in sand. His cot creaks as he adjusts a leg that has fallen asleep. Then the sound of swiftly running steps. Suddenly darkness erupts into light. The entire inside of his tent is aflame. Helplessly, he imagines the flames become as docile as long-stem candles.

★ ★ ★

I'm a boy: twelve years old. What do I know about handling grief? I don't know anything. I don't know how to talk about it. Do I walk it off? Do I put it in the closet, behind the clothes that I never wear, in a shoe box, with his cigarette lighter, and a small conk shell that he bought for me on one of our beach trips? Perhaps I put my grief in the shell, and when I want to listen to it, to him, I can lift the shell out of the box and put it to my ear. I can hear the sounds of surf, the splash of salty water, and I can conjure the image of him near me. But the truth is why would I want to do that? What I want is him. Nothing less. I don't want the memory of him. I don't want a photo image. I don't want a story about him by a distant cousin who I don't know at all, and don't care to know. I don't want someone to tell me what he was like as a boy, how I look like him, how I remind them of him when he was my age. What does any of that mean to me? The truth is some days I wish I never knew my father. That he never existed. That Iraq never existed.

Some days I wish I never existed.

# JOHNNIE COME LATELY
★ ★ ★
*Kathleen M. Rodgers*

Letter to the Editor
*Portion Telegraph*
November 2007

Another boy from our community has been killed in Iraq. As I stood by the War Memorial at Soldiers Park and watched his procession come up Main Street on its way from the airport to the mortuary, I couldn't help but think of a young guardsman from Portion named Steven Tuttle.

*Tutts*, as my two sons call him, was terribly disfigured a few months ago—most of his face got blown off—when his Humvee crossed paths with an IED. Before he deployed, Steven worked part-time for Farrow & Sons…driving that very hearse that now carried the remains of a fellow soldier. Steven's mother, a single parent, had to quit her job so she could be with her only child as he recovers in a military hospital in San Antonio. Sometimes there are worse things than death.

Sometimes there's just death.

My dad died in Vietnam when I was six. The bomb that killed him wasn't called an IED. But a bomb's a bomb, and it blew him to bits just the same. Although I barely remember him, I can't forget him. His death was the great tragedy of my childhood. It sent my mama over the edge.

My youngest son just enlisted in the Army. He's still at basic training, but you can imagine what goes through my mind. Now Veterans Day is coming up. Everywhere I go I hear people say,

"Thank you for your *sacrifice*," when talking about the war dead or injured. The more I hear this, especially from folks who don't have a *dog in the fight*, I want to scream, "HEY, I don't want my son sacrificed for anyone. Not you. Not the fat cats in Washington...

And damn sure not me!

Johnnie Kitchen,
one P.O.'d mama

# The Neighbor's Yard

★ ★ ★

*Brian Seemann*

You could say my husband's patriotic. He's the first one on the
block to hang the flag on Memorial Day or the Fourth of July.
At ballgames, he removes his hat and sings the National Anthem.
Whenever a group of boys returns home from a tour of duty, he
drags me to Camp Mabry or up to Fort Hood to welcome every
one of them home. Waving a tiny American flag, he makes sure to
shake every soldier's hand. If there's a food drive or a collection
for clothes to send overseas, he has me bake something or go
through the closets. And if he ever sees a man or woman in
uniform, he doesn't hesitate to salute. He goes a little overboard
sometimes, sure, and I have to remind him that those boys have
no idea our son once had been in the service. He says that isn't the
point. Those boys are heroes, he tells me, and they deserve all the
respect we can give. Most of the time I don't bother to disagree.

It's a Sunday and I'm in the front yard, watering. It's the
time of year when everything needs a drink at least once a day
if not more, and I'm finishing one flowerbed as my husband
brings his lawnmower back from the yard next door. I'd seen
him talking to the realtor earlier, and after he pushes the mower
into the garage and comes to the front of the house, I ask him
what it was all about.

"New neighbors come tomorrow," he says.

We've hoped a nice young family would move in soon, and I
ask if our dreams have come true.

My husband squints. "Sort of."

"What's that supposed to mean?" By this point, I've shut the water off and started climbing the steps onto the front porch to get out of the May sun. I take off my gardening hat and wait for my husband to join me.

"It's a family, but it's minus a husband right now. He's overseas, so the mom's by herself with three kids."

"Three kids," I say, shaking my head. I can't imagine. I run a hand through my hair. It's graying, and I notice a few strands float to the wooden boards below. I'm only forty-seven. My hair's turning gray and the idea of three kids is foreign to me.

"Military man," he says. "Those are good men." My husband never enlisted, and I think he always regrets it. When our son decided to serve, my husband beamed for weeks.

We're quiet for a while. We sit like this a lot, side by side, looking out onto our front yard. My husband shifts in his chair. He's not a deep thinker, but I can see he's putting something together.

"You know… I'm going to keep mowing their yard. See if I can't lend an extra hand." Since the last neighbors moved out, he's been pushing the mower next door every Sunday. It's a nice gesture, I tell him, but I'm sure our new neighbor might want to take care of things herself.

"But why not?" he asks. "It's the neighborly thing to do, especially for a soldier's family."

"Maybe she's got family, a brother or somebody, to take care of it. I'm not saying it isn't nice, but you don't need to do more than you have to."

"I wouldn't mind at all." He stands and heads inside to wash up.

I put on my hat and go back into the sun. I get the water going and turn the nozzle onto the flowers. Some of them take to the water. A few of them droop, their petals giving out under the brunt of the spray.

One week later, my husband, home from church, runs the mower over our yard before taking it across the driveway. I'm out front again, hunched in the flowerbed, deadheading irises. The sound of the mower turns faint as he pushes it toward the far side of our neighbor's yard. In a minute, he's by the driveway again, wiping his brow. No matter the heat, he always wears long-sleeved plaid, blue jeans, and leather boots. Like me, he can be stubborn.

I wave as he turns the mower around. He doesn't see me. When he gets something in his head, it can occupy him. I've seen it before, and I wonder, like I always do, if it's worth it. I return to my flowers, realizing I need to cut the stalks. There are pruning shears in the garage, and I go to retrieve them. At the side of the house, I can barely hear the mower. Inside the garage, I rummage through my husband's messy workbench. There are hammers, screwdrivers, empty cans, you name it. I find what I'm after and head back around the side of the house. I can't hear the mower anymore, but the closer I get to the front of the house, I can start to hear voices.

The mower has stopped. A Hispanic woman stands in front of it, her arms crossed, and she seems to be explaining something to my husband.

This must be our new neighbor.

I admit, I've meant to walk next door in the past week and say hello, but I'd been busy. The few times I'd thought about it, I'd look out the window only to see an empty driveway. I figured she was gone, and I'd wait until later. I'd forgotten every time, and now, I'm a little nervous, knowing I have no excuses.

"I understand…" my husband's saying, his hands hanging from the top of the mower. He's sweating and his face is red. "I'm just trying to give you a hand."

The woman looks in her mid-thirties. Her black hair's down to her shoulders. She's pretty, in a way. She tells my husband, and I get the sense she's repeating herself, that she's thankful that he's mowing the yard, but she'd rather do it herself.

"I can take care of this," she says, turning now to see me at her side.

I introduce myself, and she does the same. Her name's Marta. When Marta speaks to me, she offers a smile. She doesn't extend this to my husband. She looks back to him and again asks him not to mow her yard.

We've been married twenty-seven years and I know almost immediately when my husband's upset. He gets a crease between his eyes and he'll bite his lower lip. He's doing this as he looks at Marta. He mumbles something underneath his breath that I wish he hadn't said. Marta gasps like someone's struck her. Unfortunately, it's something I've heard my husband say before, but that doesn't mean I'm not disgusted.

"*Leland*," I say.

My husband looks at me, a little dumbfounded.

Marta says something in Spanish that sounds hateful. She stomps across her yard to the front door, and before going indoors, she turns to tell both of us to stay off her yard. The door slams behind her, and the two of us are left standing on a yard that isn't ours.

"I'm going inside," I say.

My husband follows me to the house. I can hear the wheels of the mower tread through the grass, and I try to ignore the sound. Once I'm inside, I realize I'm still holding the shears, and I leave them on the countertop.

Later, after he's put the shears and the lawnmower away and come inside, my husband looks out the window, and when he begins to talk about how he's only doing a favor, I tell him to keep quiet.

Honestly, I just don't get the patriotic stuff. And this business with the neighbor's yard? He's got this idea that the more he does that sort of thing, the better off things are going to be. I mean, this Marta thing, for example. He thinks he's doing the right thing because her husband's fighting halfway around the world. He's got an obligation, he'd tell you. But not once will he stop to think of what someone actually wants. He only thinks about what people *should* want. Thirteen months ago, things were different. We were the ones receiving all the help. People felt accountable somehow, and they reminded us that our son died as a hero for our country. That was when my husband started putting all this patriotic stuff in his head.

"I don't care what she said. I'm going to mow that yard again." My husband's looking out the window in the living room. Half a week's gone by, and the yard next door looks half-chewed up and spit out. I'm embarrassed every time I see it.

"Just look at it. It looks terrible. If she's not going to cut it then I will. I don't care if she gets angry. She oughta be thankful I'm willing to do it."

I'm sitting on the couch across the room. There's a picture of our son on the wall from when he graduated high school two years ago. He'd gone off to boot camp a month after the picture was taken and before we knew it, our only son had been shipped out. Never had he been so far away from us. He sent us emails and pictures. We were worried but hopeful, and when we had the chance to hear his voice on the phone, we could sense his exhaustion, but we could also detect the sound of our son growing up. We were proud of him and of who he'd become.

So when we got the news, we were devastated.

My husband, to this day, insists we call our son a hero. I'd rather we just call him our son. It's the one thing I know he always was. My husband wants to keep a picture in the living room of our son wearing his military dress uniform, but I refuse to let it happen. The only pictures I'll look at are the ones of my son as my son.

My husband continues to look out the window at the neighbor's yard.

All I can do is watch him and wonder why a patch of grass means so much.

Every Sunday my husband goes to the early service at First Baptist. He's home by 9:45, and after changing clothes and having a glass of iced tea, he drags the mower out of the garage and starts in the backyard. Today, when he arrives home, he moves through the house without saying a word. I'm reading the paper, and I can hear him pace the living room. I imagine he's beside the window, staring next door. Soon, I'll get lunch started.

My husband finishes mowing the backyard and takes a break before doing the front. He stands at the counter and sips another glass of tea. I've got chicken salad and bread on the table, but he ignores it. I can see that he's putting things together in his head. "It doesn't make any sense," he finally says. "I oughta be the good guy for this."

I tell my husband that I love him, but he's wrong.

He only shakes his head.

I watch from the porch as he begins to mow the front yard. Something inside me is trying to figure him out. It's been that way for a while. I wonder why my husband must be so stubborn about something so small. He pushes the mower back and forth across the lawn. If I watch him long enough, it seems he's simply following the same path over and over.

When we'd gotten the news about our son, we both broke down. For weeks, we were a wreck. But it was my husband who eventually began to deal with it first. Before I was ever able to cope with what had happened, my husband had the American flag outside the front door.

As I knock on the door, my husband disappears behind the side of the house. The engine noise fades, and I wait. A young girl finally answers, peeking her head out. I can hear talk from inside.

"Mama," the girl says. She has to repeat herself before the other talk settles. I hear footsteps coming to the door.

"Yes?"

It takes some effort for me to talk my way in. Marta's been watching my husband, and I can see her aggravation building. I hate to think of what could happen between her and Leland, and that's why I'm here. She offers me a seat in the living room, and before she joins me, she goes to the window and peers out onto my yard. After a moment, she takes a seat across from me.

"My husband can be very stubborn," I say, hoping to draw Marta's attention away from the outdoors.

"They can be that way, can't they?"

I smile as to agree. I point to a photograph on the wall behind her. "Is that your husband?"

She nods. "He left a month ago for his third tour."

We sit without saying anything. I can hear the buzz of the mower moving across my front yard. My husband should be close to finishing. I clench my fingers into a fist. I start to tell Marta about my husband and his patriotism. I tell her how he gets these ideas worked up in his mind. I talk about the drives we take into Austin or up to Killeen to greet soldiers when they return home. The look on her face doesn't say much, but she seems to understand my frustrations. I don't want her to get the idea that I hate welcoming home those soldiers. I just want her to know that after a while, I just don't want to do it anymore.

Outside, the grating mower blade continues. No matter how many stories I tell, Marta's got at least one ear on what's going on outdoors.

A pair of boys dash through the room behind us and into the kitchen. Their voices are loud, commanding one another. Before Marta can say one word to them, they've vanished. In no time, we're alone again.

"Do you have any children?" It's not often I hear this question. No one who knows me and Leland would ask such a thing. But there's usually someone who hasn't heard the story.

"We had a son who died in combat."

For the first time, Marta responds to something I say with more than just a polite nod of her head. She tells me she's sorry.

It's never fun to turn a conversation like I've just done, and I know I'm blushing. But this is what happens when you start to open up to someone. You're exposed. As I'm sitting here, though, there's another thought inside. There's a thrill of letting go, of telling the truth. There's something that makes me want to tell the entire story.

"Honestly…" I start. "My son didn't die in combat."

Marta, who's been leaning towards the edge of her seat, sits upright.

"He'd been over there for a couple of months. We thought everything was going okay…" I have to stop for a second. When I do, I can see the concern in Marta's face. "But one day they found him, a rope around his neck. There wasn't anything they could do. He was already gone."

Marta covers her mouth and again, she says she's sorry. "That's so sad."

Telling this story aloud, I can recall hearing the news and the image that had stuck in my head. My nineteen-year-old boy, hanging lifelessly, a rope digging into his skin. I pictured him now, his mouth open, his eyes staring into mine. But the rope, that was the one thing I couldn't shake. I'd had so many nightmares, each one of them ending with me failing to reach up and cut the rope and set my son free. Each one of them ended with me unable to save my only child.

"My husband would never tell you that story," I say to Marta. "He'd rather not think of what really happened. Instead, he'll go on about my son, the hero. Patriotism and serving your country..." I trail off, not really sure what I'm trying to say. I can't shake the image of my son now that it's back.

There's a moment where Marta and I just sit and look at one another, and then comes the sound of the mower firing up just outside the front of the house. Marta sits alert, and I turn to the door. The rumbling noise of the engine fills the room.

Marta stands and goes to the front door.

"Marta..."

I follow her. When she opens the door, the sound of the mower is louder, and my husband is just beyond the front steps of Marta's house. He turns and sees us standing here, and he looks surprised. I imagine he's absolutely stunned to see me standing inside our neighbor's house, and the face he makes is one I've never seen before. But then he continues to push the mower. He'll keep going until someone comes out to stop him.

But it won't be Marta. She stands in the doorway, watching him guide the mower across the lawn. "It's okay," she says. "Let him mow." She sounds sympathetic, and this frustrates me.

I step down from the porch and walk around the side of Marta's house toward our garage. Once inside, I search the cluttered workbench for the pruning shears. I remember them being here a week ago, and after some poking around, I find them and move back to the front of Marta's house. My husband hasn't stopped mowing, and Marta still watches from the porch.

Everyone seems to have finally gotten what they've wanted. Except me.

I shout at Leland to turn off the mower. He's a few feet away from me. I shout again, and now he shuts it off.

"What?"

"Stop it."

He looks at me, and I can tell that nothing's making sense to him right now.

"Our son…" My hand is at my throat, wiping away the sweat. "He hanged himself, Leland."

My husband approaches me, but I duck and go to the side of the mower. I snatch the ripcord from the body of the machine and slide it between the shears. The cord feels rough in my hand, but it snaps quickly.

"What the hell are you doing?" My husband has his arms raised, and behind him, I can see Marta disappear behind a closing door. It's only the two of us now. My husband's waiting for an explanation as I head back to the garage. I begin to think of what I'll tell him first. I'll start by telling him that I want only a son, not a hero.

Behind me, I can hear the wheels of the mower slowly moving through the grass toward the garage. When I turn around, I see my husband is carrying the severed end of the cord, and I can only begin to hope that he'll soon understand why that means so much to me.

# THE THINGS HE SAW

★ ★ ★

*David Abrams*

They said he was lucky. The eye had not lost all its internal fluid, which would have led to its permanent collapse. Another millimeter to the right—one piece of shrapnel colliding with another to alter the course of his history—and the puncture would be bigger. Probably would have gone all the way to the brain. It was all in how you looked at it. Could have gone either way. Let's keep things in perspective, they said. He was one lucky soldier.

Lucky. Yeah, right, motherfucker.

The first photo he ever took over there was snapped two minutes after the C-130 touched down at Baghdad International Airport: his buddy, Specialist Tim Dietrich, unbuckling himself from the seat harness and groaning about how the canvas webbing would no doubt leave a permanent crease in his ass. Dietrich's Kevlar is tipped forward, casting a hard shadow across the bridge of his nose. You can still see the grimace, though.

He hadn't used a flash, so everything came out grainy. That's how most of his portfolio was: grainy. That's how he remembers Iraq: dim and grainy.

Dietrich's hand is wrapped tight around the barrel of his M-16. In the dark of the C-130, lit only by the blackout lights, his knuckles glow.

If he could go back there to the belly of that plane and say one thing to those soldiers, humid with their fears and bravado, he'd tell Dietrich to relax, to loosen the death grip on his rifle. He'd tell all of them none of it mattered, not in the long run.

Dietrich would be gone in just under a month. All four limbs simultaneously amputated in a blizzard of shrapnel from a roadside bomb. He only has one other photo of Dietrich, but this is the one he prefers, the one where you can see his knuckles.

It was just something he did, taking pictures. Tried not to let it distract him from the mission. He assured First Sergeant that he was infantry, first and foremost. Playing Joe Shutterbug was just a hobby of his.

"All right, but the minute it becomes a problem, I'll snatch that thing right out of your fucking hands and smash it to fucking bits right then and there. We clear on that?"

"Perfectly clear, First Sergeant." And they'd had no more trouble from that point on.

Some of the others ragged him for it, but they shut up soon enough when he gave them photos they could send back to their wives and girlfriends, proof it wasn't all fun and games over there in the desert.

Some days, he can still feel the ghost of the camera pressed against his right eye. In those moments, everything feels like it's coming into sharp focus through the Nikon lens. In, out, in, out until the edges settle into a crisp outline.

The rest of the time, everything is blurred and distorted, like he's opening his eye underwater. The light gets refracted at an odd slant and fucks everything up. He can make out shapes and color and letters, as long as they're the size of billboards.

He can no longer see his photographs—except in the vaguest, grainiest way—but he carries the details in his head. He's got his favorites thumb-tacked to his barracks room here at the medical hold company and he can still see the frozen moment captured in the click of the shutter.

Jackson, for instance, cradling that kid in his arms. There was no hope for the little girl, but Jackson had gone on rocking her all the same. He had three kids of his own back at Fort Drum, and they all knew what that could do to a guy over here. You started taking shit like this personally. One lousy, fucked-up counterstrike from Brigade Artillery and pretty soon you're picking your way through the rubble of a schoolhouse, shouting one word, "Fuck!" over and over like it would make a difference, tossing chunks of bricks left and right not caring who got hit. And some days, you ended up on the ground like Jackson, rocking back and forth, a little girl's brains smearing the belly of your shirt, but you're not even there. That blank, drained look in your eyes says you're half a globe away hugging someone else. That's what shows up loud and clear in the photo.

He lifts his patch and dabs at the dead eye with a handkerchief. He still has the eyeball and they think they can work with what's left. Cornea transplants and all that shit.

Whatever.

At least they were able to save the camera. It sits on the bookshelf in the corner of his room, battered but not broken. His body absorbed most of the blast. He sacrificed a sliced-open calf, a ripped ligament and a collapsed eye for the sake of his Nikon. Not so much as a crack on the lens.

Doesn't matter, though. He hasn't put his eye to the viewfinder since he's been back. He's afraid of what he won't see.

On his barracks wall, there's the one of Staff Sergeant King in the stairwell. He's just made it to the first landing and he's looking up the spiral of the stairs, his M-16 raised, like he was expecting trouble to come tumbling down any minute. There's a skylight at the top of the stairs and Staff Sergeant King's face is all lit up while the rest of the squad huddles behind him in the darkness, panting in anticipation of what's waiting for them.

This is one of his favorite photos. It's totally spiritual the way that light hits Staff Sergeant King.

Lucky, the doctors had called him. And why not? He was alive and five of the other ten in that Stryker—including Staff Sergeant King— were dead. Nothing but smoldering puddles of melted flesh and bone.

The bomb punched the breath from his lungs, jarred loose three teeth, sent all ten bodies colliding in a jumbled mess inside the Stryker like they were in a blender. Nineteen tons lifted twenty-one inches off the road in Mosul. Fan-fucking-tastic. He wishes he'd been standing outside of the Stryker to get a shot. *The* Shot. The Pulitzer-in-waiting. Nineteen tons and ten men (nine, if you were able to subtract him from inside) tossed like a salad, blood mixed with diesel fuel, a wedding of metal and bone.

He has a photo of a wedding. It isn't tacked to his barracks wall, but he has it around here somewhere.

It's not much of wedding photo. Nobody's smiling, no conga line, no champagne and cake anywhere in sight. Jackson's in it, so are Butterfield, McNaughton and Linley. They're all standing over the bride—what *used* to be the bride—and none of them are smiling. If you weren't there that day, it's hard to tell what they're looking at: a careless pile of white lace all in a heap, splayed legs and arms. But nothing where the head should be. No, the bastards took that with them, apparently.

"Sunnis," Captain Blowser said that day. He spat the word like it was a loogey he'd dislodged from his throat.

They'd pulled up in the Stryker too late. The Sunnis had already melted from the scene. They came, did their work with AK-47s and machetes, then got away while the blood was still dripping down the walls of the wedding tent.

The groom is somewhere outside the frame of the shot and now he tries to remember if the Sunnis left him intact. Doesn't matter. The bride is the focus of the photo.

From that pile of lace, your eye travels up to the faces of the men surrounding her. Who knows what Jackson, Butterfield, McNaughton and Linley were thinking, but it's a pretty good bet they were wondering whether this hajji bride was a total babe or a total dog. No way of telling with the head gone.

There's another one of Linley. He's stripped to his T-shirt, cigarette dangling from his lips—very Brad Pitt, a la *Fight Club*—eyes squinting from the smoke as he glares at the camera. He's flipping the bird, but the finger, too close to the lens, is out of focus. That's cool, though. As long as he got Linley's eyes. They're the important thing here. They say "Fuck you" all on their own.

There's one of another time they were on Hajji Clean Up Duty. This one is of a Shiite restaurant gutted by a suicide bomber. A swift, lethal fire erupting from a backpack right at the height of tea time—or whatever they call it over there.

Part of the ceiling is gone and hot sunshine floods the charred interior. Viscera is smeared across the floor. Tables and chairs, inextricably married in a tangle of chrome legs and plastic cushions, rest against a back wall where they have been propelled by the blast. Bright packages of crackers, tins of tea and cellophane-wrapped candy are still neatly arranged on a shelf next to a register, waiting for someone to come along and make a purchase. A man, presumably the owner, stands in a still-smoking door frame—the door is gone, thrown halfway down the block. Hajji looks like he could cry. But he won't. He won't cry. He is through with crying. Now he is just good and goddamned angry at Sunnis and Americans alike.

At least that's what comes through in the photo.

Next to that picture is the one of the suicide bomber from that same attack.

A head. Two legs which appear to be sprouting from his neck. A hand, fingers twisted and broken, in the region where you'd normally find the right hip bone. That's it. Nothing else. Everything in the trunk of the body—skin, bone, muscle, organ—has been vaporized, a brick-red mist splashed through the dust and rubble of the restaurant. His eyes are squeezed shut, as if in the final reflex before he pulled the det cord. His feet on the end of those neatly-severed legs are turned in opposite directions—one up, one down. If you didn't know better, you might mistake his legs for arms, his feet for hands. He looks like a meaty jigsaw puzzle of parts—with those feet-hands, he looks like a child's drawing of a traffic cop, one hand saying "Stop!", the other beckoning "Go!"

★ ★ ★

There's one of a private whose name he forgets. A cherry who joined the brigade just before they shipped out. Guy was dead less than two weeks after they got here, so this must be one of his earlier photos, before he started paying closer attention to stuff like composition and focal points. This one is more of a snapshot, really. Kid is on a rooftop pulling security while guys from another unit are down below kicking in doors and grabbing suspects by the collar. This kid's time is already ticking away, but he has this look on his face like he's all tough and shit, but you don't believe it because of the way he's holding his mouth. He's just one AK-47 burst away from breaking into a full-scale blubber, complete with tears and crying for his Mommy.

What was his fucking name anyway? *Damn.*

In the distance, a Blackhawk hovers over the neighborhood, ready to track down the hajjis who break and run. It's two blocks away, but in the photo it looks like it's right above the New Guy's head, buzzing like an insect ready to land and sting. Dead Man Walking has no idea what's about to hit him.

It's funny how photos can fuck with your perspective like that.

Like the one of the sheik arguing with Captain Blowser. In the photo, you can't even tell the two of them are deep in disagreement over where the new sewage line for the village should be dug. The U.S. engineers have one idea, the villagers have another.

The way Captain Blower is pointing his finger at the sheik, he could be saying, "You da man!" In the photo, the sheik is reaching out as if to shake Captain B.'s hand. In the photo, it sure looks like smiles, the way those teeth are exposed.

Cover photographer **STAFF SERGEANT RUTH PAGAN** hails from Charleston, South Carolina, and joined the Army in 1999. She serves with the 2nd Brigade Combat Team, 4th Infantry Division, in Fort Carson, Colorado, and has been deployed three times, to Kuwait, Iraq and Afghanistan.

About the cover photograph, she says, "This picture was taken Christmas day. Our mission was to go by Chinook to about five different outlying forward operating bases and deliver duffel bags of goodies. The FOBs were very isolated so being able to bring our fellow soldiers these baked goods was a treat for us. The photo I was able to capture was at the end of the day and the guys were walking out into the field to wait on our Chinook to arrive."

# AUTHOR BIOGRAPHIES
## AND STORY NOTES

**DAVID ABRAMS** is the author of *Fobbit* (Grove/Atlantic, 2012), a comedy about the Iraq War which *Publishers Weekly* called "an instant classic" and named a Top 10 Pick for Literary Fiction in Fall 2012. It was also a *New York Times* Notable Book of 2012, an Indie Next pick, a Barnes & Noble Discover Great New Writers selection and a Montana Honor Book. One of his stories also appears in *Fire and Forget* (Da Capo Press, 2013), an anthology of short fiction about the wars in Iraq and Afghanistan. His short stories have appeared in *Esquire, Narrative, Salon, Salamander, Connecticut Review, The Greensboro Review, Consequence,* and many other publications. He earned a BA in English from the University of Oregon and an MFA in Creative Writing from the University of Alaska-Fairbanks. He retired from active-duty after serving in the U.S. Army for 20 years, a career which took him to Alaska, Texas, Georgia, the Pentagon, and Iraq. He now lives in Butte, Montana, with his wife. His blog, *The Quivering Pen*, can be found at: www.davidabramsbooks.blogspot.com. Visit his website at: www.davidabramsbooks.com.

### Note about "The Things He Saw"

The year I spent in Iraq was a visual one. As a media relations NCO with Task Force Baghdad in 2005, one of my many duties was to establish a catalogue of photos from the journalists in our line units as well as images from Combat Camera teams. Every war since the mid-1800s has depended on the medium of photography to serve as a sad reporter from the battlefield. Even though the wars in Iraq and Afghanistan sometimes played out in YouTube videos, the historic totems we'll take from these wars are primarily still photographs, from the crude Polaroids of the hooded, electroded victims of Abu Ghraib to the heartbreaking rows of flag-draped coffins in the cargo holds of transport planes. We remember our time in the desert in camera clicks and eye blinks. As I sat at my desk in Baghdad, the mosaic of the Iraq War streamed in to me in bloody bits of dpi and pixels. Now, at the distance of eight years, all I have are shutterburst memories, flickershot movies of images—some of them mundane like the faces of my co-workers tapping at keyboards in our cubicles and the array of steaming food lined up for us at the dining facility; but some of those mental pictures I brought home with me are the horrible ones I'll never be able to shake: the meaty, scattered parts of suicide bombers, the empty sandals piled in the street after the tragic stampede at the Al-Aaimmah bridge. This is representative of my combat tour in Operation Iraqi Freedom—the mundane mixed with the macabre. When it came time to write "The Things He Saw" (the title a not-too-sly reference to Tim O'Brien's classic story of Vietnam, "The Things They Carried"), I had no trouble calling up images to paste in this verbal photo album.

ZOEY BYRD has published stories in *Home of the Brave: Stories in Uniform* and *Best New American Voices 2001*. She is certain that this is the year she finishes the novel she keeps claiming to be working on. She currently lives in Honolulu.

### Note about "Rangers Lead the Way"

I was called to write this story—out loud. On Memorial Day 2009, I went to Section 60 in Arlington Cemetery where military members killed in Iraq and Afghanistan are interred. What a shock it was to hear every mother I met name the unit where her son was assigned, the exact village and province where he was killed, and the details of how he died. Like a sponge, I sucked it all in, and then I went home and cried my eyes out for a good week as if I had been told over and over and over again those awful words, "I regret to inform you...." That first night, I woke up out of a dead sleep and sat straight up in bed because I'd heard a voice say, "Rangers lead the way." It was not a dream. I swear. The next night, I woke up to "Hey." I appreciated the brevity. This wasn't a dream, either. If it were a dream I would have felt fear and anxiety. Instead my reaction was, "Who are you and what do you want?" I also smugly thought, "Bug off. I'm not writing your story." The third night, in between crying fits, I was reading a Rumi poem in which the lover describes watching his beloved sleeping. At that moment I heard the story start to write itself. "Dammit," I thought. "Okay, I'll write your story, but I'm writing my version." They were like, "We know. That's the version we're giving you." Ever since then, I've chosen to consciously acknowledge the presence of the dead in my life and their need to get involved. I'd like to take a moment to let them know I heart them. That is one of the best ways to write, I think. The good news is no one has dared to wake me up again in the wee hours of the morning saying stuff. That's just too weird.

As a side note, the day of the deadline for submitting this story I heard a chorus of voices say, "Send the story! Send the fucking story." I was like, "No, it sucks and it's too long. I have to cut 5,000 words. It might be a novel." They said, "Cut the fucking words." The only option was to cut Melissa, Seth's girlfriend, out of the story. "But I love Melissa," I said. "She's really cool and goth and works in a record store in Tacoma, and Seth might love her, too." "Cut her!" they said. "You have enough women in the story." So that's how Melissa ended up on the cutting floor and how Seth ended up not marrying Rosa and not becoming a lawyer who plays golf on weekends and lives in a big house in Houston.

CALEB S. CAGE graduated from West Point in 2002 with a degree in History. He was commissioned as a Field Artillery officer assigned to the 1st Infantry Division with which he served as a platoon leader in the city of Baqubah, Iraq in 2004. He co-authored a book with Gregory Tomlin entitled *The Gods of Diyala,* which is based on their experiences in Iraq and was published by Texas

A&M University Press in 2008. Cage is a founding editor of *The Nevada Review*, a journal dedicated to the literature of his state.

## Note about "Soldier's Cross"

Though "Soldier's Cross" is thoroughly a work of fiction, some of the scenes and ideas came from my first deployment as a platoon leader in Baqubah, Iraq in 2004, as well as my upbringing in Nevada. As a platoon leader, I had a great time with my guys when we got to hang out during down time, but during combat, I had to deal with the prospect of losing them, of having to catalog and ship their personal effects home, of having to tell their parents. As many other wartime writers have examined, this tension causes great frustration. In me, it caused me to question the military's rigid authority and it caused me to struggle with the concept of truth and a higher power. The iconic image of the soldier's cross that nearly everyone who has deployed to a warzone knows—the boots, the rifle, the helmet, and the dogtags—captured these tensions for me from the first time I saluted one for one of our fallen soldiers.

**JON CHOPAN** teaches creative writing at Eckerd College in St. Petersburg, FL. His first short story collection, *Pulled from the River*, was released by Black Lawrence Press in December of 2012. His writing has appeared in *Hotel Amerika, Glimmer Train, Post Road*, and *Epiphany*.

## Note about "Men of Principle"

When I wrote "Men of Principle" I was thinking about the guys I grew up with, about my brother and his best friend Nick. In many ways Nick is the main character in this story, a Marine who served in Iraq, a good guy who has clear convictions about justice and how justice is handed out. The general frame of the story, three guys looking for a bad guy, is my brother's story, but I wondered how the story would take on new weight if a veteran were the one seeking revenge. I was interested in what his actions might come to say about the war in Iraq, how they might parallel the war. Mostly, I am interested in masculinity in America. I am interested in how men act, in how they carry themselves in the world. Men of Principle is a story, for me, about that, about how we might do things, at times, because we believe they are right even though we realize, in the moment, or after that fact, that they are wrong.

PAUL CRENSHAW's stories and essays have appeared or are forthcoming in Best American Essays 2005 and 2011, anthologies by W.W. Norton and Houghton Mifflin, and numerous literary journals, including *Ecotone*, *Glimmer Train*, *North American Review*, and *Southern Humanities Review*. He teaches writing and literature at Elon University.

### Note about "Came a Flood"
I had written several short stories involving characters affected by the wars in Iraq and Afghanistan, and several others with the two girls who become the main characters in "Came a Flood" and who are rather loosely based on my daughters. I had an image of the house, and the stream flowing through the back yard, and from there I diverted the stream into the house. Then I just had to figure out why anyone would do that, and the story came together.

TRACY CROW is the author of *Eyes Right: Confessions from a Woman Marine*, recipient of the 2012 Florida Book Awards bronze medal in general nonfiction. She is assistant professor of creative writing at Eckerd College in St. Petersburg, Florida, and the nonfiction editor of *Prime Number Magazine*, a Press 53 publication. Her essays and short stories have appeared in a number of literary journals and been nominated for three Pushcart Prizes. Under the pen name, Carver Greene, she published the conspiracy thriller, *An Unlawful Order*, the first in a new series to feature a military heroine.

### Note about "An Unlawful Order — Chapter 1"
This is chapter one from a military conspiracy thriller, *An Unlawful Order*, released under my pen name, Carver Greene. The novel is based on actual events of helicopter crashes, a cover-up conspiracy,

and deaths that occurred during my ten years as a Marine Corps combat correspondent and public affairs officer. The sequel, also based on actual events, takes place in Okinawa, Japan, and involves the role of the Japanese mafia—the famed Yakuza—in the white slavery market. Chase and Joe reunite in a harrowing search for their friend. The sequel will be released in 2014.

JAMES R. DUNCAN is an author and screenwriter in Tampa, FL. He is a contributor of fiction for the 2012 Bread Loaf Writer's Conference, a participant of Writer's in Paradise for 2010 and 2011, and an alumni of Los Angeles' ScreenwritingU Pro Series. He has completed several short stories, and has two novels and a screenplay in progress.

## Note about "Sacramentum"

As a story, "Sacramentum" attempts to wrestle with the concept of certain people being brave enough to give their lives for an ideal, yet often times, for individuals who do not appreciate it. In the dark of night does that sacrifice become regret, if there is no love ever received for the effort? Or does giving everything for truth, regardless of the outside world, actually make someone more whole in the end? The story's main character, Tom, is also a central character in my novel-in-progress, The Severed Sun. The Severed Sun wrestles with the same questions, including if Tom can rise to be a hero yet again for a world that now largely sees him as an outcast.

ROLAND GOITY lives in the San Francisco Bay Area, where he writes in the shadows of planes coming and going from SFO. His stories can be found in *Fiction International, The Raleigh Review, Word Riot, Compass Rose, PANK, The MacGuffin*, and many other fine journals. He edits *WIPs: Works (of Fiction) in Progress*, where he interviews authors about their current book projects in conjunction with publishing excerpts of their work.

## Note about "Sand Trapped"

I wrote "Sand Trapped" in 2009 as the War in Afghanistan

approached its eighth year. To me it seemed my country had lost sight of what it meant to "support the troops," and wasn't showing proper concern regarding a number of war-related issues, particularly how multiple deployments were wreaking havoc on military families. The story's focus on things back home was influenced by an excellent feature I had read in the *Los Angeles Times*, which described the ordeal of a young military wife who, feeling isolated, turned to drugs and let her life spin out of control.

KEVIN C. JONES' work has been featured in *The New York Times, Ink Pot, r.k.vr.y, Prime Number, Monkeybicycle, The Cobalt Review, The Atticus Review, O-Dark-Thirty*, and the anthologies *Home of the Brave: Stories in Uniform* and *Boomtown: Explosive Writing from Ten Years of the Queens University of Charlotte MFA Program*. A former Marine, he lives on Florida's Gulf Coast where he teaches writing and literature.

### Note about "The Edge of Water"

This story started with an image of a young boy with his dad at the beach and went from there. It wasn't a military story to start with. I was just writing about someone post-trauma. Later on, I reworked it (considerably) into the Iraq story by merging the original bones with a narrative about a woman who blew up a Marine squad on patrol that I couldn't make it work on its own. It's about trauma, and fathers and sons, and the ways in which people try to make sense of senseless things. Things that, more often than not, they'll never really understand, even years later. At least, that's what it is to me. To paraphrase Deleuze, a story is only an assemblage. A little machine that doesn't work without a connection to its reader. There is no difference between what a story is about and how it is made, because writing is always the measure of something else.

BROOKE KING served in the United States Army, deploying to Iraq in 2006 as a wheel vehicle mechanic, machine gunner, and recovery specialist. Her combat experience has led her to focus on the involvement of female soldiers, giving perspective and insight about how women have fought in combat and war. Her work has been published in the *Sandhill Review* with a forthcoming publication with University of Nebraska Press. Currently, Brooke is attending Sierra Nevada College's Master of Fine Arts program and is working on her first novel.

## Note about "Mourners of the Dead"

"Mourners of the Dead" is loosely based on an encounter I had with an Iraqi woman during my deployment in Baghdad 2006. The story depicts how both soldiers and Iraqi civilians were affected by the war. So often in war, compassion is lost and humanitarianism is forgotten. I hope that through the story of these two women that one can see that such simplicities in life are not left for dead and that in the mist of chaos and wreckage, we as humans can be there for each other when words simply are not enough to comfort one another from the horrors of war. With this story, I hope to show how with a single embrace, complete strangers are able to find a sort of peace, even as they sit surrounded by a war zone where the conflict still raged on.

JACK KING's fiction has appeared in *Epiphany*, *Gemini*, *Forge*, and the *Oklahoma Review*. His nonfiction has featured in *Info World*, *ISSA*, and other IT journals nobody reads for fun. He is a Gold winner in the MWA Short Fiction contest in 2012, and first place in the MWA Novel contest in 2006. When not fixing his wife's laptop, he works as a cloud computing engineer for a large consulting firm in the Baltimore/Washington area.

## Note about "Kill Box"

The genesis of this piece came from the idea of war as a career for a civilian contractor, and the implications of fighting by day and having dinner with the family at night. Having worked for nearly fifteen years as an IT consultant for various DoD agencies, I've been exposed to my fair share of troubling realities ranging from work on the Army Suicide Prevention database to compiling an IED incident casualty system to highlight improvements in armor that can save lives. As our armed forces shift reliance to automated and remote capable weapon systems, we move the trauma of war back to the homeland and into the board room. I believe the psychological implications will leave a lasting epitaph that will ring through generations to come.

FRED LEEBRON's novels include *Out West*, *Six Figures*, and *In the Middle of all This*. His stories have appeared in numerous literary magazines and have received a Pushcart Prize and an O. Henry Award. He directs writing programs in Roanoke, Charlotte, and Europe.

### Note about "The Idiot, or Life in Wartime"
I started this story because I wanted to write about something political, as I rarely engage in political debate and I was tired of sitting on the fence about something that was happening right now. Ironically, entering the story only got my character on the fence, and so I followed it to see what would happen to him thereafter. Later, I wrote a longer version of the story for a film director who had optioned the rights so he could more easily write the feature screenplay. Then Obama was elected and that was that.

COURT MERRIGAN is the author of *Moondog Over The Mekong* (Snubnose Press) and he's got short stories out or coming soon in *Needle*, *Weird Tales*, *Plots With Guns*, *Shotgun Honey* and *Noir Nation*. He is currently shopping a novel, *The Broken Country*. Links at http:/ /courtmerrigan.com . He runs the Bareknuckles Pulp Department at *Out of the Gutter* and lives in Wyoming with his family.

### Note about "The City of Screams"
Rattlecreek is a rather thinly disguised Whiteclay, Nebraska, a town which lies 200 feet across the South Dakota border from the Pine Ridge Reservation. Pine Ridge is officially dry; 12,500 cans of beer are purchased a day in Whiteclay, mostly by Oglala Indians. Meanwhile, Shahr-e Gholghola, Afghanistan, also known as the City of Screams, was conquered by Genghis Khan in the 13th century and every single resident slaughtered. My father, a great champion of the Afghan people, traveled to this city and reported

that the locals referred to the massacre in the present tense, as though blood still streamed down the streets of the abandoned city. So I wondered, what would happen if an Oglala serving as a soldier was mistaken for a Mongolian and nearly killed by Afghans seeking revenge, putting him in mind of the atrocities his own people suffered? And what if that wounded Oglala returned home to come afire with that same lust to avenge history?

My gratitude to my brother Nate Merrigan and sister-in-law Beth Bellinger Merrigan, veterans both, for the fine-toothed vetting of this story for military accuracy.

JOE MILLS is a faculty member at the University of North Carolina School of the Arts and has published four collections of poetry with Press 53: *Sending Christmas to Huck and Hamlet, Love and Other Collisions, Angels, Thieves, and Winemakers,* and *Somewhere During the Spin Cycle.* More information about him can be found at www.josephrobertmills.com.

### Note about "At the Veterans Hospital"

Sometimes I don't remember the words of a book I've read long ago, but I'll remember the experience of reading it: where I was, what season it was, what time of day, how I carried it around, how it felt holding it in my hands, in short, the physicality of the experience. What happens when there is no longer an actual book to hold? What happens when there is no longer a hand? And what might this mean for "religions of the book"—Christianity, Judasim, Islam—and for those of us for whom reading is such a fundamental metaphor in the shaping and articulation of our world views that sometimes we cease to recognize it as a metaphor at all?

THOMAS VINCENT NOWACZYK was born and raised on the south side of Chicago and dropped out of high school during his senior year to join the US Marines. He served on active duty from February 1976 through December 1986 as both infantryman and award-winning military journalist. He is a graduate of the Basic Broadcaster Course (with Honors) and the Electronic Journalism course from the Defense

Information School, Ft. Harrison, Indiana. He also holds a Bachelor of Arts degree in Humanities from Shimer College, Chicago, and studied British Literature in Oxford. His work as a military journalist earned him a Department of Defense Thomas Jefferson Award for Professional Excellence: a Distinguished Performance Award from the Marine Corps Combat Correspondent's Association; and several other honors. He currently lives in San Francisco, CA, with two Harley Davidson motorcycles and a Martin guitar.

### Note about "Killing Time in Kandahar"

"Killing Time in Kandahar" grew out of an exercise in a writing craft class by venerable Bay Area writer, Laurie Ann Doyle, through UC Berkeley Extension. I realized I had a unique opportunity to craft a story about the experience of being a Marine at war in a workshop full of participants with little or no military exposure. Their feedback was essential in helping me find ways to make the military environment more accessible while simultaneously heightening the reader's emotional investment. I am of course indebted to my classmates for the lesson.

KATHLEEN M. RODGERS' work has appeared in *Family Circle Magazine*, *Air Force*, *Army & Navy Times*, *Family: The Magazine for Military Families*, *Fort Worth Star-Telegram*, *Albuquerque Journal*, *Clovis News Journal*, and in four anthologies: *Because I Fly*, by McGraw-Hill, *Lessons From Our Children*, by Health Communications, Inc., *Stories Of Faith And Courage On The Home Front*, by AMG Publishers, and *Hearts of Steel*, by Military Writers Society of America. Her debut novel, *The Final Salute*, won a Silver Medal from Military Writers Society of America and is an Amazon Bestseller in both Kindle and paperback format. She is seeking a publisher for her latest novel, *Johnnie Come Lately*.

### Note about "Johnnie Come Lately"

This is an excerpt from my recently completed novel, *Johnnie Come Lately*. This passage appears as a Letter to the Editor penned by my protagonist, Mrs. Johnnie Kitchen, whose son has just left for basic training.

MAX RUBACK is a high school reading teacher and girls basketball coach for the Coconut Creek Lady Cougars. He is a graduate of the MFA program at Florida International University and has published fifty stories in various literary magazines.

## Note about "Seven in the Morning"

The story included was a part of a larger story I had been working on for about a year. The story wasn't working as a whole, and I revised and cut and added and revised for months without much emotional progress along the way. So like an old car that you sell off for parts, I did the same with the story, in a flash sense. Three flash pieces were subsequently published from the one story that just wasn't working, one of which was "Seven In The Morning."

BRIAN SEEMANN currently lives in the Austin, Texas area. He earned an MFA from Wichita State University, and has won the William J. Stuckey Memorial Prize for Fiction. His fiction has appeared in *Regarding Arts and Letters*, *Forge*, and *Fast Forward*.

## Note about "The Neighbor's Yard"

The origins of this story started in my own front yard. A few summer's back, I mowed not only my yard but also my neighbor's yard; her husband was away on duty, and I cut their grass mainly out of neighborly kindness. That's the only connection reality has with the fiction of this story—everything else grew from my mind as I pushed the lawnmower back and forth in the one-hundred degree heat. The story went through very few drafts, surprisingly, and after a few suggestions from two outstanding fellow writers, it was finished. I can't say that I understand what people like my narrator feel, but I can empathize, and that's probably where this story really comes from. I didn't lose anyone to the wars in Iraq and Afghanistan, but because of World War I, my mother was without a father by the age of nine and I, of course, never met my grandfather. War is a necessary evil in this world, unfortunately, and it seems the longer one tries to reason with such an idea, the less time one has to enjoy the beautiful things the same world has to offer.

PAUL STROEBEL is a six-year army veteran who served with the 82nd in Iraq and Afghanistan. He holds a B.A. in Writing form Methodist University in Fayetteville, North Carolina, where he runs writing workshops for a Veterans' Writing Collective and has compiled a bibliography of veteran's literature from the last one hundred years of modern warfare.

### Note about "Antidote"
The work is influenced by James Jones as well as the author's experience. It is also informed by the events prior to and after the experience of war. Survivors' guilt, PTSD, as well as disillusionment complicate the war story. While any of these individual events could be a tragedy, together they are a chronicle.

DANIEL TAYLOR was born, raised, and currently resides in Monmouth, Illinois. He served four years as an infantryman in the Army with the 172nd Stryker Brigade Combat Team in Ft. Wainwright, Alaska. In that time he was deployed for 16 months to Iraq and after a brief trip home, served 9 months in Afghanistan with the 1-178IN, Illinois National Guard. He's attended Carl Sandburg College, recently graduated Western Illinois University with a B.A. in English, and plans to enter an MFA program. In addition to a large group of friends and family, he enjoys great support from his wife Jessica, and their three sons, Ethan, Riley, and Connor.

### Note about "Half-Smiles"
"Half-Smiles" started after my unit was extended in Iraq for four more months after we had already served 12 months. The entire unit moved to Baghdad to help quell the sectarian violence that had erupted in 2006. There was a transition period and I found myself with about a week without any operations. I used to write stories as a kid and I always wanted to get back into writing. I had an idea for a story bouncing around my head so I thought to myself, why not write something and why not make the character a war veteran. What I started writing ended up being the basis for "Half-Smiles." Originally, the story was supposed to be a first chapter of a novel, an introduction to the character, Connor,

while he was fighting in Iraq. It focused on a firefight and was heavy on action. After I left the Regular Army, I took a creative writing class and it influenced me to pursue an English degree. At school, I found myself in another culture and I found that the students had a lot of misconceptions about the military and were ignorant of its people. It motivated me to write about "real" service people, to tell the good and the bad, but to do it faithfully. As my education progressed, I realized that the real story of Connor and his buddies was after the firefight. I wrote my first draft of a new story titled "Half-Smiles."

JIM WALKE grew up in Michigan and still has near-freezing lake water in his blood. Following college he was a stage actor for a decade or so, living in and touring dozens of states while getting paid very little to swing swords and kiss pretty girls. The promise of health insurance finally dragged him to a halt, and now he helps Virginia Tech write very large biomedical research proposals from his tiny turquoise house in South Carolina. On the weekends he heads up into the mountains with Kipling, his young dog of dubious provenance. www.jimwalke.com

### Note about "Monster"

In the South, people will lay out their lives on the side of a pickle jar on the gas station counter, with a simple plea for help. Cancer, fiery accidents, cancer, kidney failure, murder, drowning and cancer again . . . always with a picture and a reliance on the kindness of strangers. That particular form of confession crossed up with a famous photo of a burned young Marine in his dress blues next to his very young bride to create this story for me. "Monster" may be the best thing I've written to date. It was rejected by 42 of the finest literary journals in the land. It took me that long to figure out that it was more of an early chapter than a short story. The novel is in the works.

ROBERT WALLACE has received an Emerging Artist grant from the Durham Arts Council, and a Writer's Fellowship from the NC Arts Council. He has had fiction and nonfiction published in various journals and newspapers, including the *Bryant Literary Review*, *Wellspring, Aethlon, The O. Henry Festival Stories,* and the *Raleigh News*

*& Observer*. His work has also been in several anthologies, including *Racing Home: New Short Stories by Award Winning North Carolina Writers*. His story "As Breaks the Wave upon the Sea" was the 2010 winner of the Doris Betts Fiction Prize. Wallace's first novel, *A Hold on Time*, was published in 2007 by Paper Journey Press. *First Kiss*, a ten-minute play, recently had a stage-reading at Wake Forest University.

**Note about "I Demand to Know When You're Coming Home"**
I have been writing a series of stories about the wars in Iraq and Afghanistan, each of them told from a different point of view, some with multiple narrators. I wanted to tell a story from the perspective of a young child. It is hard to describe the grief of a child losing a parent, perhaps even more so due to war. Oftentimes we think of a child acting out their grief because a child may lack the ability to put their grief into words. That is the common conception. But I think the loss could very well be insular in nature, so much so that grief could become claustrophobic. I wanted the reader to feel this boy's pain and terror—and how grief can feel like it goes on forever.

Editor **JEFFERY HESS** served six years in the U.S. Navy aboard the fleet's oldest and then newest ships before going on to earn degrees in English and Creative Writing. He's the editor of the award-winning anthology, *Home of the Brave: Stories in Uniform* (Press 53) and his writing has appeared in numerous print and online publications. He lives in Florida where he's completing a novel and leads the DD-214 Writers Workshop for military veterans.

# PERMISSIONS

# A Note from the Editor

Most sincere thanks and appreciation to everyone who served in the United States armed services or has been affected by someone who did. Without you the world would be a drastically different place and these stories would not be possible.

I'd also like to thank all the immensely talented writers who contributed stories for this anthology. Thank you for your belief in the project and for making my job so enjoyable.

I'm forever grateful to my publisher at Press 53, Kevin Watson, the nicest guy you could ever meet and an indefatigable proponent of the short story.

Many thanks to Sheryl Monks and Sally Drumm for ushering me into anthology editorship a number of years ago.

Thanks also to Dennis Miller, Jennifer Gustafson, Pinckney Benedict, Mark Fleeting, Matt Flaherty, Tracy Crow, Tim Wright, and with a hat tip to Carol "Dee Dee" Turner, for their patience, wisdom, and support.

And as always, debts of gratitude that I'm incapable of repaying are due to all my friends, my parents, my entire family, and my wife, Lauren.

Thank you all very much.

Jeffery Hess
Editor

# DD-214 Writers Workshop

A portion of this book's proceeds will help fund the DD-214 Writers' Workshop (established 2007), an independent, weekly workshop in the Tampa Bay area.

The DD-214 Writers' Workshop seeks to provide instruction, encouragement and assessment to military veterans of any age who wish to write.

All writing workshops contain classroom lecture and critiques in a friendly environment of encouraged participation with a student to faculty ratio not to exceed five to one. Every workshop is suitable for beginning, intermediate and advanced writers. Each workshop addresses the craft of writing across experience levels and across genres of fiction writing, non-fiction writing, screenwriting, and poetry as student submissions dictate.

Workshop group meets once per week for six consecutive weeks (excluding adjustments for holidays). For more information, visit: www.DD214Writers.org.